*'I hope you're not thinking of staying here a...'*

Ria said to Grady.

'No need to think about it, it's all arranged,' ...
'I'm staying.'

'Grady, this is my house. You can't stay here!'

He shot her a cocky grin. He liked her anger, enjoyed it far better than the worry in her eyes that had been tearing him apart. 'Afraid you'll be overcome with lust and jump me in the night?'

'Hardly,' she muttered, jerking her gaze away from him.

'Afraid *I'll* jump *you?*'

'Just don't say any more,' she warned, but her lips twitched and her cheeks were pink.

Grady suddenly felt hopeful. Maybe there was such a thing as a second chance after all.

Dear Reader

Welcome to Silhouette Sensation® in the new millennium. As always we've got plenty of terrific reading for you, so come and forget the daily grind with us—indulge yourself!

Let's start with a very special man, January's **Heartbreaker** from Sharon Sala—*The Miracle Man*—he's the kind of guy most women would choose to father their child—if only they dared!

*The Tough Guy and the Toddler* by Diane Pershing pretty much speaks for itself, and *Like Father, Like Daughter* from Margaret Watson kicks off a set of linked books from this talented writer. Look for *For the Children* in March.

And last but never least, is favourite author Paula Detmer Riggs with a cracking read about a cop and his ex-wife whose son is abducted and how, once the boy is found, they become *Once More a Family*.

Enjoy!

The Editors

# Once More a Family

## PAULA DETMER RIGGS

SILHOUETTE
SENSATION

*Silhouette, Silhouette Sensation and Colophon are registered trademarks of Harlequin Books S.A., used under licence.*

*First published in Great Britain 2000 Silhouette Books, Eton House, 18-24 Paradise Road, Richmond, Surrey TW9 1SR*

© Paula Detmer Riggs 1999

ISBN 0 373 07933 8

18-0001

*Printed and bound in Spain by Litografia Rosés S.A., Barcelona*

## PAULA DETMER RIGGS

discovers material for her writing in her varied life experiences. During her first five years of marriage to a naval officer, she lived in nineteen different locations on the West Coast, gaining familiarity with places as diverse as San Diego and Seattle. While working at an historical site in San Diego, she wrote, directed and narrated fashion shows and became fascinated with the early history of California.

She writes romances because 'I think we all need an escape from the high-tech pressures that face us every day, and I believe in happy endings. Isn't that why we keep trying, in spite of all the roadblocks and disappointments along the way?'

# *Prologue*

Hot damn, he felt good!

Finally, after thirty-six years, three months and two days of never quite measuring up, Grady Hardin, the sorriest, ugliest, dumbest of the five Hardin brothers had done something right.

Damn near half the narcotics division of the Lafayette PD had battled for the promotion to captain of the newly created drug interdiction department. In spite of the two reprimands for insubordination in his service record and a tendency to smart-off to the wrong people when his resentment of authority got the best of him, he'd snagged the prize. Since his father's retirement from the force last year, only his straight-arrow big brother Kale outranked him.

He owed it all to his sweet Ria, he decided as he rocketed his candy-apple '69 Charger along the narrow country road. Marrying Victoria Virginia Madison nine years ago had been the best thing he'd ever done in his lazy, self-indulgent life. His lady loved him, though God alone knew

why he'd been so blessed. Maybe a good deed in a former
life. He sure as shooting didn't have much to offer a lady
like her in this one.

He wasn't all that bright, he was clumsy as an ox, and
he tended to stumble over his tongue when he wasn't with
other cops. Which is why he tended to shy away from talking to women. But somehow she made it easy. Maybe because she laughed at his jokes. Or asked him questions that
made him feel she really cared about the answers.

His brothers had darn near swallowed their tongues when
they'd gotten their first look at her. She was flat-out beautiful, with sparkling moss-green eyes, a sweet smile, and a
sassy rear end.

She was also the sweetest, kindest, strongest woman he'd
ever met in his life. Wanting to earn her respect had given
him a reason to stop messing up his life and do something
with all that potential everyone kept nagging him about.

Three years ago, when she'd given him a son—and then
insisted the little boy carry his daddy's name, James
Grady—he'd nearly burst with pride. He'd vowed then to
make her—and Jimmy—proud.

Since he was alone, he let out a Hoosier version of a
rebel yell, and then because it felt so good, did it again.
Feeling as giddy as a prisoner suddenly released for good
behavior, he shoved his favorite Marvin Gaye cassette into
the player, checked the mirrors and floored it. The souped-
up V-8 beneath the big hood responded instantly, adding
the deep-throated growl of unleashed power to the soul-
stirring beat of rock and roll.

A white-faced heifer grazing near a rusty fence looked
up from a batch of sweet clover, and Grady waved at the
pretty little Hereford. Damn, but it was a beautiful day in
Indiana.

The first day of summer.

Grady loved summer. As a kid, he'd been wild to escape

the miserable boredom and daily humiliations of the classroom, his clumsy hands itching to wrap around his favorite fishing pole. Lying on his back by the river with his line in the water and the breeze cooling his face, he was freed from the restrictions of a brain that didn't quite work right.

On days when the letters on the page remained a hopeless jumble, no matter how hard he tried, he'd skip out during the lunchtime break and head for the woods.

Grady still remembered the tanning he'd gotten one sunny day in May when Mason Hardin had tracked him down in his favorite spot on the bank of the Wabash. His butt had been sore for days, driving his brothers into gales of laughter every time he tried to sit down. But it had been the disappointment in his father's eyes that had finally gotten to him. So he'd stopped playing hooky and worked to bring his usual collection of D's up to a respectable C average. He'd even given up his dream of becoming an Indy champion and followed family tradition by becoming a cop.

No one thought he'd last a week in the police academy. Brother Kale figured forty-eight hours max. He'd heard rumors his father had declined to take the bet. Grady'd had a few doubts himself. Bending his will to someone else's idea of discipline had never been high on his to-do list. On the other hand, giving up on a commitment was even lower on his personal hierarchy of desirable character traits.

Besides, he loved goading those mean-as-sin instructors into red-faced fury. Seeing the frustration in their eyes had been worth the pain of the brutal training. The more they figured he'd wash out, the harder he dug in. By the time he graduated he'd earned a reputation as a tough SOB with a sneaky left jab.

No one was surprised when he ended up working undercover in the murky world of drug addicts and pushers. Hell, he had a sneaking suspicion most of the watch commanders were relieved he hadn't ended up in their division.

He grinned as he thumped the heel of one hand against the wheel in time to the music. The tender stalks of corn shooting up on both sides of the road flashed by in a blur of green, and wind flavored with sunshine slapped at his face.

The quick flash of a strobe in his rearview brought him down to earth with a familiar thud. Just what he needed—another speeding ticket on his record.

Damn.

A glance at the speedometer had him grinding out his favorite obscenity, the one that had had him spitting out soap when he'd been a kid.

Hell and blast, the old Charger still wanted to run. So did he, damn it. His butt had been glued to a chair behind a desk for a solid week without a day off. Before that he'd been cooling his heels in a courthouse corridor, waiting to testify. He was so wired he was ready to blow.

Resigned to his fate, he heaved a sigh and signaled that he was pulling off. Tight as a tick, the county-mountie hugged his bumper all the way to the shoulder.

"Fun's over for today, Trouble," he muttered, tossing a guilty grin at the scrawny black and white kitten peering at him over the edge of the box on the passenger seat. "We've been busted."

Accustomed to the drill, he killed the engine and leaned across the gearshift to grab his registration from the glove compartment.

"Act innocent," he ordered the cat, who answered with a plaintive meow. Damn thing was just about the sorriest looking critter he'd ever seen. Far as he'd been able to see, it didn't have much of a personality, either. Probably had worms as well as an ugly face and a mangled leg.

The bill at the emergency animal hospital had had him sucking in hard. He was still working on the argument he planned to lay on Ria—after he'd softened her up with flowers and a promise to do all the cooking at the lake for the entire two weeks they would be at the cottage.

He'd rather eat dirt than cook.

Why the hell hadn't the damn cat crawled under someone else's vehicle after he'd been hit? he thought sourly. A entire parking lot full of wheels, and Trouble chose his.

Still, Jimmy had always wanted a pet, he reminded himself as he watched the cop climb out of the cruiser and walk toward the Charger. Just his luck. The guy was a bruiser with a cocky walk and an impeccable uniform. Straight-arrow all the way. Grady had a sinking feeling he wasn't going to talk his way out of this one.

Though he was tempted to deal with this one eye to eye, he stayed put. Cops got real nervous when drivers left the vehicle. Especially guys his size driving a muscle car on a deserted road. For all the trooper knew he had a trunkful of dope and a semiautomatic under the seat.

"Afternoon, officer," he said when the trooper stopped a few feet away. Standard traffic stop procedure, Grady noted with satisfaction. Too far to be knocked over by the car door, far enough to get to his weapon fast. He squinted at the silver name tag pinned to the starch-crisp shirt. He knew a lot of state cops, some by name, some by reputation. He opened a file for Officer Jansing to the list he kept in his head.

"The Indy 500 was last month, buddy."

Now *that* was original, he thought as he tossed the guy a friendly grin. "You're telling me. I dropped two big ones when the rookie from Portugal took the checkered flag."

Unmoved, Jansing narrowed his gaze behind the Rambo shades. His heavy Hoosier twang marked him as a longtime native. "License and registration, please."

Resigned to paying for his fun, Grady handed over the registration, then flipped open the leather case containing both his driver's license and professional ID.

"James Grady Hardin," he read aloud from the registration now clipped to his board, then frowned and glanced up curiously. "*Captain* Hardin, Lafayette PD? The guy who took down that scumbag drug lord, Rustakov? The one they call the Mad Russian?"

"'Fraid so."

Jansing swallowed hard, reminding Grady of himself when he'd busted a deputy chief for being drunk and disorderly in a topless bar. Twenty-four hours later he found himself called on the carpet for being disrespectful to a superior, something that was wasn't going to happen to this eager youngster.

"Sorry for not recognizing you right away, sir. Me and the other guys were rooting for you when you were in intensive care."

"I appreciate it."

"Too bad the DA couldn't get the Mad Russian himself, instead of settling for that wimp son of his," the trooper declared in a disgusted tone. "But like the sarge says, it's an election year."

"Your sergeant's right. A prosecutor who blows a high-profile case is dead meat."

It wasn't the first time DA Ray Harrangh had gone for the slam dunk instead of the hard slog. Grady had all but gotten down on his knees and begged, but Harrangh had his eye on the governor's chair.

"Heard Rustakov is trying to wrangle his son a new trial."

"Won't happen. Sergei's gonna be an old man before he walks through those big iron gates."

The officer's grin had a cynical slant. "Nice to win one now and then."

"Yeah."

Russian-born Boris Rustakov had made a fortune smuggling heroin into the slums of Moscow before coming to the States with his son, Sergei, leaving his wife and daughters behind. His MO was a particularly nasty one. He targeted college campuses, using young, good-looking pushers to pass out junk at fraternity parties. In some kind of perverse reversal of status, heroin had become the drug of choice among the well-fed, well-tended students.

It had taken Grady a solid two-years of crawling around Lafayette's underbelly to set up the sting that brought the bastard down. The trial had ended last week. Sergei Rustakov was on his way to do fifteen hard ones, thanks to twelve hardworking citizens who considered the attempted murder of a policeman a serious crime.

Grady agreed. He'd been the one who'd taken two slugs from Sergei's .357 Magnum. The damage had been massive, the blood loss severe. He shouldn't have lived. Even the doctors had been surprised when he'd survived. The wicked scar puckering one side of his chest had made a vivid impression on the jury. Grady's testimony had sealed Sergei's fate.

Justice had been a long time coming. For the past twenty-four months, he'd spent more time on the streets or in smoky bars than he'd spent at home. Ria had been patient at first, but when he'd missed both Jimmy's third birthday *and* their anniversary dinner, she'd turned prickly. He couldn't blame her. Hell, he knew he'd been a lousy husband and a worse father.

But all that was over.

Life was looking up. He had fourteen days to spend mending fences.

The officer watched a cattle truck rattle by, leaving a ripe smell of fresh manure behind, then returned his gaze to Grady again. He looked acutely uncomfortable. "The thing is, sir, I clocked you at ninety-eight in a fifty-five zone."

"That's about right," Grady admitted. "Figured with

this nice stretch of road, no cross streets, I'd blow out some carbon.''

The trooper grinned. He was younger than Grady at first pegged. ''Beg pardon, Captain, but I radioed in this stop which puts me in a real bind. I really should issue a citation.''

Grady admired Jansing's integrity. ''Write it up, officer. I deserve it. You had me cold.''

''Yes, sir.''

The man's relief was obvious as he hastily bent his attention to the citation form. Grady checked his watch. He'd promised Ria he'd be home early enough to help her pack, but he'd gotten hung up. He'd meant to call. Damn, he had to start thinking like a husband instead of a cop.

The trooper, too, checked his watch, then scrawled the time and his signature on the citation before handing over the clipboard. ''Guess you know where to sign.''

''Guess I do.'' Grady scrawled his name and took his copy and ID before passing the board through the window again. Habit had him glancing at the fee schedule on the back of the citation.

''Ouch,'' he muttered as he folded the flimsy and tucked it into the pocket of his shirt. ''Looks like I'll be holding it down for a while.''

The trooper fought a grin. ''It's been a real honor meeting you, sir. Cops like you make us all proud.'' He flipped a crisp salute before turning on his heel to stride back to his cruiser.

After tucking his wallet into his pocket again, Grady glanced to his right where the half-grown cat was still watching him with unblinking eyes, clearly unimpressed. Careful not to make a quick move, he rubbed the scruffy fur between its ears. The kitten yawned.

''Hey, show some respect, Trouble. You're riding with

a gen-u-ine hero. Got my name in the paper and a nice shiny medal to prove it.''

The trooper waved as he drove past, and Grady tapped the horn before fastening his seat belt again. The big car protested the snail's pace, but he bit the bullet and kept to the limit all the way home.

Ria's van was in the driveway instead of the garage. The side door was open, a laundry basket of Jimmy's favorite sandbox toys on the floor. Item one on her list of things to be taken to the lake. Ria was compulsive about being organized.

''Stay cool while I soften her up,'' he told the cat before slipping out from under the wheel. After retrieving his briefcase and the bouquet from the back seat, he headed up the brick walk he'd laid the summer after they'd bought the big old farmhouse. At the end near the porch were Ria's prized rose bushes. Damask, Ria had called them when they'd first seen the place. Like that made them special.

While she'd been burying her face in the blossoms, he'd been mentally adding up the cost of repairs the neglected structure would need before it would be even marginally fit for habitation.

He'd had his arguments all ready, lined up all neat and tidy like recruits at muster—and then she'd lifted her gaze to his. As soon as he'd seen the dreamy look in her moss-green eyes, he knew he'd just bought a house. He'd signed the papers the next day.

He had his key in the lock before he realized the front door was ajar. He felt a tightening across his shoulders before he remembered the basket of toys. At least he was in time to carry the bags to the van for her.

Hiding the flowers behind his back, he nudged the door wide and walked in. He smelled dinner. Something with spices and tomato sauce. The TV was on in the family room at the back of the house. He recognized the music. Jimmy's favorite *Winnie the Pooh* video. The little dickens had talked his mom into letting him watch that sucker again, even though Ria had sworn she could recite the dialogue in her sleep.

"Ree? Sweetheart?"

There was no answer. Nothing but the muted sounds of Christopher Robin and his buddies. His mood spiked a little higher. When Jimmy was watching Pooh, nothing distracted him. Grady closed the door and twisted the deadbolt, then headed upstairs, already undressing Ria in his mind. Better yet, maybe she was grabbing a quick shower, the way she did sometimes when Jimmy was glued to the tube.

His mood heated at the thought of finding her naked and wet, her skin dewy from the steam. He figured he could shuck his clothes in two seconds flat and be inside her in three. His usually proper lady liked it that way sometimes. Fast and wild.

"Ria? Honey? Haven't you finished packing yet?"

There was no answer, and the smile in his mind died. "Ree, answer me."

Several stacks of neatly folded clothes lay on the bed next to a suitcase already half-full. The door to the walk-in closet was open, as was the bureau drawer where she kept her panties and bras.

He raked the room with a trained gaze, his mind icing at the edges. She wasn't in the bedroom. Nor, he discovered, in the master bathroom. Damn.

Worried, now, he dropped the flowers next to the suitcase and unsnapped the holster holding his .45. Moving quickly, his mind already ticking into well-worn grooves, he headed down the hall to Jimmy's room.

The door was ajar, the room beyond silent. The fear came hard and fast, like the slug that had taken him down. Almost as quickly, he blocked it out.

Heart thudding, he drew his weapon. Standing to one side, he used his free hand to nudge open the door. He saw the pint-size bed shaped like a squad car, small shirts and shorts, neatly folded.

He edged inside, then went cold. Ria was lying on the floor, in the fetal position. Her face was obscured by the dark curtain of tumbled hair. His heart wedged in his throat as he knelt down, his hand already reaching for her pulse.

She moaned then, and stirred. His hand shook as he lifted her hair away from her face. Her forehead was gashed, her eye already turning black. Blood oozed over half her face.

"Ria, baby. Wake up."

Her lashes fluttered open, and she stared up at him, her expression blank. And then suddenly, fear contorted her face, and she jerked.

"Oh, God, Grady," she cried, panic in her voice. "I heard a noise and...Jimmy! Where's Jimmy?" She darted a frantic look around the room, her fingers clawing at his arm as she struggled to sit up.

Grady gathered her into his arms and folded his body over her. "Calm down, baby. I need you to be strong for a minute, okay? I have to call this in."

"No, no, I have to find him!" She was amazingly strong all of a sudden, a mother desperate to find her son. His heart tore.

"Hold tight, sweetheart. I'll be right back."

Moving fast, his mind focused, he methodically checked each room, calling his son's name, opening closets, looking under beds and behind furniture.

Eyes narrowed, weapon ready, he circled the outside, checked the garage, the van, behind bushes.

Holstering the .45, he raced inside and up the stairs. Ria had made it to the bed where she sat bent over, her hand pressed to her head and her eyes closed. Concussion, he thought. And a stomach full of queasy eels.

He knew the signs.

He was halfway across the room when she jerked up her head and cried out. Her already-pale face turned a sickly gray.

"Ree, listen to me," he soothed as he dropped to his knees and took her icy hand in his. "Sweetheart, I need you to think back."

She blinked, then visibly swallowed down the nausea. "I'm…better," she whispered.

"Did you see anyone?" he asked slowly, carefully.

"No, no…one."

"A car in the drive?"

She shook her head, then winced.

"Did you hear a voice? Male, female?" He paused, his fear growing rapidly. "An accent?"

She blinked rapidly, her breathing shallow and too fast, but she made a valiant effort to control the panic. "I…nothing. I was packing…I heard Jimmy running down the hall and poked my head out to tell him to slow down." Her lips trembled, and she pressed them together for a moment.

"Take your time," he ordered, his mind already zoned into procedure.

"Jim-Jimmy told me he'd come up to get Pooh so they could watch his video together. I went back to my packing. I'd just opened your sock drawer when I heard Jimmy cry out. I called to him, but he didn't answer." She paused to take a deep breath, her hands clinging to his. "I walked into his room to check on him, but he wasn't there and then…I heard an odd swishing noise."

She flinched at the memory, and he went cold. "That's all I remember."

He drew his handkerchief from his back pocket and gently blotted the fresh blood from her temple. "Do you remember what time that was?"

Biting her lip, she considered. "It was past three when he got up from his nap. I dressed him for the drive to the lake, and I didn't want him getting dirty so I said he could watch Pooh one more time. Maybe…maybe twenty minutes later."

Give or take, two hours.

"Oh, Grady!" she cried, her eyes dark with dawning horror. "Why is this happening? Who…who would want to take our baby? Who?"

"We'll find him, sweetheart," he said as he scooped her gently into his arms. "I swear to you, we'll find him."

It was then, while trying to comfort her, that he saw the scrap of newspaper, lying next to one of Jimmy's sneakers. The clipping had been torn from the front page of the *Lafayette Journal-Courier*. Headlines screamed Sergei Rustakov's conviction. Scrawled in red pen across the picture of Sergei being led away in handcuffs were the words,

You were warned, policeman. Now you suffer as I suffer. You will never see your son again.

# *Chapter 1*

*Six months later*

The kidnappers had been pros. It was as though the earth had opened and swallowed their son. Once a KGB colonel before Glasnost had put him out of a job, Rustakov had always chosen his thugs with as much care as he'd once chosen assassins for the motherland. He'd layered his organization so well no one knew more than two or three other members.

In spite of thousands of man-hours put in by dozens of dedicated professionals over the past six months, the case was as cold as it had been on the day he'd found Ria on the floor.

Grady leaned back in his chair and closed his eyes. He was so tired the letters on the screen were jumping around worse than usual. It was so bad he'd had to sound each word out in his head, the way he'd done when he'd been learning to compensate for the dyslexia that had made his childhood a living hell.

Even Trouble had given up and abandoned his customary spot next to the monitor for the basket Ria had fixed for him near the heater vent. After some initial infection, the cat's leg had healed perfectly. Ria's pampering had turned the scrawny stray with a death wish into a fat, spoiled lap kitty.

Ria's lap, anyway.

These days, whenever Grady tried to pick him up, the ungrateful animal hissed and bared his claws. Not that Grady blamed him. Nobody had to tell him he was rotten company.

His family had started visiting Ria when he was at work. At the station house, everyone kept their distance. The officers under his command had taken to ducking into doors when he walked in.

Because of his reading problems he'd always been a plodder. He'd had to be, working longer hours than anyone else. These days he put in a good twelve hours a day behind his desk, sometimes more. The brutal hours tired his mind so that he was able to sleep a few hours every night. Most nights, anyway. But not even the long hours or the physical work he'd taken to doing around the house eased the grinding ache in his chest that was there when he woke up and still there when he went to bed.

Maybe it was time to take a few days off. Even though the weeks surrounding the end-of-year holidays were coveted vacation time, he had enough seniority to swing it. Heck, he was a detective captain now. Top brass, according to his baby brothers. He was entitled to some downtime.

And do what, hotshot? Listen to Ria chatter brightly about everything and anything but their son? Watch the big-screen TV that was supposed to be Jimmy's big Christmas surprise and think about the stack of Jimmy's videos gathering dust? Make a snowman and remember last Christmas when he and Jimmy had pelted Ria with snowballs?

In two days it would be Christmas. The enormous pine tree in the living room glowed with dozens of twinkle lights, strung with the same fierce absorption Ria brought to even the most inconsequential task these days.

Grady hadn't wanted the tree, or the bright decorations, damn near each one evoking memories of happier times. Or the elaborate family dinner she was hosting in two days' time. Ria had insisted. She needed to keep busy, she'd told him with a smile that invariably tore him to shreds. So he'd listened to her debate about menus and table settings and schedules—then he'd gone out and chopped wood for hours. Anything to keep from thinking too much.

Even though he understood what was driving her, he hated to see her wearing herself out. He guessed that polishing silver and baking yeast rolls from scratch was better than sitting on Jimmy's bed, holding the pillow that still carried his scent the way she had for weeks and weeks after their little boy had been stolen.

Grady hadn't been in the room since the crime scene tape had come down. There was no need. He'd memorized every empty inch on the day he'd found Ria on the floor.

He and Ria rarely spoke about their son. When they did, he usually ended up picking a fight so that he could stalk out. He could handle her anger. But the terrible grief she was trying to hide was slowly tearing him apart. Worst of all were those times when the phone rang and she bolted to answer it, both fear and hope alive in her eyes. It was becoming more than he could handle. God help him, he sometimes wished she hated him.

After those first rocky days during which he was running mostly on rage, coffee and drags on borrowed cigarettes, he'd ruthlessly pared his emotions to the ones that kept him from falling apart—rage, mostly.

He worked, he slept when he could, ate because he had to, and put in endless hours, talking to anyone and everyone he could think of who might have information to offer.

Over and over he reminded himself that good police work was more about tenacity and hard, slogging work than brilliance. The system was often ponderous and slow, but it worked more often than most civilians realized.

Tonight he'd added a good two dozen more printouts to the inch-high stack already on file. Tomorrow he would make calls to the contacts listed on the sheets and repeat his story one more time.

He'd spent so many butt-numbing hours sitting in the dimly lit den, staring at the flickering images on the computer screen while methodically searching the various web sites on the Internet devoted to missing children he'd been forced to start wearing reading glasses to keep from suffering blinding headaches. Just his luck the headache had hit anyway, pounding like a sledge inside his skull. Maybe a drink...

Suddenly he realized he wasn't alone. Ria was standing just inside the door to his den with her dark hair mussed from the pillow and her pink fuzzy slippers peaking out from the hem of her flannel robe. Her arms were crossed over her too-thin waist, and her eyes were drowsy smudges in her pale face.

"Grady, it's nearly 4:00 a.m."

Her soft voice was flavored with the musical vowels of the south, a legacy from the years she'd spent growing up in a series of foster homes in Louisville. In spite of her impoverished background and a mother who'd gradually spiraled into madness, she carried herself like a lady. Folks just naturally watched their manners when she was around.

Even his rambunctious brothers cleaned up their language in her presence.

"Go back to bed, honey," he urged, his voice rusty. "I just want to get through the rest of these leads."

She directed a weary glance at the file folder on his desk. "You've been through them so many times the paper is transparent from handling. If there was anything there, you would have found it."

Her confidence in him broke his heart.

"We just need a little luck, Ree. Someplace to start. Maybe a guy pumping gas who sees a little boy in the back seat and then remembers the flyer he's just taped to the station window. Or a mom in the park someplace watching a bunch of kids playing and sees a new kid who looks a lot like the picture on the milk carton she'd picked up at the market earlier."

He shifted in his chair, wanting to beg her not to give up on him. To give him a little more time. But what good would that do? So far he was working on maybes and might-bes.

"One of the staffers at the children's hotline gave me a list of private investigators who specialize in missing kids. A couple have pretty impressive records."

Looking anything but convinced, Ria padded across the patterned rug she'd found in a little antique shop near Lake Freeman. She waited until she reached the circle of the light cast by the desk lamp before asking in the quick, nervous voice he'd come to expect from her, "You think that might help? Hiring a…a private eye?"

He couldn't lie to her. He also couldn't admit he was so desperate at this point he was seriously considering a call to a psychic recommended by a sheriff in Fort Wayne.

"Guys who work private have more time. Instead of twenty cases screaming for attention they can work one at a time."

She drew a breath, her gaze fixed on the papers and folders littering the big desk. She smelled pretty and delicate, like the roses that were her pride and joy. His gut knotted as the memory of the last time he'd bought her flowers.

"Can we pay for a detective and still offer the reward?"

The department had started a fund to augment the forty thousand he'd been able to raise by cashing in his retirement policy and savings. After the first of the year, Ria was going back to work for the Indiana Department of Social Services in order to add her salary to the fund.

"I've talked to Ted Ford at the bank. He's pretty sure we have enough equity in this place for a loan."

She hugged herself more tightly as she leaned forward, her face soft as she gazed at the photo of Jimmy in the flyer. A grinning, happy three-year-old in a miniature Indianapolis Colts jersey, standing in a patch of summer sunshine. Grady had taken the picture himself, only a few days before their son's disappearance. Everyone who saw it remarked on what a good-looking little boy he was. The spitting image of his dad.

Taller than average, he had broad shoulders and a sturdy build already showing the promise of a muscular physique. His hair was one shade lighter than Grady's own dusty blond, his eyes the same odd shade of golden-brown that all five of the Hardin brothers shared. His heart ached with a mixture of fatherly pride and anguish. If anything happened to his son, he wasn't sure he'd come out on the other side sane.

"I can still see the look on his face when you brought home the shirt," she murmured, her voice breaking.

"Jersey," he corrected, just the way he'd laughingly corrected her that day. Right before he and his son exchanged a smug "what does a woman know about football anyway" look.

*Teach me to throw, Daddy,* Jimmy had begged, his eyes as bright as new pennies. But Grady had set a meeting with a snitch, and the man had been waiting.

*This weekend,* he'd promised. But he'd been setting up a buy that weekend.

*Next Sunday for sure.* He'd been twelve hours into a stakeout when he'd remembered the promise he'd tossed off so casually.

He'd learned later that Jimmy had stood on the porch all day, with his football in his hand. Waiting.

He drew a hard breath. He wasn't sure he could hate himself more than he hated himself at this moment.

"Did...did he ever learn to throw a spiral?" he asked, his gaze riveted to his son's smile.

"After a fashion. He...he wanted to surprise you when we were at the lake."

He felt the sting of tears behind his eyes and lowered his gaze. "I, uh, just have a few more web sites to check. I'll be up in a minute."

"Please, Grady. I'm tired of sleeping alone." She touched his shoulder, something she did so rarely these days he flinched.

Ria carefully withdrew her hand and stepped back. "We can't go on like this." The pain in her voice tore at him, but somehow he couldn't make himself move. "I can't handle losing my son and fight for my marriage, too."

The emotion that gripped him felt too much like the panic of a cornered animal. Somehow he fought it down. "Our marriage is fine, Ree. I'm just...tired."

"I'm tired, too," she said softly, but with enough steel in her tone to have him glancing up. She waited until his gaze found hers before continuing. "I'm tired of fixing meals you don't eat, tired of watching the man I love work himself to death so he doesn't have to feel. I'm tired of living with a man who cringes whenever I touch him."

"For God's sake, Ree," he muttered, his jaw hard. "You should know better than that."

Ria ignored the stiff plea in his tone, her patience finally and irrevocably exhausted. For weeks—months—she'd been powerless to keep this strong, honorable man from flaying himself alive for something that wasn't his fault. Day after day he drew deeper into himself, aging before her eyes. She'd tried everything she could think of to help him. Nothing worked.

She decided she had nothing to lose. Her marriage had been slipping away for years now due to Grady's constant work. Yet the thought of ending it was so painful she'd pushed it farther and farther into the back of her mind.

"But you know what I'm tired of most, Grady?" She moved closer, crowding him, forcing him to listen. "I'm tired of wondering how long you plan to hide behind those walls of self-pity you've built around yourself."

Something dangerous leaped into his eyes, and alarm raced through her. It was a look she'd never seen before, a look she suspected was as much a part of him as the ugly black gun that rode his hip. For an instant she wondered if she'd pushed too hard.

He'd shown her anger before, but never this icy fury. She took a breath, made herself stand steady. But then, as she watched, he slowly absorbed the anger, drawing it inside like a banked fire.

"I'm trying to find our son," he said in a voice as controlled as the rage. "Is that so wrong?"

"Of course not! But what happens if you don't? Are we going to spend the rest of our lives creeping around the house like mourners at a funeral? Not speaking his name, preserving his room like a shrine?"

He shoved back his chair and stood. His jaw was tight, his gaze fixed on the papers he shoveled into his open briefcase. "This conversation is pointless. We'll only end up saying things we'll regret."

He was shutting her out again. Deliberately, coldly ignoring her needs. She realized she preferred the anger.

"It's almost Christmas. Jimmy should be here, yes! He should be making his list for Santa and helping me bake cookies. I miss..." She felt her throat close, and paused to clear away the sudden burst of tears. "I pray every night that...that wherever he is, he's being treated well."

His face contorted, and for an instant he looked destroyed before he pulled her into his arms.

"Don't, Ria, please don't."

She fought the resurgence of tears, even as her body trembled. His big hand stroked her back, while the warmth of his body seeped through her robe. It felt so good to be in his arms again. To forget for a few moments that they'd been drawing farther and farther apart. That his obsession with proving himself as good a cop as his father and brothers wasn't driving them inexorably apart.

"Remember the first Christmas we spent in this house?" she murmured against his chest. "I was pregnant with Jimmy and we hung this tiny stocking for him on the mantel. And then you made a big fire and we made love in front of the hearth."

His breath was ragged. "You caught cold."

She choked a laugh before pulling away. "And you fed me chicken soup and virgin hot toddies."

His mouth slanted, and his face softened—and then, suddenly, she saw the flash of guilt. When Jimmy was born, he'd fought tears as he'd sworn to take care of them both. He felt he'd failed, and it was destroying him.

If she lost him, too...

"Make love to me, Grady," she pleaded almost desperately. "It's been so long. I need to be close to you."

Grady heard the quick little catch in her voice and knew what it was like to be staked out and bleeding.

It wasn't that he didn't want her. God knew he did, sometimes so desperately he'd ached with his need for her. But it seemed wrong, somehow, to feel pleasure while the room down the hall remained empty.

"Ree, it's late—"

"Don't push me away. Not tonight."

Asking for what she needed shouldn't be so difficult, she told herself as she drew back. Grady was her husband, the man who'd taught her how wonderful physical love could be.

They'd made love countless times in dozens of places. Jimmy had been conceived in a patch of clover on a deserted island in the middle of Lake Freeman while Fourth of July fireworks had burst overhead.

In spite of the growing distance between them, they'd always had a wonderful sex life. Grady was a tender, thoughtful lover. When he was touching her, kissing her, he allowed the gentle, tender side of his nature to emerge. That was the man who'd won her, the man who'd looked at her with so much longing and love she'd felt like the luckiest woman in the world.

She needed that man now. Needed him desperately.

She was used to fighting long odds. The statistics she'd studied in graduate school predicted that she would end up like her mother—uneducated, pregnant, on welfare. Instead she'd put herself through six years of college, graduating with honors and a satisfying number of job offers.

She'd also been a virgin when she'd married Grady.

Now she was fighting long odds again. Odds that said the distance between the two of them had grown too deep to be bridged. That the love they'd shared before his job had come between them was dead.

Her hands shook as she worked the knot of her robe.

When the sash hung loose, she slipped the heavy flannel from her shoulders and let it fall to the floor. Her gown was cotton jersey, soft enough to reveal the contours of her breasts.

His eyes turned hot, and his chest heaved as he drew in a ragged breath.

"I need you tonight, Grady."

Holding his gaze, she reached for the button at her throat, but he lifted his hand to push hers away. His fingers were too big and too rough to be deft. As he eased the gown from her shoulders, the calluses snagged on the thin material.

She shivered, not from the cold but from desire. It was wildly exciting to know that this tough man with the hard edges and brutally scarred, powerful body wanted her.

He lowered his head, and his kiss was hard, just shy of angry. Yet his tongue was sweet as he drew it slowly along the curve of her mouth, sending slow waves of the sweetest sensation spiraling through her. Her legs went watery, she clung to him, her fingers pushing against the lean, hard muscle of his neck. Her pulse was roaring in her ears, and fire flickered low and deep inside her.

She felt the give in him, the sudden release of control. He growled deep in his throat, a feral urgent sound that ran along her nerve endings like a current.

Need slammed into Grady like a series of vicious punches. The control that was his only defense shuddered, then broke. He buried his hands in her hair, holding her still for his mouth. He used his tongue, his lips.

A dark, angry emotion raced through him as he opened his mouth over the tender curve of her neck. He didn't know if it was love or hate or something in between. He only knew she was making him feel again, and it hurt. Yet, he couldn't stop kissing her, couldn't stop wanting her.

She groaned, her hands frantic, jerking his shirt free of

his jeans. Her finger raced over his belly, sending ripples of sensation through him.

His body swelled. The pressure inside him was close to unbearable. His skin burned for her. His blood throbbed. He was too close to shattering now for patience.

He let her go long enough to swing her into his arms. He carried her with powerful, impatient strides to the thick rug in front of the living room hearth, now cold. Later he would build her the fire she wanted. Later he would soothe and pet. Now there was only the need to bury his pain in that soft willing body.

He jerked her gown to her waist, then glanced up. Her face was pale, her eyes glazed, her lips swollen and parted. His hand fumbled with the buttons of his fly. Too aroused to strip, he hooked his thumbs in the waistband and jerked the material to his thighs.

His need was a living thing. He'd been so lonely, so lost. Only Ria could heal him. His body surged free, and he moved over her. He closed his eyes and thrust into her.

She cried out, her body arching. And then he was pounding into her. She trembled, cried out. Through the haze of desire he realized she was sobbing.

He froze, struggling to contain the need clawing him. Her eyes were squeezed shut, her face lined and pale. Slowly he withdrew with shuddering slowness, trying not to hurt her any more than he already had. A hot knot formed in his gut as he shifted to her side. His hand shook as he drew the gown over her legs, his heart contracting when he noticed the discoloration of bruised skin.

Sick inside, the self-loathing sharp and twisting, he fastened his jeans, then leaned down to brush her hair from her wet cheek. He used his fingers to wipe away her tears, then bent to brush his mouth over her temple.

"Forgive me," he begged, his voice raw.

Her smile was terribly sad. "It's over, isn't it? What we had."

He couldn't quite meet her gaze. "We've hit a rough patch, Ree. What's happened is hard on both of us."

"No, it's more than that." She sat up and pulled up her legs. Her face was unnaturally pale. "Somehow we've just lost each other. When we had Jimmy, it didn't matter as much, but now…" She paused to draw breath. "We're just two people who share a house and some very precious memories."

She was ending their marriage, and all he could feel was relief that he no longer had to face her every morning.

# Chapter 2

*Two and a half years later*

Grady spotted the federal narc the instant he stepped off the tarmac into the gloomy interior of the Imperial Valley International Airport's only terminal. A good-looking Latino of average height, with a wiry body and enough attitude to make even the toughest barrio hustler scurry for cover, he'd been leaning against a pillar just beyond the glassed-in waiting area, eyes hidden behind dark shades.

As Grady approached, the man straightened and moved into his path. It was a smooth move, a subtle power play. Though Grady was a head taller and a good fifty pounds heavier, this was the narc's turf, the narc's rules.

Play it his way or not at all came through loud and clear.

Grady decided he liked the little guy's style.

"You looking for me?" he asked, meeting the eyes that were scrutinizing him through the smoked lenses.

"I am if your name is Hardin."

"That's one of them. I prefer Grady."

"Fair enough." The man's grin flashed as he offered his hand. "I'm Cruz. Cruz Mendoza. Welcome to Calexico."

"I appreciate the lift," Grady told him as they shook hands.

"Glad to do it. Guys like me usually see the dirty side of this business. It's nice to be part of a happy ending."

"It's not happy yet," Grady reminded him as they walked past a line of check-in counters, most of which were still empty. The bone-jarring, stomach jolting commuter flight from LAX was the first of the day.

"Don't get me wrong, Captain, but you look like a man in desperate need of coffee."

Grady summoned enough of a smile to keep the man's goodwill. After twelve hours en route, two delays and three flights, he was feeling a little punch-drunk. "Thanks, but I'm already wired."

The truth was he would kill for a sip. Hell, even a whiff of caffeine would give him a high these days. But for the past couple of months his gut had taken a strong dislike to the stuff.

"Is that it for luggage?" Mendoza asked, indicating the worn, olive drab duffel bag passed down from his dad who'd been a sailor during the Korean War.

"That's it."

Grady arched his aching back to work out the kinks, then slung his duffel over his shoulder and walked with the agent out of the terminal into a blaze of summer sunshine. It had been drizzling in Indiana when he'd left. A sodden, gray, miserable day in a long string of miserable days.

He fished a pair of shades from his shirt pocket and slipped them on. A hot southwestern wind flavored with grit slapped him across the face as he followed the wiry agent to a dirty brown Jeep with pitted fenders and a broken taillight parked in a red zone.

"Border Patrol found it stuck in the mud a few miles

west,'' Mendoza said with a wry grin. "No VIN, no plates. Blends in real good south of the border.''

Grady tossed the duffel into the back and slid into the bucket seat. The Jeep smelled like damp sweat socks and stale hamburger grease. A desert emergency kit was tucked into one corner of the cramped space behind the seat. A dark blue windbreaker was shoved into another. Between the two was a jumble of boots, dirt-encrusted sneakers and a faded DEA ball cap.

Oblivious to the litter, Mendoza slipped easily behind the wheel and slammed the door. "The couple picked up with the boy are at the county jail. I figured you'd want to talk to the prosecutor who caught the case, so I made a tentative appointment to meet her at noon at the courthouse.''

"Thanks.''

"Bastards lawyered-up first thing. Some high-powered suit from LA.''

"What about bail?''

"Two mil. They'll be a while making it.''

"I'll want to see them.''

"Figured you would,'' Mendoza said with a satisfied grin. "You want to head for the motel first?''

Grady glanced at his watch which he'd set to Pacific time someplace over the Rockies. It was a few minutes past seven. "If it's all the same with you, I'll like to see the boy.''

"Figured you'd say that, too.'' Mendoza turned the key, fired the engine. "He's with a foster couple at the far edge of town. Good people.''

The narc checked the mirror, then sped off, leaving a cloud of fumes behind. So much for California's clean-air act, Grady thought as he shifted position, trying to stretch the kinks out of his legs.

Too many hours jammed into a series of economy-class seats with his chin damn near resting on his knees had

numbed his backside, while the endless hours of not knowing had slowly, inexorably twisted his gut into a searing
knot. Taking shallow breaths against the pain, he dug into
the pocket of his windbreaker for the antacids that were his
constant companion these days.

He was supposed to be in Indianapolis for a statewide
meeting of police captains and inspectors this morning. No
doubt he'd hear about that from the brass when he got back
home. At the moment he didn't give a rat's ass. His obsession to prove himself worthy of the Hardin legacy had
been the worst mistake of his admittedly misbegotten life.
Right now, this instant, he'd willingly trade his captain's
bars for his son's safe return. Hell, he'd even turn in his
badge if that would bring Jimmy home again.

The first time he'd snagged a "maybe" from a kiddy
cop in St. Louis, he'd felt honor bound to call Ria to let
her know. And, yeah, maybe he'd wanted her to know he
wasn't sitting on his duff, licking his wounds and feeling
sorry for himself.

It hadn't surprised him when she'd insisted on going with
him. Though she looked as delicate as the lacy veil she'd
worn over her shimmery brown hair at their wedding, she
had the soul of a warrior in that tidy little body. When life
took a punch at her, she doubled up those small hands and
fought back.

Sometimes, though, no matter how many punches you
landed, you couldn't win. When the child had turned out
to belong to someone else, the disappointment had ripped
open a lot of wounds for both of them. Since then, he'd
checked out the leads alone.

Twelve times in the past three years he'd climbed on a
plane in response to a "maybe" from a fellow cop who'd
seen the flyers he'd mailed out by the hundreds every
month. Twelve times he'd walked into a strange room with
his heart in his throat and his gut in a knot. Twelve times

he'd walked away disappointed, fighting to keep from pounding his fists into hamburger.

The divorce had been final for more than two years. The farmhouse belonged to someone else now. He and Trouble shared a place near the Purdue campus. Ria had rented a town house overlooking the Wabash. As far as he knew, she lived alone. His parents never talked about her love life. He sure as hell never asked.

She was a career woman now, the administrative director of the Wabash Women's Center, which she'd founded a little more than a year back with two friends from grad school.

He'd read about the opening in the paper. The mayor herself had cut the ribbon. Everyone in his family had been there but him.

He hadn't been invited.

When the two of them met at family functions, they were polite to each other. When they spoke about something related to the search, they did it by phone. She'd stopped asking him if there were any clues, any leads.

Each time he'd had to disappoint her, the hope in her eyes had dimmed a little more. He was terrified that someday that hope would be gone forever.

"The foster parents are expecting us, right?" he challenged, his voice a shade too rough. Mendoza shot him a measuring look before nodding.

"Social worker'll be there, too. Guy by the name of Tsung. I got hold of him on his cell phone right before your plane landed, gave him an ETA. He's bringing the report from the kiddy shrink."

"Has...the boy said anything?"

"Not much beyond crying for his mama. I mean, the piece of human slime he *thinks* is his mama." Mendoza's voice was surprisingly gentle. Grady liked him for that. "You ever been to this part of the country before?"

Mendoza continued after a couple of minutes of tense silence during which Grady sucked on chalk and took stock of his surroundings.

"Nope."

Mendoza braked to keep from ramming the back of a slow-moving truck, whose bed was piled with watermelons. Pickers were already in the fields lining the road, their backs bent as they moved down the rows. In the distance a biplane swooped low, leaving a trail of white behind.

"I grew up here. Picked my share of tomatoes before I got smart and hit the books."

Grady heard the rueful note and sympathized. "Reminds me of northern Indiana." Lots of fields, lots of dust and plenty of backbreaking labor for not much pay. "My brothers and I used to pick up extra money summers threshing hay." He could still feel that maddening, itchy feeling between his shoulder blades where the chaff invariably settled, no matter how tightly he tied the bandanna around his neck.

"Sorry about the lag time on notification." Mendoza flicked him a quick look. "Budget cuts hit us hard this year, and we're short three agents in this district. Me and my partner have been in Mexicali for the past week, which is why I didn't get to the arrest report until yesterday."

Grady didn't want to think about other times, other places when overworked public servants just might have overlooked a vital clue. "System works slow sometimes. Sometimes it doesn't work at all. This time maybe we got lucky."

In response to a tip, Border Patrol had checked out a couple from San Diego by the name of Wilson. The guy who'd dropped the quarter swore the "Wilsons" were seasoned moles, real pros at smuggling junk into Calexico from the Mexican sister city of Mexicali.

The drug-sniffing shepherd had found the neatly wrapped

bricks of heroin in the hollowed-out seats of the late-model van and called DEA. In the back seat had been a six-year-old, blond, brown-eyed male who'd given his name as Steven Wilson.

The couple claimed to live in San Diego, but the local authorities hadn't been able to scare up any school records or next of kin. The alert caseworker from child welfare had flagged the case for further investigation.

The arrest report had sat on Mendoza's desk for ninety-six bleeping hours. Hours that must have seemed like a lifetime to a scared little boy stuck in a foster home with strangers.

"As soon as I saw the boy, I knew there was a strong possibility he was the kid in the picture you sent." Mendoza slowed to let a rust-bucket pickup chug past before turning into a narrow street lined with stucco and timber duplexes. "Your son was three when he was kidnapped, right?"

"Right."

"Damn amazing what computers can do these days." Mendoza shook his head. "Showing what a three-year-old would look like at six. Impresses the heck out of me, that's for sure."

"Actually, that particular picture was real. My dad took it of me when I was six."

"Yeah? Guess that means your boy looks like you?"

"Darn near identical. My wife…ex-wife…had our baby pictures framed side by side. Not even my folks could tell which was which."

But Ria could tell. She claimed it was a mom thing. Part of the bonding process. Ria had been big on bonding. Hell, she'd even bonded with her rose bushes. Her prized babies belonged to someone else now.

"It was the half-moon birthmark that jogged my memory," Mendoza confided, braking for a stop sign. "Remembered reading about it before in the memo my boss sent around about a year back. Said you'd called him direct to ask us to keep an eye peeled. Then when I read the new flyer, it clicked.''

Grady reached for the roll of antacids again. How many similar calls had he made? Hundreds? Thousands? Damn near maxed out his Visa card paying toll charges. If he had to, he'd beg the bank to raise his credit limit—and work security to make the payments.

''Tell me about this couple you picked up,'' he said, glancing Mendoza's way.

''Not a lot to tell yet, Captain.'' The agent checked the mirror, then pulled out to pass an ancient VW bus with Mexican plates. ''IDs are in the names of Moira and Lance Wilson, good forgeries, but phony. Anglos, both of them. Mid-thirties, fancy label, teeth-bonded types. Claimed to own a gift shop in Old Town San Diego, and in fact they do have part interest, though some guy named Barger runs it. Retro-hippie type, no known record. Way I figure it the 'Wilsons' bought into the shop in order to use the buying trips as a cover for their trips south. Had the back of the van piled with pots and wrought iron, typical Mexican exports. Claimed to be man and wife—until the computer spit out a long list of aliases. Don't know for sure what names are on their original birth certificates, but we're checking. Far as we can tell, they've never made it to the altar—at least not together. There's also no record of children born to either of them.''

Grady fought a surge of excitement. Mixing emotion with logic was a rookie mistake. He'd taken a bullet once because he'd ignored that basic fact.

''You dig up anything to suggest a link to Rustakov?''

''Not yet.'' Mendoza braked, checked for traffic, then swung the Jeep into a driveway on the left. ''This is it,'' he said as he cut the engine. "In a few minutes you'll know."

"Nights are the worst. I...I hear her c-crying, and I get up to go to her but—" Brenda Benteen's voice broke, and she buried her face in her hands.

Several of the other women seated in a ragged circle around the basement room fought their own tears. The newest member of the group, Anne Williams, a strikingly beautiful high-school senior who'd once dreamed of being Miss America before she'd had an illegitimate stillborn child, bit her lip as she passed the tissue box to the now sobbing Brenda.

Seated across the room, Ria waited for the woman to regain her composure and thought about the support group that had gotten her through those first terrible months after Jimmy's disappearance.

The paralyzing grief was gone—time's greatest blessing—but the pain was always with her. There hadn't been a day pass when she didn't think about her child and wonder if he was happy and healthy. His memory was with her constantly, even now. His lopsided smile, the soft brown eyes that sparkled with life and happiness, the sturdy body that was always in motion.

Going back to work had saved her.

Wabash Women's Center had started small, offering support groups for newly divorced women and single moms, plus confidence workshops and counseling, which Ria as a licensed social worker ran herself. Tova Jones, Ria's best friend and fellow Purdue alumna, ran the job-training program which included career planning and placement. Internist Dr. Katherine Stevens ran the open-door clinic. Volunteers and teacher interns from Purdue supervised the preschool and day care programs.

Since the center had been Ria's idea, her fellow directors

steamrollered her into acting as chief administrator, which was a fancy title meaning she got to spend fourteen hours a day juggling the bills and scrambling for donations—when she wasn't filling in for the volunteers who helped staff the day care center or counseling new clients.

Brenda had first come to Healing Friends three months ago, her eyes still red and swollen, and her face pasty white from lack of sleep. Her attendance had been sporadic since then. In spite of Ria's encouragement and support, however, the painfully shy twenty-three-year-old waitress had never been comfortable enough to say more than her name. Instead, she'd sat with her gaze focused on the hands she kept tightly folded in her lap, listening intently to the others as they poured out stories of pain and loss and grief.

Tonight, however, something seemed to have broken inside her, and words spilled out almost too fast for her to control. Ria considered it an extremely positive sign.

"I'm s-sorry," Brenda mumbled as she scrubbed tears from her blotchy cheeks.

"Never apologize for sharing your emotions," she told Brenda gently but firmly.

"Heck, no, honey," exclaimed the imposing woman sitting to Brenda's right on the shabby brown sofa.

Calpurnia Glendon was six feet two inches of exuberant, outspoken, gloriously flamboyant female who was fond of brilliant colors and large, clunky jewelry she designed herself. Eighteen months earlier, on Christmas Eve, she'd lost her husband and twin sons in a fire. She'd been in the group from the beginning and now acted as Ria's co-facilitator. "Me, I blubbered my eyes out for the first six weeks I was here."

"Actually, I think it was more like eight," Ria said, thanking her with a look. Callie grinned before she turned back to Brenda, who was now busily kneading the used tissue in nervous fingers. "It's all right, Brenda. Take your time. We're here to listen."

Brenda nodded, then cleared her throat. "Missy was just lying there, like…like a little doll baby. I'd just gotten her this little pink sleeper, and she looked so sweet. Even…even Monk thought she looked real nice like. 'Wake up, little lazy bones,' I said, and then bent down to kiss her on the little tuft of hair, like I always did, you know? And then I noticed she…she—" She faltered to a stop, her face twisting with anguish.

Ria ached for the suffering woman. The other seven women in the support group waited, their expressions uniformly solemn.

"Is Monk your husband?" Annie asked in a timid voice.

"For almost a year now." Brenda dropped her gaze to her hands. "My mother, she keeps saying he's no good because he didn't want the baby at first, but he's a real good guy, Monk is."

Callie snorted. "Get your head outta the clouds, girl. The man threatened to *leave* you if you didn't stop coming to our group here."

Brenda brought her head up to glare at the older woman. Ria dropped her gaze, hiding her surprise. Callie and Brenda had obviously spoken outside of class. It happened that way, sometimes. Callie took her responsibility seriously and often phoned members of the group when they were absent, to check on them.

"I told you, Callie," Brenda declared with a rare passion, "he didn't mean it. He just gets these moods sometimes. From all the stress and stuff he went through in Desert Storm. And he has terrible headaches, he can't sleep and or eat and the littlest noise hurts something awful, which is why I know he sometimes—" She broke off to bite her lip.

"Sometimes what?" Ria probed in a gentle tone.

Brenda darted a nervous glance around the room before dropping her gaze to the tissue she was shredding. "Nothing," she muttered, her shoulders stiff.

"He hits you, don't he, girl?" Callie declared, her voice flat.

"No! That's a mean thing to say."

"Ain't mean if it's true."

"Well, it's not!" Brenda twisted in her chair, her face contorting. "You're just like that policeman, trying to make me say things about Monk that aren't true."

Ria caught Callie's quick glance. "What policeman, Brenda?"

Brenda started. "The one the paramedics called when they…after…" She stuttered to a stop, her face losing the color her outburst had brought to her cheeks. "The cop, he kept asking me did Monk ever lose his temper with Missy? I told him Monk yelled sometimes, but it's like, he's got a right, you know? Him working so hard to provide for me and the baby and all."

Ria felt a chill. "Are you saying the authorities think Missy might have been murdered?"

Brenda flinched. "The coroner, he said it was natural causes. You know, SIDS?" She glanced up, her expression beseeching and a little lost. The other women nodded their understanding.

"At least your husband hung around," Annie said in a thin voice. "My boyfriend split as soon as he found out I was pregnant. Quit school and joined the Army."

"How about your folks?" Sylvia asked quietly.

From the corner of her eye Ria saw the relief that passed over Brenda's face as the group's focus shifted away from her. For the rest of the hour Brenda stared in silent misery at the floor, alone with her own memories. As soon as the meeting ended, she bolted from her chair and headed for the door.

Ria had been giving Annie a hug when she saw Brenda rush past. "Excuse me a minute, Annie," Ria said, hurrying after the fleeing woman.

She caught up with her an instant before Brenda reached the stairs leading to the ground floor.

"Brenda, wait!"

Brenda spun around, her face ravaged by tears. "It wasn't my fault, Ria. Missy was almost out of diapers, and I had to go to the market for more. She usually slept a couple of hours, so I figured I'd be back before she started to cry."

She swiped at her wet cheeks with a trembling hand. She was clearly agitated, which was understandable. It was the raw fear in Brenda's pale blue eyes that had alarm bells ringing in Ria's head.

"Did she cry a lot?" she asked with a gentle smile.

Brenda nodded. "It wasn't so bad when Monk was on the road, but when he's home, he needs his sleep, you know? 'Specially after he's been out on a long haul." She stopped, her gaze darting past Ria's shoulder. "I've got to go." Before Ria could stop her, she turned and raced up the stairs.

"There's bad stuff going down in that girl's life," Callie said as she reached Ria's side. "Might be we don't see her again."

"We can't force her to come, Cal. All we can do is be supportive when she's here."

While Callie collected several foam cups that had been left under the chairs, Ria emptied the coffee urn into the sink in the small rest room at the end of the hall and wiped it clean.

In the room opposite, Tova was conducting a job skills seminar. One floor up in what had once been the living room, dining room and kitchen, Kate was holding evening clinic. The Center was open until nine. Ria rarely made it home before eleven.

"I sure do hate what I'm thinkin'," Callie murmured as they climbed the stairs side by side.

When they reached the foyer, they stopped. The door to the clinic's waiting room was open, and Ria noted that most of the seats were filled. For the past six months Kate had been lobbying for a physician's assistant, but the budget was already stretched tissue thin.

Callie shifted her huge tapestry purse from one shoulder to the other. "When are you doing your back-to-nature gig? Tomorrow?"

"No, early Saturday morning." She flexed her tired shoulders. "I still can't believe I'm starting off my one and only vacation by spending two nights in a tent with ten other females."

The annual Big Sister-Little Sister campout was to be held in a state park near the Illinois border. As the deputy director for the greater Lafayette area, she'd felt obligated to participate—even though the ten-year-old girl who was her Little Sister had just come down with chicken pox and wouldn't be attending.

"I read this story once, about this fer-de-lance that crawled into a man's sleeping bag in the middle of the night and curled up on his belly. One twitch and the guy was dead. He had to lie there frozen for hours until the sun came up and the snake got too hot and finally crawled away." She shuddered. "I know I won't get a wink of sleep."

Callie chuckled. "I hope you like s'mores and rock music, girl, 'cause you sure are gonna get your fill of both."

"I thought about coming down with a sudden case of twenty-four-hour flu, but Betty Lou Sanberra would just knock down the door to my town house with those line-backer shoulders of hers and haul me out of bed."

Callie's grin was merciless. "Knowing you, you'll be right in the thick of things, roastin' weenies and sittin' around the campfire, telling those tired old urban legends about guys with hooks stalking lovers in parked cars and folks waking up in a bathtub full of ice and finding out they mislaid a kidney."

Ria had to laugh. She suspected Callie was right. "It's supposed to rain this weekend. The man at the sporting goods store swore that the tent he sold me was waterproof, but he couldn't quite look me in the eyes when he made that claim."

Callie laughed. "If it rains, maybe they'd call it all off."

"Not a chance. Betty Lou would simply consider mud camping a challenge."

At the door they exchanged hugs before Callie pulled open the door. A gust of wind scented with rain swirled around them, and they exchanged looks.

"Pray for clear skies," Ria muttered, shooting a fatalistic look at the sky. "Start tonight."

Callie's sultry mouth twitched. "Soon as I get home," she promised, before heading into the rising wind.

Ria frowned at the thick charcoal clouds faintly visible in the fading twilight before closing the door. Tova's seminar had apparently just ended, and noise swelled from below as the attendees spilled into the corridor. In the clinic waiting room a baby cried and a child laughed.

Turning to head upstairs, she spied a waif-thin teenager helping an elderly woman who was using a walker to inch her way across the foyer. On the sunset side of eighty, Ester Cocetti lived in a tiny frame bungalow across the street from the Center. In her salad days she'd been an exotic dancer in the wild and woolly days of Al Capone's Chicago.

Now crippled with osteoporosis and arthritis and struggling to exist on a tiny pension from her husband's job as a railway conductor, she'd been Kate's first patient. Since then, the garrulous widow had adopted them.

"Ria, dear," she said, drawing to a stop. "I was hoping to see you before your vacation."

"Hey, what's happening, boss lady?" Sixteen-year-old Tina Cocetti was spending the summer with her great-grandmother. As a favor to Mrs. Cocetti—and in spite of the added strain to their budget—Ria had hired the girl to do odd jobs. To her great surprise and delight, Tina had turned into a regular dynamo.

"Good evening, ladies," she said before leaning down to kiss the papery cheek Mrs. Cocetti presented. "Is this a routine visit, I hope?"

"Oh, yes, dear. Katie does mean well, but she fusses so."

"Gram's been having chest pains," Tina contradicted, earning her a look of rebuke, which she blithely ignored. "Dr. Kate said it was the chili peppers Gram insists on putting in everything."

Ria leveled a severe look at the woman she'd come to adore. "Now, Mrs. C.—"

"Don't you starting fussing, too. I'm perfectly fine." Mrs. C. patted Ria's arm. "I'm glad we ran into you, though. I wanted to ask you about that rabbity looking girl who went running out of here a few minutes ago. Poor thing looks like she could use a good iron supplement."

"Oh, Gram," Tina muttered, her gaze on a youth about her age seated just inside the waiting room, reading a magazine. "She was just a little pale."

Ria narrowed her gaze. "What was this woman wearing?"

"A dress in the most unattractive shade of mauve, poor thing. Two sizes too large, at least. In my day we called them house dresses."

''Brenda,'' Ria murmured, more to herself than the Cocettis.

Mrs. C. cocked her head. ''Whatever her name is, she's the same woman I saw tussling with a man in your parking lot last week.''

Ria felt a sudden chill. ''Tussling?''

''Well, it wasn't really a tussle. God knows that poor thing couldn't hold her own against a flea, let alone a bruiser like the one who grabbed her.''

''I'm sorry, Mrs. C, but I'm afraid I'm not following.''

''Not at all dear.'' Mrs. C. glanced around to make sure they weren't being overheard.

The old woman puckered her brow below the fringe of white fuzz. ''It was a few minutes before seven. She was just getting out of this old Ford station wagon—you know, the kind with the fake wood on the side.'' Her lips compressed. ''Now in my day, they used real wood. Oak, I think and—''

''I hate to interrupt, Mrs. C., but I'm a little pressed for time.''

''You always are, dear.''

Tina took pity on her. ''Like Gram said, this lady was getting out of her car, and all of a sudden this big old truck comes barreling into the lot.''

Ria's stomach tightened. ''Truck?''

''Yeah, just the cab part, you know? Kinda blue-green, with a red stripe?''

Ria nodded, feeling sicker and sicker.

''Anyway, this big guy jumps out and grabs the lady by the arm and throws her up against her car. She musta hit her elbow, 'cause she grabbed it and sort of bent over. And then he was, like, yelling at her.''

Mrs. C. looked surprisingly sprightly all of a sudden as she bobbed her head in vigorous agreement. ''I told Tina to call the police, but by the time she found that blasted cordless doohickey, the man had pushed the woman back in her car and she drove off, with him following practically right on top of her.''

Ria compressed her lips. Maybe Callie was right. Maybe Brenda was being knocked around. ''Could you identify this man?'' she asked, her gaze including them both.

''Probably,'' Tina said with a shrug.

''Of course,'' Mrs. C. said at the same time. ''My eyesight is still young, even if the rest of me is moldering away as we speak.''

Ria choked a laugh. ''You're doing no such thing.''

''Ha. You haven't seen me naked.''

''Not so loud,'' Tina exclaimed, looking mortified.

Ria and Mrs. C. exchanged smiles. ''I appreciate the information,'' Ria told the old woman before giving her a gentle hug. ''And please, let me know immediately if you see that man again.''

''I certainly will. We can't have those kinds of goings-on in our neighborhood.'' Mrs. C. moved her walker a few inches, then stopped. ''If Big Al were still around, that bully would have been buzzard bait by now.'' Her face turned dreamy and her eyes distant. ''Now there was a man, Ria. There was a man.''

''Don't start, Gram,'' Tiny muttered, opening the door.

Ria helped the old woman out the door, then watched as Tina helped her grandmother across the street.

Arms crossed against a wind that was suddenly biting and angry, Ria glanced toward the entrance to the lot that was hidden behind the building. Though it was the first day of summer, she was suddenly ice cold.

# *Chapter 3*

The third of the five Hardin sons and the next eldest after Grady, Flynn Hardin had always reminded Ria of a nineteenth-century pirate, with his tawny hair flowing like a lion's mane to his wide shoulders and a gold, pirate's earring glinting in his ear. Of all of Grady's brothers, Flynn had always been her favorite, maybe because he was so much like his big brother.

"I appreciate your help on this, Flynn. I know it's not your case." Ria finished refilling both their mugs and returned the pot to the warmer before reseating herself at the table.

"No sweat, sugar. I'm honored to be asked. Gives me a chance to spend time with my favorite sis-in-law."

"Your only sis-in-law at the moment," she reminded him gently. "And an ex at that."

"Like hell." His grin was crooked, but his eyes were serious. "A piece of paper don't mean squat when it comes to family."

The old longing to belong took hold before she could shake it off. During the nightmare days and nights after Jimmy's abduction, the Hardins had put aside their own pain to offer comfort and support.

After the divorce, which no one wanted but everyone seemed to understand, they'd made it abundantly clear that she was still one of them. She was invited to every family function. Sarah still called with invitations to lunch. Mason stopped by the Center often, to share a cup of coffee and regale her with his latest bunch of corny jokes. Flynn and the others called often, just to check on her. Only Kale, the closest emotionally to Grady, had seemed constrained.

She lifted her cup and forced down a swallow of coffee. "Thanks for coming. I know you've had a long day."

"No problem." Looking deceptively lazy, he pulled a small black notebook from his pocket and flipped to a clean page before taking a pen from the pocket of his sport shirt. "Why don't you bring me up to speed on what's already happened? You said it was a case of crib death?"

"I hate that term," she muttered before pausing to order her thoughts. Dealing with Brenda's tragedy had served to bring her own into sharp focus again. As always, when the pain hit, she took refuge in precision. Compartmentalizing her mind helped keep the grief locked down tight.

"The baby's mom, Brenda Benteen, was an in-house referral from my partner, Kate."

"Kate, the Ice Woman," he said after asking her to spell Brenda's last name. "Now there's an interesting lady. Real tidy and buttoned up. Make's a man's fingers itch to undo some of those buttons."

He flashed her another grin—the wicked, slightly naughty one he and Grady shared.

Flynn and Kate had met at Ria's wedding. Kate had considered Grady's brother a lightweight—pretty face, a gorgeous body and the emotional depth of paint. But then Kate was drawn toward the slick, corporate types. Suits, Tova called them.

"Kate had been treating Brenda's baby daughter for severe colic for about three months," Ria said, "when one day out of the blue last November she got a call from one of Lafayette's finest, asking her to fax the baby's records downtown. Naturally Kate being as much a fanatic about confidentiality as she is about everything else, she asked him why, which was when the callous jerk casually dropped the news that the baby had been found dead in his crib that morning."

Flynn winced. The lingering glint in his eyes disappeared in the span of a blink. "I assume Kate sent the records."

"Eventually. Her first concern was Brenda, of course. The poor woman was a wreck. Bouncing from hysteria to an almost catatonic state and then bursting into wild tears again." Ria drew a breath. "My mother used to do the same thing. It can be…scary."

Flynn smiled back. "Yeah."

Ria let her smile fade. In her manic state Virginia had smothered her little girl with maternal attention, sometimes rousing her in the middle of the night to dance in the moonlight to a tune only her mother could hear.

Ria came to dread those once-a-month days when her mother's welfare check landed in the mailbox of their musty, dingy apartment house. With a crow of delight, Virginia would dress Ria in her best and hustle her to the first of a series of movie houses. Sometimes they would attend five movies in a row before Ria could talk her mother into going back to the apartment for a meal and sleep.

Ria had lived a life of constant fear, never knowing when her mother's mood would suddenly turn. Those were the worst times—dark, frighteningly unpredictable times, when her mom would huddle beneath the covers of her bed and sob. School became Ria's respite. Her haven. The only order and security in her life.

Her caseworker, a raw-boned, homely earth mother named Alice Mansfield, had tried to protect her, but she'd been hampered by the rules and regulations of a system unwilling to deny a mother custody of her own child—even though that mother was mentally ill.

She'd been in the sixth grade when her mother had tried to kill her by putting sleeping pills in her milk. It had made her deathly ill instead, finally giving Alice the ammunition she needed to end Virginia's parental rights.

Ria had been made a ward of the court then. Instead of placing her in a foster home, Alice had taken her into her own. Her husband, Glen, was the pastor of a small neighborhood church and the kindest man Ria had ever met. She'd lived with the Mansfields until she'd gone off to college.

Her mother had died a few days before Ria's fifteenth birthday. In many ways it had been a blessing for both of them.

"Kate gave Brenda a mild tranquilizer and stayed with her until she was able to answer questions." Ria paused, trying to remember exactly what Kate had told her. "Brenda swore the baby had been fine when she'd put her back in her crib for her morning nap. She said she'd been putting a load of laundry into the washing machine when her husband came home. He's a long-haul truck driver. I think he works for one of the local freight haulers, but I'm not sure which one."

"You have a name for this guy?"

"Brenda calls him Monk. I don't know if that's his real name or not."

"I'll check."

Ria thanked him with a quick smile. "Last night, my neighbor told me she'd seen Brenda and someone I think was Monk in the Center's parking lot.'' She went on to recount Mrs. Cocetti's story.

He digested that. ''Have you ever seen signs of abuse? Bruises, for example?''

''No, nothing.'' Ria shook her head. ''It's just something I feel, you know? Like one of the hunches Grady used to talk about.''

His smile saluted his brother before he returned the notebook to his pocket. ''It'll take me a few days to put it together.''

''You have at least fourteen before I start bugging you.''

''Fair enough,'' he said, reaching for his coffee cup. ''Here's to a great vacation.''

''Thanks.'' Ria lifted hers in salute before she took a sip.

''Guess you know Grady's thinking about relocating to the west coast.''

Shock stunned her into a temporary silence. ''You mean, permanently?'' she asked when she found her voice again.

Flynn nodded. ''A small town along the Oregon coast is looking to hire a chief of police. Apparently Grady's at the top of their list. Last I heard he was planning to fly out there over the Fourth for a look-see at what they've got to offer.''

Ria took a sip, a large one. ''He always said it was his life's ambition to become chief before Kale.''

''Yeah, those two always were pushing and shoving about something. Grady generally came out on the bottom—until he grew into his hands and feet.'' Flynn leaned back and stretched out his legs. ''Grady told me once that he'd only started to like himself when you fell in love with him. Before then, he'd considered himself a born loser.''

Stunned, Ria jerked her gaze to his face. His gaze bored into hers, dark with a truth she didn't want to see.

''Think about it,'' he ordered gruffly. ''Kale graduated from college with honors up the wazoo. The twins are music geniuses and me—'' he shrugged, then preened ''—what can I say? All-American in three sports.''

She grinned and shook her head. ''Modest, too.''

''There is that.'' He glanced down at the plate that had once contained a mound of peanut butter cookies. Now there was one lone survivor.

''Be my guest,'' she said when he lifted a brow.

''Guess I will.'' He devoured half with one bite. ''Grady wasn't special in anything,'' he continued, after wolfing down the remaining bite. ''Unless you call screwing up, in which case he was A number one.''

Outside, a siren wailed, and in the distance a dog joined in with an off-key howl.

''He told me once that he sometimes wished he'd been born crippled instead of dyslexic,'' she admitted. ''He said that when you had a visible handicap, people cut you some slack, but he just came across as stupid.''

''Which he's not,'' Flynn said quietly.

''Yes, anything but.'' Grady could add a column of figures in his head faster than she could total them on a ten-key. He could remember the lyrics to songs he'd only heard once or twice. And he could read the needs of her body with the sensitivity that took her breath.

Ria stood up, too agitated suddenly to sit still. Heart pounding, she stalked past him to retrieve the coffeepot from the warmer.

She was just about to refill the mug he extended when the phone rang. The answering machine picked up on the second ring.

''Aren't you going to answer?'' Flynn asked over the drone of her terse message.

''Not unless I have to. I'm on vacation, remember?''

''Ree, are you there?''

At the sound of Grady's distinctly husky voice, she froze, her gaze darting to Flynn's. Before she could move, Grady spoke again. "Brace yourself honey, okay? It's about Jimmy."

"Do you hear the Charger?"

Without waiting for an answer, Ria jumped up from the easy chair by the fireplace she'd never used and crossed the living room to the bay window overlooking the street.

"Grady has different wheels these days," Flynn said from the sofa where he'd been for the past hour, playing solitaire on the coffee table.

Astonished, Ria turned to find him watching her with hooded eyes. "Where's the Charger?"

"He sold it and put the money in the reward fund. These days he drives a banged-up pickup he'd bought from impound and fixed up."

She took a careful breath before returning her gaze to the empty thoroughfare. Grady had spent hundreds of hours rebuilding the muscle car from the chassis up. In many ways he and his speed machine were exactly alike. Big, fast. Potentially lethal.

She remembered the first time she'd seen him climb out of that car and stalk toward her. She'd been working her way through grad school waiting tables in an Italian restaurant at night and on weekends. When one of her fellow waitresses had been raped, Ria had been dismayed to discover just how pitifully limited the resources for rape victims had been.

Consequently she and Kate, who'd been in her first year of med school, had helped found a hotline for victims. In order to raise money, one of the sororities had come up with the idea of a calendar featuring local hunks. One of Grady's younger brothers, Davon, had been dating a member of that sorority and, as a prank, had given them Grady's picture to use.

It had been taken one hot day in August when he'd been

practicing with his grandfather's old Carbine. He'd been wearing threadbare cutoffs that barely covered his tight buttocks and a Lafayette PD ball cap pulled down low. His huge chest had been bare and sweat glistened on the curve of broad shoulders, running in meandering rivulets over the hard-packed musculature of his upper torso.

The photographer had caught him in the act of slipping shells into the chamber, his eyes narrowed against the sun as he'd looked up, his mouth a split second into a grin. One big hand caressed the barrel of his rifle in a pose so erotic Ria had felt the impact all the way to the soles of her ratty old sneakers.

A feeling like a warm melting sigh ran through her as she remembered the way her mouth had gone dry and her hands had curled around the stiff glossy paper.

The calendar had sold out. Mr. August had become an instant favorite. Ria had been on the phone when he'd come charging into the hotline's cramped office, brandishing the calendar, his jaw hard and his brown eyes sparking with outrage.

He was being ragged within an inch of his control by his fellow officers, he'd bellowed at her the instant she'd hung up. All because of a damn picture taken two years earlier and used without his permission.

Because she was alone and a little intimidated, she'd jerked her spine a little taller and ripped into him.

"So what?" she challenged. "It's for a good cause. Or don't you care?"

His tawny brows drew together, and his chin came up. "Hell, yes, I care. That's not the point."

"Then what is?"

"I'm a cop, damn it. It's tough enough going against bad guys who've got better firepower and faster cars, without having a damn suspect drooling all over the arresting officer."

She fought the grin that tickled the corners of her mouth. "You have bad guys drooling over you?"

His mouth slanted just enough to tease a shallow dimple into one lean cheek. "More like one professionally bad *girl* I busted on the stroll near the bus station. Gave me this come-hither grin before going on and on about how August was her favorite month, it being so hot and all. Offered me a freebie—and then slapped my butt when I was giving her the Miranda."

Ria choked on a laugh. "Did it hurt?"

"Only my dignity. It so happened the duty sergeant saw the whole thing." His voice was more rough than resonant and was lashed with something that sounded suspiciously like humor.

She knew now she'd started falling in love with him at that moment. And when he'd asked her for a date, she'd accepted.

After the divorce she'd tossed the calendar in the trash, then got up in the middle of the night to retrieve it from the barrel she'd already set out for pickup. It was in the bottom of the trunk where she stored her wool sweaters.

She drew a ragged sigh. "He told me he'd be here in two hours," she said as she paced back to the chair she'd just left. "It's been two hours and ten minutes."

"Maybe he got stuck in traffic." He put a red nine on a black ten.

"At 1:00 a.m.?"

Flynn turned over the last card, frowned, then let out a long-suffering sigh before admitting defeat. "Are you sure I can't fix you a drink?"

"I'm too nervous. It'll just make me sick."

"Wine then?" he suggested, shuffling with the easy skill of a Vegas dealer. "I saw some Grand Marnier behind the Scotch. How about a couple of fingers to take the edge off?"

"The only thing to do that will be seeing my baby again."

The cards slapped the table's glass top in a steady rhythm as he laid out the hand. Only then did he glance up.

"Ria, remember what Grady told you? The boy doesn't have any memory of his life before he was abducted."

"Not consciously, maybe. But I've saved all of his things. His books, his Matchbox cars. His Pooh bear." She nodded, folded her arms across her middle and nodded again. "You'll see. He can't help but remember Pooh."

His dark eyes held hers, his expression a little pitying. "He thinks his name is Steven Wilson." He paused to add far more gently, "He didn't recognize his own dad or the picture of you Grady had in his wallet."

She drew a breath. "It's an old picture. From college. My hair was longer, for one thing, and I was much thinner."

Of course Jimmy would remember his mommy, she reassured herself as she jumped up to return to the window.

"Maybe I should have had you pick up a hamburger when you went out for groceries," she murmured, leaning closer to the window in an effort to see headlights at the far end of the block. "Jimmy always liked hamburgers—" She broke off, her heart taking off suddenly as a dark-colored pickup truck suddenly came into view below. Even before it slowed she knew.

"Oh, God, they're here," she whispered, her gaze riveted to the truck turning into the residents' parking lot.

Flynn surged to his feet and hurried to join her by the window. Her heart thumping wildly, she watched Grady park next to Flynn's vintage XKE, then climb out. He paused to grab a couple of bags from the back, then circled around to open the passenger door.

Her breath dammed in her throat. "There he is," she exclaimed eagerly as a boy climbed down. "Flynn, it's

Jimmy. Oh God, it's really my baby.'' She pressed closer, desperate to see her child's face. But she was too far away to make out his features. ''He's gotten so tall.'' Her voice broke, and she bit her lip. ''He's all arms and legs.''

Beside her, Flynn cleared his throat. ''Looks like the kid hates haircuts as much as his old man does.''

Ria choked out a laugh, but her gaze remained glued to the man and the boy walking toward the entrance to the building. They were so much alike, both long and lanky, with the same wide shoulders and loping walk.

''I'm so scared, Flynn,'' she whispered when they disappeared from view.

He slipped a brotherly arm around her shoulders and gave her a quick squeeze before he let her go again. In unison they turned to face the front door.

Grady had never been inside Ria's new place. Never even driven by, although he'd had the new address scrawled in his Rolodex next to her new phone number. A couple of times when he'd found himself in the area, he'd been tempted to stop by, just to make sure she was settling in.

Like she would actually let him in, he thought bitterly.

It was a decent neighborhood, a mix of town houses and single-family, moderately expensive homes. The area had average crime stats, mostly break and enter. Just in case, he'd had a quiet talk with the desk sergeant in charge of scheduling, and, in the way of cops everywhere, had let it be known he'd consider it a personal favor if the guys on the street kept a close watch on this particular complex. Specifically the pretty, dark-haired lady in Unit B in Building 2. And in the way of cops, the sergeant had understood that in granting that favor he was entitled to a favor in return.

So far Sgt. Gruen hadn't called in the marker. Maybe he

never would. Cops didn't take kindly to attacks on one of their own.

"Nice place, huh?" he said as he guided the reluctant child up the steps to the second floor. "Real classy."

Jimmy grunted something unintelligible, his gaze fixed on the carpeted risers. Talk about stubborn; this scruffy six-year-old with hot, angry eyes could give lessons to a barn-yard mule. In the three days since Grady had walked into that small pink bungalow in Calexico—and damn near lost it in front of a roomful of strangers when he'd recognized his son—Jimmy hadn't voluntarily said more than a couple of dozen words to him. This from the kid who had once started his day chattering about everything and anything, rarely stopping until he fell into bed at night.

He glanced down at the unhappy little boy. "Your mom is pretty emotional, so she's probably going to cry all over you," he told the boy as they headed up the carpeted stairs leading to the second floor. "When you're older, you'll realize women do that a lot. Sometimes at the darnedest times. Best thing to do is just suck it up and let her vent."

The boy flicked him a sullen look. "She's not my mom," he grumbled in a surly tone that set Grady's teeth on edge. "I don't know why I have to be in this stupid old place, anyway."

"Because this is where you belong."

At least part of the time. They hadn't worked out a cus-tody agreement in the divorce settlement. He'd had to fight to get Ria to accept half of their assets, though he would have willingly given her everything he owned. But no way would he give up access to his son.

When they reached the landing, Grady put a hand on the boy's shoulder and drew him to a stop. When he had the kid's undivided attention, he crouched down so they were face-to-face, eye to eye.

He hated the defiance he saw there, but he understood

it. Maybe he even respected it. In Jimmy's world, he was the bad guy, the stranger who'd taken him away from the parents he loved. The boy was fighting back the only way he could.

"No matter what anyone has said, you *are* my son. All you have to do is look at my face, then look in the mirror. Your name isn't Steven Wilson. It's Jimmy. Jimmy Hardin." He kept his voice soft, but with enough bite to make the point stick. "Maybe you don't want to believe that, but it's as true as true can be."

Jimmy's eyes flashed. "It's not! My mom and dad wouldn't lie to me! You're the one who's lying. You put them in jail, and I *hate* you!" He tried to jerk away, but Grady wrapped a hand around the boy's bony shoulder to keep him rooted.

"Think a minute, son. I've explained about the man who had you kidnapped and why. Tomorrow, your mom and I will show you the videos we took of you when you were a baby." The memories he'd locked away came flooding out. "After we took you to the circus on your third birthday, you announced that you were going to be a clown when you grew up. Clowns made people happy, you said. And happy was a good thing. You said your name wasn't Jimmy anymore because that wasn't a clown's name. So your mom and I started calling you Jimbo."

Something flickered in the boy's eyes before he dropped his gaze. "My name is Steven Allen Wilson. You can't make me say it isn't."

In spite of the bravado, his lower lip trembled a little, and he clamped it still between his teeth. Grady had to clench his jaw to keep from begging the boy to forgive him for pushing too hard too fast. Patience, he reminded himself. He and Ree had gotten their son through colic and a hellish series of ear infections, and they'd get through this.

"It's okay to be scared, and it's okay to be mad at me.

You can even hate me if it makes you feel better—although I hope you won't, because I love you.''

Jimmy started at that, his eyes widening visibly, as though the concept was foreign to him. Damn, Grady thought, clamping down hard on the need to swear long and hard. Couldn't those pieces of human garbage have spared a few minutes to show a lonely little boy some affection?

''I love you,'' he repeated more softly, and with more force, just in case the boy was having trouble getting his mind around the idea. ''And your mom loves you, too. So much she was like to die of grief when you were taken from us. Which is why I want you to be real polite when you meet her.''

He waited a beat while the boy absorbed that. While he waited, he told himself it would be all right. He and Ria had had Jimmy for three solid years. Sweet, happy years when the big old house was filled with laughter. Somewhere in the boy's psyche the memories of those years were waiting.

Still, he wasn't about to kid himself. It was going to take time to get past the lies the Wilsons had fed him.

*Set limits of acceptable behavior and stick to them,* the therapist had advised. Children needed boundaries. Especially children dealing with life-altering situations. When everything else was shifting and changing around them, a child needed a lifeline to hang on to. Something solid and reliable. And safe.

Grady had to admit it made a weird sort of sense. He'd been heading down a long road to some serious trouble until his father had laid down the law. In some perverse way he and his dad had been closer after that.

But damn it was hard. Instead of playing hardball with the boy, he wanted to snatch up his son and hold tight.

"Are we straight on this, son?" he asked quietly when, finally, Jimmy met his steady gaze again.

It wasn't really a nod, more like a flicker of his eyelashes, but pressing the boy for more would only serve to dent the kid's pride. Most likely it was pretty stiff. Had to be, he decided as he stood. The boy was a Hardin, wasn't he?

*Chapter 4*

Ria heard voices outside her door, then an impatient knock. Her heart started slamming like crazy, and her knees jellied.

"Oh, God, I thought I was handling this so well, but now...I'm petrified," she whispered, clutching Flynn's arm.

"Hang in, Sis. It'll be okay." Flynn gave her another quick squeeze, an even quicker grin, and then strode quickly to the door. He paused, braced his shoulders and opened the door.

Flynn was between Ria and the boy, so all she saw were the frayed hems of faded jeans and boy-size, scuffed high-tops that looked much too big for her baby. Suddenly she couldn't seem to breathe.

"Hey, Bro, welcome back," Flynn said, his voice rough.

"Thanks, kid." Grady cleared his throat. "Jim, this big ugly guy here is your Uncle Flynn."

"Hi-ya, Jimbo." Flynn's voice was very gentle, very gruff. "I sure am happy to see you."

The boy mumbled something she didn't catch. Apparently Flynn did, however, because she saw him exchange a quick look with Grady who shook his head.

"Damned if he doesn't look exactly like the picture you sent out," Flynn muttered, rubbing the back of his neck. "Mom is gonna be flat-out amazed."

"Hear that, Jim? Uncle Flynn here thinks you and me look alike."

"Don't, neither. I look like my grandpa Wilson. Mama said."

Mama? she thought as she took a few steps forward. As though sensing her approach, Flynn stepped away from the door. Grady dropped a hand on the boy's shoulder and guided him over the threshold.

Joy burst inside her as she whispered his name. The boy jerked his head in her direction.

"Hello, baby." Her voice was a thread.

"Say hello to your mom, Jim." Though Grady addressed his son, his gaze was on her.

Instead of speaking, Jimmy dropped his gaze, determined, it seemed, to ignore her. She understood his feeling all too well. She'd been deposited on her share of doorsteps in the middle of the night, too. As she'd done then, he was shutting out what he couldn't change.

"Are you hungry?" Mindful of her own miserable unhappiness whenever she'd had to adjust to a new set of foster parents, she kept her tone light and her voice quiet. "I can fix you a peanut butter sandwich or maybe some cocoa and cookies. I have oatmeal with icing." Those had been his favorites. Maybe they still were.

He looked at her then, his expression closed, his eyes sullen. "You got a bathroom? I gotta take a leak."

"Remind me to have a talk with you about your language," Grady muttered before Ria had a chance to reply. Beside her, Flynn made a valiant effort to stifle a grin.

Ria ignored them both. "Through that door there and down the hall, sweetie. Second door on the left. The light switch is on your right."

Jimmy flicked her a wary glance before heading off down the hall. In the sudden silence, she heard the door close and the lock click.

"Reminds me of the time you got your mouth washed out with soap for saying something graphic in front of Great Aunt Marvel," Flynn mused, his grin the devil's own. "Mom said you foamed at the mouth for a week."

"Mom's pulling your chain, Little Brother," Grady muttered before turning to close the front door.

Tension radiated from him like a dark, smoldering aura. Ria felt it, too, sizzling along her nerve endings, like the feeling she had when a sudden summer storm rumbled in over the lake. It was always that way now, when the two of them were in the same room, which was one of the reasons she turned down more invitations to family gatherings than she accepted.

As though he felt it, too, Flynn glanced her way and winked. Katie was wrong, she thought. Grady's brother was anything but shallow.

She thanked him with a shaky grin, but the nervous energy that had been building for hours was making her feel light-headed. So much had happened so fast.

"Ready for that wine now, Sis?"

She rarely drank, preferring to experience life exactly as it came her way. It was a fear of losing touch with reality, she suspected. Deeply ingrained by years of watching her mother's slow, painful spiral into a world of black nightmares and euphoric delusions. At the moment, however, a little blurring along the edges of that reality couldn't hurt.

"A small glass," she decided aloud. "There's an open bottle of white in the fridge. Callie left it the last time she came to dinner."

"Gotcha." He shifted his gaze to Grady, who had left bags next to the front door. "What about you, slick? I'm pouring, in case you're interested."

"Maybe later."

Flynn nodded. "One small white wine comin' up for the lady," he said before heading toward the kitchen, which was at the other end of the long, narrow living room.

"Sorry we're later than I figured," Grady said when they were alone. "Took me a while to get the truck out of long-term parking. Some joker had stolen my battery."

Her smile trembled before she compressed her lips. "It's okay. Flynn kept me company. I don't know what I would have done without him."

"Yeah, he's a real thoughtful guy, my brother. He always sends his girlfriends flowers before he dumps 'em." He rolled his shoulders, then glanced around, more instinct than curiosity, she suspected.

His rough-hewn textures were the same as before—the chiseled-from-stone jaw, the arrogant cheekbones, the aggressive mouth with the subtle hint of sensuality few woman could resist. The blatant, in-your-face masculinity was the same, too. As fiercely powerful as it had ever been on that sun-washed autumn day when he'd first leveled that beautifully intense gaze in her direction. Yet he was different, too, she realized as his mouth slanted into a brief half smile.

His thick sun-streaked hair with the unruly waves that taxed the skills of even the most skillful barber was now dusted with silver at the temples. The faint worry lines above the strong bridge of his nose had deepened to permanent creases. Beneath the cocky sweep of this brows, the nut-brown eyes that had once twinkled with irresistible mischief were somber, even guarded, with hints of bitterness and an inward-turning anger in the dark pupils. It was the face of a man who had suffered, and suffered deeply.

"Are you okay?" he asked gruffly after bringing his gaze back to her face.

"A little dazed by the suddenness of this all," she admitted. "But it's a good feeling." She laughed a little and hugged herself. "No, it's a *great* feeling." She took a stuttering breath. "Oh, Grady, he's so beautiful, isn't he? And so tall. Of course, we knew he'd be above average in height, even with my shrimp size pulling down the mean." She laughed, again, then sobered as Flynn's gentle warning replayed in her mind. "He really doesn't remember us?"

"Doesn't seem to." Grady directed a quick look toward the hall. "He's scared, Ree. He'll be more relaxed tomorrow."

"It'll take time, I know that. But we have that now, thank God."

"Yeah, thank God."

He lifted a hand to rub at a spot on his belly just above the waistband of his low-slung jeans. Beneath the soft cotton of a dark blue T-shirt, his body was still impressively conditioned. A virile, attractive man in his prime. For a moment she forgot she no longer loved him.

"He's pretty whipped," he said, dropping his hand to his side. "A storm over the Rockies made us late into O'Hare and we had to run for it to make the flight to Indianapolis. Otherwise I would have called you from Chicago. Given you more notice."

"Why didn't you call before you left California?" It was one of the questions that had been nagging at her since she'd heard his voice on the machine.

"I figured it would be easier on you if you only had to obsess for a couple of hours instead of five or six. More, if we got hung up or had a flight canceled."

"I don't—" She broke off to smile ruefully. "I suppose you're right," she admitted, darting a glance in the direction of the hall. "What's keeping that child, anyway?"

"Want me to check on him?"

"No." She frowned. "Give him another minute or so."

He nodded, then stifled a yawn. "Sorry about that. I've been bunking on a couch belonging to the DEA agent who scared up the lead. Damn near wrecked my back. I was working up an excuse for moving to a motel when the okay came through from Children's Services to release Jimmy in my custody. Three nights of that torture was about all I could handle."

Grady knew he'd blown it even before her face went still and her eyes clouded. Just when he'd begun to think they could get through a conversation without cutting at each other, he'd screwed up.

"*Three* nights?" Her voice was deceptively casual. "When, *exactly,* did you find out about Jimmy?"

He had a feeling he wasn't going to enjoy the next few minutes worth a damn. "Late Monday afternoon."

She reflected, then narrowed her gaze. "Let me get this straight. You're saying you deliberately kept my son from me for *three* days?"

"*Our* son. And there were reasons, Ree. Good reasons."

"What kind of reason could possibly justify that kind of cruelty?" she challenged in a low, angry voice that had Flynn stopping dead in his tracks halfway across the living room, a glass of wine in each hand. A quick warning glance from Grady had him retreating to the kitchen without a word.

"You can rip at me all you want when we're alone, but right now our son doesn't need any more uproar in his life." Grady said when they were alone again.

"You're right. What matters now is the welfare of our son and—" She heard the bathroom door open, and broke off.

Side by side, yet anything but united, they watched the child they'd created in an explosion of mutual pleasure edge into the room. Ria gave a little cry of alarm when she saw the boy's face. He wasn't just pale. He was green. Drops of sweat as large as tears stood out on his forehead.

Grady's heart kick-started into raw panic as Ria rushed to the boy's side.

"What's wrong, sweetheart?" she asked gently. "Are you sick? Are you going to throw up?"

"Already did," Jimmy muttered, then slanted her a sideways look that was a mixture of defiance and misery. "I kinda ruined the rug."

"It'll wash," she assured him as she tested his temperature with a hand to his forehead. Grady caught the quick flash of fear in the gaze she raised to his face.

"Fever?" Grady asked, his gut twisting.

"I'm not sure. He's a little warm, but it's a hot night." She smoothed back her son's silky hair, only to have him jerk away. "It's okay, sweetheart. Mommy will make it better."

"Not my mom," Jimmy grumbled, slanting her a sullen look. It was like acid on an open wound.

"Something wrong?" Flynn asked as he came up from behind. He took one look at Jimmy's face and frowned. "Uh-oh. Looks like we've got us a sick puppy."

"It's probably the flu," Ria said as she got to her feet. "Our clinic's been jammed with cases. But just to be on the safe side, I'd better give Kate a call."

Grady took a breath. The knot in his belly was on fire again. "Think we should give him something, just in case he has a fever?"

Ria considered. "Let's take his temperature first. Kate will want to know how high it is."

"Right. Okay." He stuck his hands in his back pockets, then pulled them free again. "Maybe we should dunk him in water, like you used to do when he had those ear infections."

Ria considered, then nodded. "You run the water while I call Katie. Make sure the water's not too cold, though. No more than tepid." She shot a glance toward the canvas satchel by the door. "Are those his things?"

"Yeah. I bought him the basics for the trip. I figured you'd want to take him shopping. You always got a kick out of that kind of stuff."

Her lips curved briefly. "He'll be more comfortable in his jammies." In charge now, she glanced at Flynn. "The thermometer's in the medicine chest in my bathroom."

"Which one's yours?"

"Through the bedroom at the end of the hall."

That answered one question, Grady thought as he scooped his son into his arms. Ria and Flynn weren't sleeping together, if he didn't even know where her bedroom was. Not yet, anyway. And if he had anything to say about it, not ever.

Grady had taken his share of punishment. More than most, he figured, mopping his dripping face with one of Ria's fat yellow towels. And damn near all of it deserved. He figured he'd even skated on a few things. Most times he'd managed to tough his way through. Losing Jimmy had been a hard one to take. Losing Ria had come close to breaking him.

This time God in His infinite wisdom had come up with a real lulu to test this poor sinner's patience. Feeling a lot like those martyrs he'd learned about in Sunday school, he swiped the towel over the worst of the puddles on the floor and considered the bit about reaping and sowing. That, he decided, was Jimmy. His father's son right down to the bone.

Tell him to sit, and he stood. Tell him to stop splashing and he drenched the bathroom. Payback in spades.

The Big Guy in the Sky had to be laughing big-time,

which Grady figured he deserved. He was just grateful no one else was watching.

He tossed the towel aside, thought longingly of the rookie cops who jumped when he even breathed in their direction, and told himself there was more to being a good parent than a ready willingness to die in defense of your family.

Limits, he reminded himself. Tough love.

He sighed. Suck it up, hotshot. Get it done. He narrowed his gaze at the kid glaring at him from the pale yellow tub. The kid who looked anything but sickly at the moment.

"Splash me one more time, and you'll be eating this washcloth," he warned, putting just enough bite in his normally quiet voice to get the kid's attention.

The boy sneered. "Go to hell!"

Grady counted to ten. Then added a few seconds before grabbing the washcloth again. "The doctor said twenty minutes in tepid water, you're damn well getting twenty minutes. Now shut up and enjoy it."

"I'm not a baby," Jimmy complained, jerking away from the washcloth.

"Then stop acting like one," Grady said with the last of his patience. He'd come close to losing his temper a dozen times in the last ten minutes.

Sick or not, his son needed a reality check, and soon. He winced inwardly at the thought of his father's reaction if he'd pulled some of the stuff Jimmy tried on him. Like jabbing him in the gut with a bony elbow when he'd tried to help the kid out of his shirt.

His belly was still aching.

He checked his watch and bit off a sigh. Five more minutes.

"You used to like your bath," he said as he reached for the shampoo on the ledge surrounding the tub. The memory stabbed, reminding him of the years they'd lost. All those sweet times they should have had, all the laughter and cuddles and father-son talks, gone forever.

He felt his breath catch. Someday maybe, in the far distant future, he might find a way to forgive himself. At the moment he simply didn't know how. So all he could do was try to make things right from now on.

"You, uh—" He paused to clear the thickness from his throat. "You had a basket of toys we kept under the sink. Rubber ducks and boats, stuff like that. Your favorite, though, was a boxlike thing with all kinds of doors and buttons and dials that attached to the side with suction cups." He tried a smile and got a bored look.

Kid's a hard nut, he thought, squirting shampoo into his cupped palm. Damn stuff was pink and smelled like roses.

Just like that, his libido gave him a sneaky kick.

This was Ria's scent, Ria's shampoo. She used it in this tub.

Naked.

He nearly moaned at the image that shot into his mind. A ripe, lush body, suntanned thighs. Lush breasts tipped with dusky nipples that poked through the froth of suds sliding over her skin. He remembered how she'd moaned when he'd traced that same slow slide with his mouth, how she'd shivered when he'd used his tongue on her.

His mind stuttered, his body already heavy before he was able to shut down the memory. It was a measure of his fatigue that it took longer than usual.

Jimmy's temperature had been a little over a hundred. "Probably a twenty-four-hour bug," Kate had said over the phone. Just in case, however—and to appease an anxious mom, Ria suspected—she'd promised to stop by in the morning on her way to the hospital for early rounds. In the meantime she'd prescribed a half tablet of Tylenol every four hours and a diet of juice, water and Popsicles.

Ria had just carried a glass of orange juice into the den that also served as her guest room when she heard a bellow of little-boy outrage coming from the master bathroom. After hastily depositing the glass on the nearest flat surface, she raced down the hall.

"What's wrong?" she demanded as she jerked open the door, her racing heart all but bursting in her chest.

Two irate males glared at her from eyes that were nearly identical. Jimmy's hair stuck up in wild spikes of dripping lather. Grady's hands and arms were covered with soapsuds, and there was a swipe of frothy white along his jaw. His shirt was soaking wet and plastered like a second skin to his chest. He looked hot and frustrated—and disturbingly virile.

"It seems your son doesn't like to have his hair washed," he declared, biting off his words.

"Grady, for heaven's sake, he's sick!" she exclaimed, holding on to the doorknob while she reined in the panic still surging in her system.

"Sick, hell. He just tossed his cookies. I used to do it all the time when I got nervous."

"He's still just a child. You're upsetting him."

"The hell I am." Grady's eyes heated. "Look at this place. I sure as sh—shooting didn't make this mess."

"He started it," her son declared hotly, drawing his legs into a tight ball against his chest. Outraged male modesty in a six-year-old. She wanted to laugh and cry at the same time. She'd diapered his bottom about a million times in the past—and kissed it every single time. Right next to the tiny dimple just above the swell of his buttocks. Grady had a similar dimple—and a tight, hard butt that was anything but boyish.

She scowled, stunned at the rush of desire the image had evoked. Ignoring them both, she jerked another towel from the rod and tossed it at Grady's head.

"I expect this place to be spotless—and dry—before you leave it."

Grady's mouth slanted. "Yes, ma'am."

"That goes for you, too, James," she declared hotly before backing out and slamming the door.

Water sloshed against the sides of the tub as Jimmy uncoiled, then sat up. "Your wife was really mad," he said in an awed tone that had Grady swallowing a chuckle.

"Yeah she was that, all right," he said, more than a little awed himself. Ria never yelled. Foster kids who made scenes got booted out, she'd told him once. "Only the thing is, son, she's—" Grady broke off, reluctant to load Jimmy down with news of his parent's split while the boy was still so raw.

"She's what?" Jimmy demanded, back to the sullen tone that made Grady's teeth ache.

"She's going to skin both of us if we don't hop to it."

The boy crossed his skinny arms and glared. "Not me, dude. Cleaning and crap like that is for chicks."

Grady sighed. "We're definitely going to have that talk about your language real soon, son. In the meantime, we have work to do."

Tough love, he reminded himself, as he dunked the boy's head under the soapy water.

Jimmy came up sputtering and spitting, looking a lot like his mom when he'd dunked her in the lake that first time. Grinning at the memory, one of many he took out and polished up to keep him from diving into a bottle during the blackest of the black nights, Grady pulled the plug and turned to grab for another towel.

When he turned around, he took a soap-slimy washcloth full in the face.

# Chapter 5

It wasn't in Grady's nature to pace. It reminded him too much of a hamster he'd had as a kid, running endless circles in a little wheel until the little beggar went psycho from sheer boredom.

When he had energy to burn, he used it productively. Like tearing into an ailing V-8 and making it purr for him the way a woman's finely tuned body purred under a slow hand. Or sanding the sleek curve of a fender until it was as smooth as the inside of a lady's thigh.

When he was pissed off, he went looking for something—or someone—to hit. Preferably someone bigger and younger and sneakier, like Flynn or one of the twins. But when he was wired on adrenaline, like now, he went completely still, inside and out.

It was a trick he'd learned from an old-line flatfoot named O'Sullivan who'd been his first partner after he'd pinned on his detective's shield. A guy got high, a guy made mistakes, Sully had drummed into him until he'd heard it in his sleep. It didn't matter what kind of chemical pulsed through his system. Adrenaline, rage, booze, they were all the same—pure poison to a man who needed a cool head and a clear eye.

Because he was short on sleep and long on nerves, he propped a shoulder against the wall opposite the fridge and watched his brother work his way through an entire bag of oatmeal cookies, washed down with enough coffee to float a decent-size ship.

The sanctimonious joker who claimed that denial was good for the soul probably drank herbal tea, he decided as he rubbed absently at the bonfire in his gut.

"What the hell is she reading the kid, *War and Peace?*" Grady grumbled, shifting only his eyes toward the far end of the town house where the murmur of voices was faintly audible.

He heard the thud of Flynn's coffee mug hitting the counter. "Don't know, Bro, but after she stopped dancing around the kitchen and hugging the bejabbers out of this old boy, she spent a good half hour rummaging through boxes in the storeroom downstairs before she hauled up a stash of books and toys." Flynn chuckled. "Made a big fuss over this ratty old bear that looked in need of fumigation. Started crying all over again."

"Jimmy forgot and left it out in the rain one time," Grady muttered, then he whipped around to face his brother. "What the hell do you mean, she hugged you?"

The glint in Flynn's eyes looked like a "gotcha," one brother ragging another just for the sheer fun of it. Just in case, Grady narrowed his gaze. "I might have slowed down a step or two, but I can still take you, Little Brother."

"Don't doubt that for a minute, Big Brother." Flynn's grin was just a shade too innocent for Grady's peace of mind.

"Just so's you know."

"Wouldn't mind going a few rounds, though. Just for the hell of it." Flynn's grin faded. "You figuring on angling for a second shot at winning the lady?"

Damn, Grady thought, grinding his teeth. Was he really that easy to read? "It's been on my mind some, yeah. You got any opinion of my chances?"

Flynn lifted his mug and sipped, his brow furrowed in thought. Behind the lady-killer charm and the easy laughter, his brother had a way of seeing through the thickest armor into the heart of a person. Grady had come to trust Flynn's judgment more than his own admittedly flawed perceptions of human nature.

"Three hours ago I would have said they weren't worth a damn," Flynn said at last. "But since she didn't boot you out on your keister when you hit her with that three-day bombshell, I figure you for an outside shot."

Grady let out the breath he'd been holding. "I've beaten worse."

"Guess you have at that." Flynn drained his cup, then rose to stow it in the dishwasher. "You gonna call the folks first thing in the morning?" he asked when he'd finished.

"Yeah, no reason to wake 'em up now."

"Mom will be steamed you didn't."

"Dad would be steamed if I did. Of the two I'd rather handle Mom."

"Not me, Bro. I'd rather go toe-to-toe with the old man any day of the week than explain myself to Mom."

"Wimp."

"Hotshot."

Drop twenty years and the two of them would have been pushing and shoving their way through a list of favorite insults. It took Grady a few beats to realize why he suddenly felt young again. Jimmy was home safe and sound. The problems that lay ahead could wait until tomorrow.

Tonight he wanted to savor the sheer joy of having his son back.

"Thanks for hanging around," he said when he realized he was close to making a damn fool out of himself. "I owe you one."

Flynn cleared his throat. "Don't think I won't collect," he said as the two of them walked through the living room to the front door. "Call if you need me."

Grady nodded, then frowned at a sudden niggling thought. "You never said why you happened to be here when I phoned."

"You never asked."

Grady narrowed his gaze. "I'm asking now."

Flynn sliced a quick look toward the other end of the room. It wasn't a good sign. "Ria asked me to look into a case one of the other homicide guys is working on," he said in a low voice. "She thinks maybe the coroner made a mistake."

"What kind of case?"

"Crib death. Six-month-old girl. The mom comes to a support group at the Center. Since Ria is—or was—leaving on vacation tomorrow morning, she asked me to drop by tonight."

Another question answered, Grady thought. It was annoying as hell to realize he'd been jealous of his own brother.

"She's the suspect, the mom?"

Flynn shook his head. "The dad. Seems the guy is ex-Army and something less than a Boy Scout. Truck driver. Apparently he's not crazy about his wife coming to meetings, so the wife sneaks away when he's out of town on a run. Ria's afraid the guy might get violent if he finds out she disobeyed him."

"Bastard," Grady muttered, running hand over the back of his neck.

"I hear you." Flynn grimaced. "Thing is, a guy with that kind of temper might just lose it with a crying kid. Maybe shove a pillow in his face."

Grady nodded. "It's happened. Too many damn times."

Both men fell silent. Grady thought back to the first time he'd walked into a child's bedroom and stared pure evil in the face. The mother had been no more than eighteen, an apathetic, undernourished drug addict, as guilty as the step-father. The guy had been a bruiser, strung out on smack. The little girl had been crying because she was hungry. The bastard used his fists.

The memory had his gut knotting, and he sucked in against the spike of hot, angry pain. "First thing tomorrow, you pull the file." The words were out before he remembered he was speaking to his brother, not a subordinate. "Sorry," he muttered when Flynn lifted a brow. "That was out of line."

"A week from now I'd have to bust you on it, but I figure tonight you're still in a state of grace, so I'll let it pass."

Grady was almost too tired to grin, but habit had him making the effort, anyway. "Put out the word, okay? No phone calls or visits until we get the logistics of this thing sorted out."

"I'll do it, but you'll owe me," Flynn said before letting himself out.


Her son was proving to be a grumpy patient. He'd balked at taking the Tylenol and grumbled about the dorky pajamas his father had picked out. Which hadn't surprised Ria all that much, given the fact that Grady slept in the buff, with the windows wide open winter and summer and an aversion to anything heavier than a sheet covering him.

Jimmy's bedroom furniture was in storage. The bed he'd loved, the twin dressers she'd refinished, the rocking chair where they'd cuddled during story hour. Tomorrow she would call the transfer company and have everything returned.

It wouldn't take much to convert the den into a room more suited to a six-year-old. New curtains, some bright posters, she decided, as she guided Jimmy to the daybed she'd made up with clean sheets. Whatever he wanted, she'd give him—and to hell with anyone who criticized her for spoiling him.

She felt a surge of happiness so great it nearly swamped her. Finally it was sinking in. Her baby was really home. Her eyes filled with tears as she smiled down at him. He didn't smile back. In fact, he hadn't smiled once since his arrival. It would take a little time and patience, she reminded herself.

"I know this seems strange to you, sweetie, but I didn't know you'd be coming home tonight," she said, drawing back the sheet to let him climb in. He studiously avoided her gaze as he scrambled onto the mattress.

Though he was visibly drooping from exhaustion, and he was still too pale for Ria's liking, she had to admit his color was better. His fever was hovering just above normal.

"You've had a long day, haven't you?" she asked gently as she sat on the edge of the bed. "And a really lousy night, poor darling. But you'll feel a lot better tomorrow."

He moved one shoulder, his gaze fixed on the knees he'd drawn close to his chest. It was about as close to the fetal position as he could get.

She recalled herself as his age, huddling into a strange bed with the memory of her mother's screams still echoing in her head. Her foster mother had brought her chicken soup and sat on the side of the bed while she ate, talking about the garden she'd planted that day.

Ria remembered being lulled to sleep by the steady drone of Mother Dee's voice. Her happiest memories were of that small, sunny house on the outskirts of Indianapolis. She'd stayed there for two years before Virginia Madison had come to claim her again. Ria remembered clinging to Mother Dee's neck, terrified of the pale, skeletally thin woman with intense blue eyes who'd come swooping into her bedroom to smother her with wet kisses.

Let him come to you, she reminded herself firmly. But the need to touch him was nearly irresistible. To appease it, she smoothed the sheet, adjusted the pillow, and inhaled the warm scent of soap and warm little boy.

She felt something tear inside her, followed by a flood of emotion so powerful it took all of the control she possessed to sit quietly instead of snatching him into her arms. Soon, she promised herself. When he was ready to accept her love.

Though he was ignoring her, she smiled, knowing he'd hear it in her voice. "I'll leave the light on in the hall, just in case you need to use the bathroom in the night."

She waited, but the boy remained stubbornly silent.

"Would you like another glass of water? Or some juice?" She paused, then gave up. "Well, good night then, sweetheart. I love you."

He glanced up then, the eyes that were nearly identical to his father's filled with misery.

"How long do I have to stay here?" he muttered.

"This is your home, now, sweetheart," she said as gently as she could. "Tomorrow we'll start fixing up this room just the way you like it."

His gaze jerked back to his knees, and his mouth took on a mutinous slant. Ria's heart ached. Inside she was dying, but somehow she managed to ask lightly, "Guess this isn't a good time for your mommy to ask for a hug, huh?"

He shot her a startled look before sinking down into the mattress and turning over to bury his face in the pillow.

Ria's hand wasn't quite steady as she smoothed his hair. "Night-night sweetheart."

Telling herself tomorrow would be better, she got up and walked to the door where she paused to look back at the boy in the bed. He was so big. Twice as big as she remembered.

Her Jimmy, she thought as she turned off the light and stepped into the hall. Blinking away the sudden tears, she closed the door to a crack behind her. She would check on him again after Grady left.

It was quiet in the rest of the house, with only the hum of the central air breaking the stillness. As she walked into the living room, she felt a familiar tension gripping her muscles. Dozens of questions swirled in her head, questions only Grady could answer.

She found him in the living room stripping off his wet T-shirt. She didn't quite suck in. After all, she'd seen this man naked countless times, had lain with her body against his, skin to skin. When they'd made love, she'd felt those powerful muscles bunch and flex beneath her. Yet somehow she'd made herself forget the physical beauty of his body.

He was older now. Broader, yet somehow even more potently male, with slab-hard muscles that she knew would feel warm and unyielding beneath her hands and an impressive symmetry of massive shoulders and tapering torso. Vitality seemed to radiate from his pores.

The sun-kissed hair covering his sculpted pectoral muscles seemed almost white against the burned-in tan. Her heart gave a lurch as she caught sight of the puckered scars that had faded with time, but would never disappear.

"Is your baby all tucked in?" he asked as she approached.

"So far, so good." She shoved her hands into the pockets of her denim skirt and looked around. "Is Flynn gone?"

"Just left." He wadded up his wet shirt, then squatted to shove it into a side pocket of the old duffel bag before rooting around inside the bag itself. Frowning, he went through three sadly wrinkled replacements before he finally settled on a pale blue polo shirt. He gave it a testing sniff, then offered her a rueful glance as he straightened to his full height.

"Agent Mendoza was partial to cheap cigars. Whole house reeked of smoke."

She was surprised to find herself smiling. "I assume he's not married?"

"Engaged. He claims they're negotiating house rules."

"What does *she* say?"

"Pretty much the same thing you told me before you agreed to taking me on. Quit or hit the road."

He pulled the shirt over his head and flipped down the collar before raking his hand through his hair, leaving it only less disheveled than before. Even dressed in a perfectly tailored suit with spit-shined shoes and a French silk tie, he looked more like a grit-and-grumble cowboy than a buttoned-up, cuff links and suspenders stockbroker sort of guy.

She walked to the window to draw the drapes, conscious that he was watching her. She'd never allowed herself to imagine him in the home she'd made without him. But now that he was here, the rooms seemed smaller, somehow and annoyingly…dull.

"Would you like some coffee before you leave?" she asked, turning.

"I'm not leaving." he said quietly, but with enough steel to tug on her temper. She took a breath, decided she was just too emotionally drained to argue and shrugged.

"Suit yourself. You have a choice of the floor or the divan."

Eyes narrowed suspiciously, he glanced behind him at

the narrow, high-backed sofa she'd bought at an estate sale and reupholstered herself. It was more Jimmy's size than his.

"How about we cut for it?" he drawled, indicating the deck of cards Flynn had left on the coffee table.

She let her lips curve. "Not a chance."

"I was afraid of that," he muttered, running his hands down his stubbled cheeks. He smiled at her then, just enough to let her know he wasn't taking it personally. His eyes had the drowsy, half-asleep look of a tired little boy, but the obstinate line of his jaw was all man. She felt her protective armor rattle a little.

"I'll get you a blanket and a pillow."

The linen closet was in the hall. On her way there, she stopped to peek into the guest room. Jimmy was sleeping on his stomach, one impossibly long arm dangling over the side of the daybed. His face was turned toward the door, and he was frowning. His cheeks were tracked with tears.

Her own eyes were suddenly brimming, and she pressed a fist against her lips to keep from crying out. She closed the door, then turned away, only to come up against Grady's hard chest.

"I was so sure he'd remember me," she said, staring at the crescent scar curling like a dimple in his chin. "It wasn't—all the times I imagined—" Her voice broke. "Oh, Grady, when I tried to kiss him good-night, he looked at me as though he...he *hated* me."

"He's worn out, honey. And it's a good bet his tummy is still pretty riled up. I've been there a time or two myself. It's a pretty miserable feeling, but a good night's sleep works wonders. It'll be better tomorrow." He pulled her into his arms and rested his cheek on top of her head.

"I know it's silly and selfish, but I want my baby back," she said in a voice that vibrated with pain. "I want to hold him in my arms and breathe in the smell of his skin. I want to rock him to sleep at night and listen to those funny little snuffling noises he makes when he's dreaming.'' She took a breath, then closed her eyes and dropped her head to his shoulder. ''Half his life, just…gone.'' She drew a harsh breath. ''Those bastards. I hope they rot in hell.''

''Shh, baby, it's okay.'' His voice was gruff, as though his vocal cords had suddenly turned to sandpaper. His body was warm and solid. The familiar scent of her shampoo contrasted sharply with the lingering smell of cigar smoke still clinging to the cotton shirt. There was another more elemental scent in the mix. A seductive, primitive hint of a sexually active male. She should have felt uncomfortable. Instead, she felt safe for the first time in months.

Years.

''I sound s-so ungrateful, and I'm not.'' She lifted her head and looked up at him through the shimmer of tears. ''It's just that my emotions keep shifting on me. One minute I'm so happy I can't breathe properly and the next I'm terrified I've lost him forever.''

''You haven't lost him, sweetheart. On some level he still knows you. It's nature's way.'' His big hand sifted through her hair, letting the strands slip through his fingers slowly.

''It hurts.''

''It's only been a few hours. Give yourself—and Jimmy—some time to sort things through.''

She managed a nod, even a small smile. ''I know you think I spoiled him, but I couldn't help it.'' Her voice broke, and she swallowed hard.

''You were loving and sweet, and you wanted the best for him. That's not spoiling him.'' Not too much, anyway. And if she pampered him a little too much, who could blame her?

Illegitimate and sickly, she'd spent the first eleven years of her life with a seriously unstable mother who'd fed her

on junk food and soda pop. By the time Ria had been res-
cued by the child welfare services and shuffled into the
foster care system, the early years of neglect had done permanent damage. Having Jimmy had nearly killed her. There
couldn't be any more babies. Ever.

Sensing her pain, he turned to rub his cheek against her
shoulder. He was afraid to move.

"Were...were they good to him? Those people? The
Wilsons?" She pulled free to look at him. In all his years
on the force, all the agony he'd seen, the despair and anguish of the victims, he'd never quite been able to seal off
his emotions. A woman's tears were the worst.

Ria's tears flat-out ripped him apart.

"Honey, you're exhausted," he murmured, his voice
embarrassingly thick. He had to clear it twice before it felt
safe to continue. "Let's save the Q and A until tomorrow,
okay?"

Alarm lanced into her eyes, and he cursed his tired brain
and rough tongue.

"No, I need to know. You have to tell me."

Grady rubbed her back, grateful that the years he'd spent
undercover had taught him how to hide his feelings. "It's
been a long road, Ree," he said quietly. "A lot of sleepless
nights. Let's not add one more, okay?"

"But—"

"Shh, you'll wake Jimmy."

She shot a fast glance toward the door, then nodded. "I'll
get your bedding."

He had to let her go then. But damn, at least he'd had a
few moments of sunshine. It wasn't nearly enough.


The sheets smelled funny in this place, and the room was
all strange, like, with scary shadows. Only Stevie wasn't
really scared. Only girls and sissies got scared.

Lance got real mad if he acted scared, and he hated it a

lot when Lance got mad. His face got all red and his voice got real loud. Sometimes Moira's voice got loud, too. Real screechy, and it hurt his ears.

Then she called him a "spoiled brat" and threatened to send him back to his real parents so they could beat him again. "They" didn't want him, she told him. "They" said he was ugly and dumb and paid someone to take him to the river and drown him. 'Cept Lance saved him and brought him home so he could be their little boy. Only he mustn't ever tell anyone else about that because then "they" would come and take him back. And beat him and beat him until he was dead. She and Lance said that lots of times, so he knew it was true.

Stevie didn't really remember much about when he was a baby. Sometimes he'd get blurry pictures in his head, but that scared him a lot so he real quick thought about something else. Now he mostly didn't get those pictures.

Moira and Lance never did mean things like hit him or make him do stuff he hated, like go to school or eat liver, and sometimes Moira even hugged him, mostly when she was coked up and all-happy.

Stevie didn't know much about golden eggs. He mostly didn't like eggs at all which is why Moira let him have pretty much anything he wanted for breakfast. Not that she noticed, anyway, 'cause she always slept in, sometimes past lunchtime unless she and Lance were making another trip to Mexico.

He liked Mexico a lot. Lance was always happy in Mexico, giving Stevie sips of his margarita and making jokes about ladies' boobies that Stevie pretended to understand 'cause that made Lance laugh.

Him and Lance were best buds, Lance said, which is why Stevie wasn't supposed to call him "Dad." It made Stevie a little sad sometimes, 'cause it didn't really seem like Lance wanted to be his father very much. He remembered once when he used to get nightmares, and he woke up yelling for his daddy. Lance got all bent out of shape and called him a crybaby and threatened to make him wear diapers.

It was okay, though, because Lance told him lots of things he didn't tell Moira, like how Moira was a bitch in heat, only Stevie wasn't exactly sure what that meant. He knew it made Lance mad. Stevie was supposed to tell Lance if strange guys came to the house when Lance was gone.

Sometimes they did. Moira told him she and Lance would get divorced if he told, and Stevie didn't want that, did he? Stevie didn't, which is why he promised not to tell, only it made him a little sick inside to keep secrets, like it was wrong or something. He hated it when guys kept showing up, sometimes when Lance was playing golf and could be home any minute. Moira just laughed when he said, "What about Lance?" and gave him money to go to the arcade at the beach. Stevie didn't much like the arcade. Real scary dudes hung out there, and sometimes bikers, so he mostly hung out at the lifeguard station.

Sometimes, when Lance was out of town with those guys who talked funny, Moira stayed out real late. His best friend, Marcus, thought it was real neat Stevie got to stay home all by himself, 'cause he could watch all the videos he wanted and eat ice cream and junk like that.

Only Stevie wasn't so sure it was neat at all. The house made funny noises when he was alone, and he kept thinking about what would happen if the house caught fire like the apartment house down the block.

Marcus's mom and dad were real strict, making him clean his room and do his homework and be in before dark. It was a real bummer, Marcus said. Nothing like how cool it was at Stevie's house. Stevie's toys were way bad, especially his computer games.

Marcus thought it was real rad that Stevie got to be

home-schooled. Your folks are really neat, Marcus said. Only they weren't really his folks, and if anyone ever found out, they'd take him away.

Whenever he thought about that, his heart felt like it was going to pound right through his chest and he couldn't breathe. He would never tell.

*Never, never, never.*

The stupid lady who asked him piles of questions in a little room in the jail kept asking him hard stuff, like where he was born and did he have grandparents. He knew he messed up on his answers, but he'd been so scared he'd gotten all the things Moira had told him to say scrambled up in his head.

The lady got a funny look on her face, and then she took him to his house where another lady fussed over him. Stuff got all messed up after that. All kinds of people came to the house, asking where he went to school and what was the name of his doctor and did he ever go to church.

No one was going to make him say nothing he didn't want to. Stevie Wilson wasn't no dumb dweeb. He knew how to hang tough. No one was gonna make him do nothing he didn't want to. Following the rules was for suckers, Lance said. Guys like you and me, kid, we're cool, he said.

A strange, scary feeling started in the back of his head, and his heart started pounding real bad. What if he never saw Moira and Lance again? What if the big blond guy really *was* his father?

Trudy, the lady at the house where they stuck him, said this guy Grady was a cop. Stevie had seen his gun at the airport when they'd gone to a special room to get permission to get on the plane.

Stevie had seen guys like him in the movies. Like Clint Eastwood in *"Dirty Harry"* which was his favorite cop show or maybe Mel Gibson in those movies, only Mel was a lot shorter and maybe not even as tough. The look around the eyes was the same, though. Like he could look right through you and know stuff you were trying to hide.

Stevie was pretty sure he didn't like Grady much. He had big hands, Stevie knew. He'd felt the calluses when the guy was washing his back. Had he really meant to kill him when he shoved him under the water?

His stomach pinched hard, and he scrambled to his knees. Holding tight to the pillow, he scooted backward until he was smashed against the curvy railings.

He didn't want to get beaten.

He didn't want to die.

*He wanted to go home.*

He wanted to be in his own bed with his own stuff. He didn't want to be in a strange place with people he didn't know. No matter what they said, he knew better than to trust them.

He wasn't exactly sure why, but he knew that guy, Grady, had something to do with Moira and Lance being in jail. Stevie had seen how everyone looked at him, like he was some important dude.

He said dumb stuff, too. Like how he loved Stevie and all.

Only Stevie knew better. He'd seen a lot of cop shows on the tube. Grady just wanted Stevie to say bad stuff about Moira and Lance so he could keep them in jail.

And that stuff about being his son, well, that made Stevie really nervous. But…maybe Grady and the pretty lady with green eyes and a soft voice only thought he was their son. Maybe, if he threw them an attitude, they wouldn't want him and they'd take him back to California.

He knew all about attitude. Talking back and using bad words. Moira had threatened to throw him off Sunset Cliffs if he didn't stop mouthing off.

Yeah, that was it. Attitude. Nobody wanted a smart-ass.

Stevie closed his eyes and hugged the pillow tighter. The

tears that had shamed him earlier started all over again, and he clamped his mouth shut real hard to keep from making those dumb slobbery noises.

He saw the light slice across the floor a split second before he saw Grady standing in the doorway. He was stripped down to his jeans, and his bare chest seemed almost as wide as the door. Stevie froze, his stomach making like a roller coaster.

Lance worked out a lot, and he had big muscles. But Grady's were bigger, and he walked like the tigers Stevie loved to watch in the San Diego Zoo. Kinda proud, like. And sort of dangerous.

"Thought you might want a glass of water or maybe some milk before turning in," Grady said as he came forward. "Me, I'd rather coffee but you have a few years to go for that."

"I have coffee all the time in California," Stevie blurted out. It wasn't quite a lie. Moira sometimes let him finish hers.

"Yeah?" Grady sat down on the bed, making the mattress sag a lot.

"All the time," Stevie repeated, hugging the pillow a little tighter.

"Guess that makes you tougher than me, because I threw up the first time I filched some of my dad's java."

"I never—" Stevie stopped just in time to keep from making a dumb fool of himself. Even so, he felt his face getting hot as fire. "It was your fault I got sick. You made me come here!"

He held his breath, waiting for Grady to raise that big hand. Instead, Grady just tugged a little on the sheet, straightening it.

"You ever been fishing, son?"

Stevie blinked. What kind of a scam was the guy pulling, anyway?

"My dad—your grandpa—gave me my first pole when I was about your age. I hated just sitting there, staring at the water, doing nothing, which is just about the hardest thing in the world for me. Thought I should be able to just toss in my line and come up with a big fat catfish. But it didn't work that way…. Took me one solid year of trying before I caught anything bigger than a minnow." Grady laughed then, crinkling up his eyes. Stevie felt a little dizzy, like the world had just tilted.

"I threatened to quit a dozen times. Broke my pole clean in two once, and then had to do chores for a month so I could buy another one."

Stevie waited, but Grady just looked at him, his mouth curved a little. "So did you ever catch anything?" he asked when he couldn't stand it any longer.

"Yep. A whole stringer of big suckers." His grin flashed, stirring up Stevie's head again. "Your dad holds the Hardin family record for the biggest catfish pulled out of Lake Freeman."

"I've never seen a catfish," Stevie admitted, intrigued in spite of himself. "Does it really look like a cat?"

"Yep. The face part, anyway. Has this big old whiskers. I'll show you one of these days."

Stevie felt a rush of panic and pulled back. "I hate fishing. Fishing's for losers."

Grady did raise his hand then, but only to put it on Stevie's knee. "One more thing I learned from my dad besides how to bait a hook," he said in a voice that was real soft and maybe a little rough. "It's called patience, son. Lots and lots of patience."

He squeezed Stevie's knee, then stood. Before Stevie could move, Grady reached down and roughed up his hair a little. The dizzy feeling flared again, and Stevie blinked.

"Good night, son," Grady said, his voice even rougher.

"I love you, and I'm glad you're home. One of these days I think you will be, too."

Stevie sat for a long time staring at the crack in the door. And then finally, he closed his eyes. The last thing he remembered was the feeling of Grady's big hand on his knee. Strange as it seemed, it made him feel...safe.

# Chapter 6

It wasn't quite six, but it was already light. Afraid that she'd only dreamed the miracle of Jimmy's return, Ria had leaped out of bed as soon as she'd opened her eyes.

Jimmy was still asleep, sprawled on his tummy at a rebellious angle. He had kicked off the covers, and his pajamas were twisted around his skinny body as though he'd spent the night wrestling with the covers. Though her eyes felt gritty from lack of sleep and the tears she'd shed, she suspected they were shining like bright stars. And inside, she felt little bubbles of happiness bursting in her chest. She loved him so much it was sometimes a physical ache in the vicinity of her heart. Her precious miracle.

She smiled as she caught sight of his bare feet. They seemed huge, compared to the rest of his body. Like a puppy's outsize paws. According to Sarah, Grady had been wearing size thirteen since the age of eleven, which was one of the reasons he'd been so clumsy and uncoordinated as a teenager.

Jimmy had taken his share of tumbles, too—most nota-
bly at the age of two and a half when he'd fallen from the
top of the kitchen counter, which he'd scaled in order to
gorge himself on the gingerbread men she'd set out to cool.
He'd been as resilient as a rubber ball. Grady had sworn
he'd actually bounced.

Her heart thumped a little too fast as she tiptoed across
the hand-woven rug to smooth just the tips of her fingers
over the thatch of unruly hair that was as thick and silky
now as his dad's.

Flynn was right, she thought, smiling through a sudden
wash of happy tears. Her baby needed a haircut. Not his
favorite thing, something else he'd inherited from his dad,
who, even as a giant of a man, had squirmed like a little
boy whenever he'd had to sit still for more than a few
minutes.

After their first and last nerve-racking trip to the barber-
shop, she and Grady had taken to trimming Jimmy's hair
themselves. It *had* taken the two of them to get him shorn—
one to do the cutting, the other to distract him with a favorite story. Since Grady still read painfully slowly, he
made up stories instead. About a famous circus clown
named Jimbo who was always having outrageous adventures.

They'd had so much, she and Grady. A fantastic son, a
funky house full of laughter—theirs and the lingering vi-
brations of other families—and each other.

If only—

No, she told herself firmly. Don't go down that road.
Think of the blessings you have now, not the ones you let
slip away.

Careful not to make noise, she closed the door and continued down the hall to the living room. She expected to
find Grady awake, perhaps out running the way he'd done
almost every morning of their marriage. Instead, to her sur-

prise, he was still deeply asleep, sprawled on his back on the floor with only the blanket she'd given him as a mattress.

His jeans and shirt were slung over a chair, his running shoes nearby. His long legs were half tangled in the sheet, the pillow in the flowered case cradled against his wide, bare chest in much the same way he'd once held her.

His lean, somewhat bony face, framed by one thick forearm crooked behind his head, was turned her way. The brutally gaunt lines of his cheeks were softened a little by thick stubble the color of wheat, but nothing could disguise the deep lines of bitterness and suffering bracketing his mouth. Lines that hadn't been there three years ago.

Like Jimmy's, his hair was tousled, the glossy, springy strands of light and dark blond, and a surprising amount of silver, blended into a provocative mixture that defied precise description. In contrast to the soft thatch, the permanent lines etched into his forehead seemed painfully harsh.

He looked worn out.

No wonder, she thought, her heart tumbling a little. Three nights on a sagging sofa and now this.

Even though the room was cool, his bare chest was covered with a fine film of sweat, giving his skin the illusion of hand-rubbed bronze, and the triangle of hair curled in damp ringlets around the tiny flat nipples.

As she stood there debating whether to wake him or not, he stirred restlessly, muttering something only he understood before drawing up one leg. The sheet fell away, and she saw that he was wearing only dark blue briefs, the thin cotton stretched taut to accommodate his sex.

He was, she realized suddenly, partially aroused, as though his dream was an erotic one. Feeling a disturbing and decidedly sexual tug in her midsection, she scrupulously averted her gaze as she tiptoed past.

Sensing an intrusion, a presence, Grady fought through

a gray wall of exhaustion, his body already reacting before his mind was fully alert. Consequently he was halfway to his feet before he realized where he was.

"Is it Jimmy?" he demanded when he saw Ria tiptoeing past. She was wearing a thin cotton robe the color of lime sherbet, and her hair was still a little mussed. His libido sneaked in a hard kick, adding more pressure to his already heavy groin.

"Good morning," she said, altering her course in order to open the drapes covering the large picture window overlooking the building's tidy front lawn. "I was on the way to the kitchen to make coffee. I tried not to wake you."

"What time is it?"

"A little past six."

Grady remembered looking at his watch around four. Two hours wasn't much, but it was better than the night before.

He reached for his jeans, far too aware of the heavy throb of arousal that he suspected had been the result of yet another dream of her. Sometimes he remembered them in stark and painful degree. Sometimes he woke with only wisps of memory. Both left him with a lingering feeling of loss.

He stretched his stiff back, then rubbed his hand over his whisker-roughened cheeks. In spite of the bath he'd gotten while cooling down his son, he felt a little too raunchy for polite company.

"Mind if I use your shower?"

Her gaze skittered to his belly, and he realized he was rubbing the fire that burned there now morning and night.

"No, of course not."

He glanced at the duffel, then narrowed his gaze her way. Her skin was pale, but her eyes had lost the sad look that had tortured him every time he'd seen her during the twenty-six miserable months since she'd stopped being his wife.

"I'm pretty much out of clean clothes. Guess you threw away all those old shirts you used to sleep in."

She nodded. "I'm afraid I—no, wait, I *do* have one that I used when I painted my office at the Center. It's fairly ratty, but it's clean—and it doesn't smell like cigar." His heart stuttered when she suddenly smiled. "If you make the coffee, I'll dig it out for you."

He decided there wasn't much he *wouldn't* do for another of those smiles. "You got a deal."

Kate arrived while Grady was in the shower. Nearly six feet tall and as sleekly stylish as a haute couture model, with short platinum curls framing a classically beautiful face and brilliant blue eyes, Kate turned heads, both male and female, wherever she went.

An avid feminist and avowed cynic, she and Ria were temperamental opposites. The Viking and the Earth Mother, Tova called them.

Born and reared in Shaker Heights, Ohio, the only daughter of a corporate CEO, Katie's upbringing had been as rich in love and security as Ria's had been impoverished. It had been her money that had bought the big old house on Wabash Drive. The operating capital, however, came from fees and donations. Twice a year they had a fund-raising reception at which Katie shone like a priceless jewel in glittering designer chic and pearls.

Everything Ria knew about the upscale side of life, she'd learned from Katie. At the moment, however, dressed in baggy safari shorts and a faded red cargo shirt with a frayed collar and an ink stain on one sleeve, Katie looked more like a harried, overworked coed than the pampered only daughter of a multimillionaire.

"Coffee," she muttered as she followed Ria into the kitchen. "Lots and lots of coffee. Make it strong."

"Trust me, it's strong," Ria tossed over her shoulder. And as black as sin.

As soon as Grady had disappeared into the bathroom with the old Boilermaker shirt draped over his shoulder and one big hand wrapped around a mug of the steaming caffeine sludge he'd brewed, she'd ducked into her bedroom to slip into shorts and a sleeveless V-necked shirt. She'd only been able to find one of her sandals, so her feet were still bare.

"It's going to be another scorcher today," Kate muttered as she deposited her black bag and a bulging purse the size of a small car on the counter. "Gotta tell you, toots, I was well and truly blown away by your call last night," she declared before braving the steam of the coffee mug Ria handed her to take a greedy sip. "Which, by the way, caught me just coming out of the shower. After I hung up, I danced around the house starkers for a good twenty minutes. Darn near wore myself out celebrating."

Ria grinned. "Now that was something I'd pay big money to see."

Katie's lips curled at the corners. "Pres seemed to like it."

Ria nearly choked on her own testing sip. "Pres?"

"Preston Woodward IV. An old friend from Shaker."

"Friend as in friend-friend or friend-lover?"

"Yes and yes." She took another longer sip, her eyes twinkling. Ria shook her head.

"So, Mom, how's your baby boy doing on this already miserably humid day?"

Ria felt her face soften. One day, maybe, she'd take his reappearance in her life for granted. But she wasn't anywhere near that stage yet. "Still sleeping like a little angel last time I checked."

Katie lifted a pale eyebrow. "How's his temp?"

"It was a fraction under a hundred at 3:00 a.m. Since he seemed so peaceful, I didn't want to disturb him this morning."

"Vomiting?"

"No, thank heavens."

Ria walked to the bleached-pine table and sat down. Kate remained where she was, leaning against the counter with her mug cradled in both hands a few inches from her mouth.

"Sound's like Jimmy's over the hump." Kate paused to take another more generous sip, her eyes narrowing in blissful enjoyment. "Next question, how's Jimmy's mom doing?"

"Still in shock, I think," Ria admitted with a laugh that came out on the nervous side. "Or maybe shell-shocked is a better description."

"From what you said last night it sounds like Hardin didn't give you a lot of notice."

Ria smiled at that. Kate had only called Grady by his Christian name once—on Ria's wedding day. It was also the only time Ria had ever seen her friend cry. Kate swore it was from sheer happiness, and since she'd been grinning as well as snuffling, Ria had taken her at her word, although a part of her wondered if Katie wasn't a little bit in love with Grady herself. Thinking of that now, she felt a familiar pang. It wasn't jealousy, of course. More like amazement. Of all her friends, Katie was also the only one who'd never said a bad word about Grady after the divorce. In fact, she'd tried very hard to convince Ria to try a separation first.

"Grady called me after they'd landed at Indianapolis. It was the longest two and a half hours of my life." She reached out to align the pepper mill with the salt cellar. "He waited three days before telling me he'd found our child, Katie. Three days!'' She felt her cheeks turning hot. ''He claimed he was protecting me.''

''Knowing Hardin, I'd say that's exactly what he was doing.''

''I'm thirty-five years old, Katherine. I don't need protecting.''

Kate's skepticism was written in large letters on her face. ''If he had called, you would have been on the next plane out, right?''

''Of course!''

''Wringing your hands, gnawing your lip raw. Your basic puddle of quivering nerve endings. Which wouldn't have done you or Jimmy any good.''

Ria shot her a disgusted look. ''Gee, thanks for the flattering description of my strength of character, Dr. Stevens.''

Kate raised her mug. ''Your character is just fine, Ms. Hardin. It's your total obsession with this whole mommy thing that's always bothered me.''

Ria bristled. ''Loving my child is not obsessive.''

''It is if it leads you to neglect your husband.''

Ria's jaw dropped. ''Is that what you really think?''

''Yes, Victoria, that's what I really think,'' Kate muttered before finishing her coffee. She was refilling her mug when Grady walked in.

Though his eyes were still shadowed, he looked more alert, wary, even, especially when his gaze found hers. His hair was damp and tousled and curling low on his strong neck. His jaw and checks had the crisp, clean look of a close shave. Though he'd tucked the paint-spattered black and gold shirt into the low waistband of his jeans, he looked more like a hell-raising street tough than a decorated police captain.

As soon as he saw Kate, the wary look disappeared and his eyes lit up. At the same time his grin flashed, a little crooked, a little reckless and with enough sexual wattage to take even the strongest, most resistant woman to her knees. Though she knew it was simply the remnants of old feelings stirring, Ria felt a powerful need to rub against that strong, hard body. Just long enough to ease the hot little ache low and deep inside.

"Hey there, handsome," Kate offered with a brilliant smile that had Ria narrowing her gaze. "Love the *Rebel Without a Cause* look. It suits you."

"Hey, gorgeous lady," he said, leaning down to kiss the cheek Kate offered.

The look Kate slanted him was playful. "Lordy, I've missed that old zing."

He looked a little startled. "What zing is that?"

"That hot little sizzle that hums through a girl when you turn on the charm."

He turned red. "You must have me mixed up with one of my brothers," he muttered as he grabbed the pot to refill the mug he'd carried with him.

"Nope." Kate shot Ria a bland look. "Ria walked into walls for a week after you kissed her for the first time."

You'll pay for this big-time, Ria told her friend with a look that had Kate's mouth twitching. "Don't you have rounds to make this morning, Doctor?"

Kate glanced at her watch. "Guess that's my cue to haul out my stethoscope and bedside manner."

"Such as it is," Ria muttered.

Unfazed, Kate picked up the handmade doctor's bag with its gold monogram that had been a graduation gift from her proud father. "So, Mom and Dad, where's my patient?"

Ria braced both elbows on the table and used her fingertips to rub her temples. From the den came the frenetic cacophony of a cartoon soundtrack. Twice she'd turned down the volume on the TV and twice Jimmy had turned it up again. Finally, she'd just given up.

Later she would worry about her son's eardrums.

It had been nearly two hours since Kate had emerged from the bedroom with a troubled expression and a blunt diagnosis. "Physically he's fine. His temp is normal, his other vitals good. But I have to tell you, I think this is one very unhappy little boy."

Utterly miserable was more like it.

The last few hours had been nothing like the joyous reunion she'd pictured over and over in her mind for so many anxious months. In fact, it was close to being a disaster. Instead of the laughing, bright-eyed, affectionate child she'd been aching to cuddle and kiss and spoil, the boy in the other room was virtually a stranger who stared at her with angry suspicious eyes—when he looked at her at all.

After Kate had left, Jimmy had picked at the pancakes she'd made, his head down and his shoulders hunched, spurning every attempt she or Grady had made to coax him into a conversation.

He didn't want to wear the shirt she'd picked out from the several Grady had bought him.

He didn't want to brush his teeth or wash his face.

He didn't want to see pictures of himself as a baby.

And for sure, he didn't want to go through the boxes of toys she'd packed away so carefully.

In short, her adorable, beloved, maddeningly stubborn son didn't want to do anything but sit in front of the TV and stare at the "stupid" screen. Stupid because "only dweebs and welfare creeps" had nineteen-inch screens.

It was that pronouncement that had stirred Grady's wrath. Fortunately, Ria had seen the firecracker heat come into his eyes in time to head him off. She had a terrible feeling it was going to be a very long day.

"Bad headache?"

Careful to keep her eyes narrowed against the obscenely bright sun streaming through the kitchen window, she lifted her head far enough to meet Grady's gaze over the remains of the breakfast neither finished. "Only a twelve on a scale of ten."

He smiled a little. His exasperation with his son was still there, mixed in with the shadows of other less-easily identified emotions in the recesses of his dark pupils. "Want some aspirin?"

"I took three while you were on the phone with your folks."

Giving up on the attempt to rub away the stabbing pulses of pain, she folded her arms on the place mat. "I'm glad you told your mom and dad to hold off on visiting. I think Jimmy needs more time to adjust."

His mouth gentled. Grady's love and respect for his parents was one of life's absolutes. There'd been a time when she'd thought herself included on the short list of those he loved. "Mom sucked in pretty hard, but Dad understood."

"When are they leaving on their rafting trip?"

"The end of the month." He rubbed the back of his neck, then flexed his shoulders. "I heard you had a vacation planned."

"Two weeks starting today. One of the reasons I called Tova so early was to ask her to tell her mom I wouldn't be using their cabin after all."

She shook her head at the memory of Tova's excited squeal when she'd broken the news about Jimmy's return. Betty Lou Sanberra had been a little more restrained, but happy for her nonetheless.

"I was hoping to have Jimmy's furniture delivered today, but the transfer company can't do anything until Tuesday."

He glanced at the clock, then leaned back and hooked his thumbs in the belt loops of his thigh-hugging jeans. The old shirt pulled taut, stretched around his torso like a second skin. He was thinner than she remembered, she decided. And he'd eaten less than she had. Jet lag, he'd said.

She lifted her mug to her mouth and drank the last of her coffee, then glanced at the pot. It was still half-full, something that was unheard of when a Hardin male was in the vicinity. Frowning, she glanced across the table to find that his mug, too, was nearly full. Instead, he was drinking the milk Jimmy refused to finish—and Grady hated milk. She was beginning to think she'd dropped into her own zigzag version of Wonderland.

"I used to hate it when my mother locked herself in her room and refused to come out," she said with a sigh. "At the moment, though, that seems like a wonderful solution."

He dismissed that with another of those soft smiles that never failed to touch her. "Nah, that's not your style, honey. You might weave a little after a left jab, but you come back strong."

At the moment she wasn't so sure she could so much as make a fist, she reflected as she heard a power mower cough into life somewhere on the grounds of the complex. She and Jimmy used to ride the jazzy red lawn tractor Grady had given her for her thirtieth birthday. He'd also given her a French silk nightgown he'd insisted she model for him in the moonlight.

Jimmy had loved that tractor almost as much as Grady had loved his Charger. Jimmy tended to drive with the same disregard for danger, too, with his ball cap pulled over his eyes like the visor of a helmet. Sometimes it had been a rocket ship, sometimes a race car. Smiling to herself, she glanced toward the window.

*Oh, Jimmy,* she thought, her heart breaking. *Why can't you let me love you?*

"They abused him, didn't they?" Her voice wasn't quite steady. "The…people who had him."

Grady glanced down. "Not physically, no. The doctor from California Children's Services who examined him agreed with Katie. He's well-nourished and healthy. On the other hand, his behavior sucks."

"He seems so…so angry."

"Wouldn't you be if you'd been ripped out of your own world and dumped into a place where people call you by someone else's name?" He got up suddenly and carried the milk carton to the fridge. "The shrink who examined him said it might take a while for him to adjust."

"There's something you're not telling me, isn't there?" she said to his broad, stiff back. "You don't need to protect me. I won't fall apart."

He turned to face her. His eyes were tired, but steady, his expression more cop than father. "If I knew more, I'd tell you, Ree. But I don't. The creeps who had him didn't give up a thing, though God knows Mendoza and I tried damn near every trick we'd learned between us."

Too tense to sit a moment longer, she got up to carry her cereal bowl to the sink. "What have you found out about them, the Wilsons?"

"Too damn little. Mendoza's still running all the aliases. Last I heard he'd come up with a half dozen for both the male and the female. At least that many arrests between them, but no convictions. Like I said, they're pros."

She turned to shoot him an angry look. "You make them sound admirable."

Grady kept his own anger tightly leashed. A man lost his perspective when his mind was clouded with rage. He made bad decisions, spit out words he later regretted. If that man was a cop, a momentary lapse in control could get someone killed. So he'd learned to turn that white hot flash of fury inward, grounding it somewhere deep inside himself until the urge to lash out eased up. But he'd come close to losing it during the hours he and Mendoza had sat across from the low-lifes who'd stolen his child.

"They're human garbage, Ree," he said, not bothering to gentle his tone. "Well-educated, middle-class scum who feed on the misery of others."

"Too bad they weren't shot resisting arrest," she declared fiercely as she turned on the hot tap with a hard twist of her wrist. Steam billowed upward, wisping the ends of her hair into flyaway curls at the nape of her neck.

She'd cut her hair since he'd seen her last, and he felt a twinge of regret at the thought of never being able to bury his face in the silky mane. It had been three years since he'd breathed in the scent of roses clinging to her skin, three years since he'd kissed her, three years since he'd felt the warm little tremors of her release vibrating beneath him.

Three years of cold showers and empty rooms and waking up each morning with a hole in his life.

"Where did they live?" She glanced up, her brow puckering. "The Wilsons?"

"Last known address was San Diego." Restless and a little buzzed on the caffeine, he grabbed the cereal box from the counter and opened cupboard doors until he found the right one. "Mendoza was going to check it out as soon as he got a warrant. Once we find out what school Jimmy went to and talk to his teacher, get the name of his friends, he might start opening up."

One of the calls he'd made while Ria had been organizing breakfast had been to Mendoza's office in Calexico. According to the female agent who'd taken his call, Cruz was having a problem tracking down Jimmy's teacher. It seemed he wasn't enrolled in the school closest to the Wilsons' home. In fact, the name Steven Allen Wilson hadn't been in the public school's database of enrolled students. Cruz was in the process of checking the private primary schools.

"How long does it take to get a warrant?" she asked as she rinsed the dishes one by one.

"Not long." He put away the syrup and the butter, then looked around for something else to occupy his hands—and his thoughts. Anything to keep him from rubbing his palms over that tight little bottom she kept wiggling at him with every swish of her dishcloth. His body gave him another of those sneaking kicks, exactly where it hurt the most. "I left this number, by the way."

The look she gave him was wary. "I hope you're not thinking of staying here again tonight."

It had been the worst kind of hell bedding down on her floor, knowing she was only a short walk away. He'd nearly paced a rut in her carpet, thinking about those skimpy summer nightgowns she'd worn, the ones with the cobweb lace that skimmed the top of her thighs every time she walked. A man would be six times a fool to willingly put himself through that kind of torture again.

"No need to think about it," he all but growled. "I'm staying." He carried the last of the dishes to the sink, then plucked the dishcloth from her hand. "Kid got syrup on the table," he said when she glared.

"You can't stay here!"

"I admit the floor's not my first choice, but I have a hunch you'd shoot that one down, so I figure to borrow Dad's sleeping bag."

Something that looked like panic glimmered in the back of her dark pupils for the span of a blink. "Grady, read my lips. This is my house. You can't stay here."

"Why not?" He finished wiping the table and walked back to the sink.

"Because it's not necessary," she muttered, snatching the cloth from his hand. "Jimmy and I will manage just fine."

He shot her a grin that felt a little cocky. He could handle her anger, even her resentment if he had to, but the worry in her eyes had been tearing him apart. "Afraid you'll be overcome with lust and jump me in the night?"

"Hardly," she muttered, jerking her gaze back to the plate she'd been rinsing.

"Afraid *I'll* jump *you?*"

Her chest rose and fell in a fast breath. "In case you've forgotten, I have a gun. A cute little nickel-plated automatic you bought me for our first Christmas. And I know how to use it."

"I have a gun, too, and it's bigger than yours. 'Course it's not nickel-plated, but—"

"Don't say it," she warned, but her lips twitched, and her cheeks were pink. He'd probably roast in hell for it, given the fact that their troubles with Jimmy were anything but over, but suddenly he felt hopeful.

Maybe there was such a thing as a second chance, after all.

# Chapter 7

Grady scrawled his initials at the bottom of the weekly report and tossed it atop the other bits of departmental busy work. Nothing put him in a foul mood faster than paperwork. He would rather face a hyped-up maniac with nothing but his bare hands than read anything more complicated than a menu.

He rotated his head, trying to work out the kinks. On his way to the office, he'd stopped by his place, fed the cat and changed clothes. Trouble had been really upset which is why the little beggar was now sleeping in his carrying box in the corner of the office. He'd thought about calling Ria from his place to ask permission to bring another houseguest, then changed his mind.

Which was his ego's way of saying he wimped out.

In the large area beyond his glassed-in office, the day-shift detectives were working the phones or dealing with interviews. Catching his eye, one of his guys lifted a thumb and grinned. Grady acknowledged the best wishes with a smile and a nod. He wasn't sure how the word had spread, only that it had, and with the usual lightning speed that never failed to amaze him.

When things shook down closer to a normal routine, he planned to throw a party for the entire squad. In one way or another each man and woman who worked under him had offered support.

In the beginning, when he'd been mostly raw nerves and raging temper, they'd hung in without even a whisper of mutiny. God knew they'd had every right to go over his head to the brass and get him kicked out of his command for cause. Instead, they'd quietly covered for him when he made mistakes, divvied up his routine paperwork, settled their own scheduling problems.

Feeling like a martyr about to be staked out for the buzzards, he picked up his pen and reached for the next report in the folder. At the same time the phone rang. Grateful for the reprieve, he snatched it up on the second ring.

Dr. Alberta Roth had a sultry voice that evoked images of damp sheets and steamy sex. The reality, however, was far more prosaic. In fact, when they'd met face to face in Calexico, the pudgy, gray-haired matron with shrewd blue eyes had reminded him of his grandmother Hardin. On a personal level he'd taken to her immediately. After an hour of watching her gentle Jimmy out of a series of tantrums, he'd wanted to beg her to come home with them.

"Sorry I wasn't in when you called earlier, Captain. I was playing racquetball with my husband." A laugh bubbled through the wire. "Just between us, I whipped his little candy butt."

Grady choked out a laugh. "My ex-wife used to whip me regularly on the tennis court. Had me begging for mercy by the third set." Mostly because he'd been watching her bottom. Half the time he'd staggered off the court so aroused he couldn't wait to get her into the shower.

When the doctor spoke again, the gloating wife had become a brisk professional. "So much for my athletic prowess. Why don't you tell me why you called?"

Grady cleared his throat. During the last meeting he'd had with her and the social worker handling Jimmy's case, Dr. Roth had given him three names of child psychologists, all within a day's drive of Indiana. After he'd leaned on her a little, she'd admitted that her first choice would be a former student intern who now practiced in Chicago.

"First thing this morning I phoned Dr. McCurry's office to set up an appointment for a consultation, but according to his receptionist, he's booked solid for the next month."

"Aha. You want me to give Patrick a call and get you in sooner, I take it?"

Grady's chair protested as he leaned back. "Yes, ma'am. That's exactly what I'm hoping."

"Is Jimmy acting out?"

"I'm not sure that's the right term, but things have been pretty rocky so far. Jim and I, well, I wasn't around much so it made sense he wouldn't remember me, but he and his mama were like a team, you know? Right from the beginning, he was his mom's son. They were, uh, bonded, I'd guess you'd call it. Did everything together. I know he was only three, but—" He broke off before he was tempted to dump his own tangled emotions on her.

"He didn't remember her?" the doctor prodded gently when the silence lengthened.

"No, ma'am. It's been rough on her. I hate to call my own son a spoiled brat, but—" He cleared his throat, but the taste of guilt remained. "If it was some lowlife threatening her, I'd know what to do, but this is way out of my area. I figure we need some professional help."

"I see." There was a pause during which Grady watched Detective First Grade DeeAnn Gregory stride with her usual impatience through the bullpen maze toward her own neat-as-a-pin desk in the far corner. Grady and Dee's husband, Terrell, had gone through the academy together. When Terrell had been killed in the line of duty, DeeAnn had immediately applied to the department herself. After a rough start, she'd turned into a darned fine investigator.

"As I recall, Captain," Dr. Roth continued briskly, "you said that your divorce from the child's mother was an amicable one. However, it's been my experience that even the most comfortable relationships undergo strain in times of high stress. Perhaps James is picking up on some undercurrents between the two of you and reacting to those."

"If you're asking me if Ria and I are snarling at each other, the answer is no."

"No offense, Captain, but children are far more perceptive than those of us who consider ourselves grown-ups. Studies have shown that they can pick up even the smallest signs of friction."

Grady saw DeeAnn approaching his office and shook his head. She held up a folder, mouthed "later" and he nodded.

"Ria and I are doing okay so far," he said, rubbing a hand over his neck. "We have to hammer out some kind of custody arrangement, but that can wait."

"Where is the boy now?"

"With his mom, at her place."

"In familiar surroundings?"

"No, not at all. The house where he grew up was sold after we split. Ria has a small place in the city now. Is that a problem?"

"Not necessarily, although research into similar cases has shown fairly conclusively that the more reminders of the patient's past life the better."

"Ria did save his toys and books, things like that. But when she tried to get him interested in going through the boxes, he pitched another fit. Flat-out told her to stop bugging him.''

He heard the sudden crackle of static. A storm somewhere in the heartland, he figured. Coming their way. The clouds were already forming, brooding black suckers that blocked out the sun.

''Has he talked much about the couple who posed as his parents?'' she asked quietly.

''Some, on the trip home, mostly. I got the feeling they pretty much let him do anything he wanted.''

''Unfortunately I had that same feeling.'' She sighed. ''Well, first things first. I can't promise to convince Patrick to juggle his schedule, but I'll try. In the meantime, I suggest you establish a routine with the boy and stick to it. Restrict the number of people he has to deal with to those who'd once been special to him in some way. You and your ex-wife, of course, and any close family members.''

''I have a big family, Doctor. Four brothers and a sister. Things can get a little hectic.''

''Then perhaps you should keep things simple for the moment.'' She sighed. ''Is there someplace where the three of you often went together? A park perhaps, or a restaurant?''

He glanced at the framed snapshot of Ria and Jim building a sand castle on a sunlit day at the lake. Sunbeams were trapped in her hair, and she was laughing as she looked into the camera.

''My folks have a cottage on a lake about a half hour's drive away. We used to spend part of every summer there. In fact Ria was packing our things for a two-week stay when Jimmy was abducted.''

''And the boy knew that?''

''Sure. We'd even gotten him his own fishing rod.''

''I think that's it, Captain, your best chance at sparking his memory.''

"Taking Jim fishing?"

"Among other things, yes. The three of you need to go to the lake and do all the things you did before. Try to replicate your previous stays as closely as possible."

"That might be a problem," he admitted, his voice tight. "Ria and I haven't told Jim we're divorced. Things were pretty hectic last night, and then today he wasn't in the mood to listen to anything either of us said."

"Maybe that's for the best. In fact…" She paused and he could almost hear the wheels turning in her head. When she spoke again, her voice was suddenly energized. "Don't tell the boy about the divorce. Not yet. Don't let anyone else tell him. Wait until he's more secure before you ask him to deal with yet one more demand on his resilience."

Grady cleared his throat. "I slept on Ria's floor last night, Doctor. Jim didn't see me, but he might. He's bound to figure out something's not right if his folks aren't—" He broke off, embarrassed as hell. The woman on the other end probably knew more about sex than he ever would, given the stories he figured she'd listened to over the years, but still…

"I take it this amicable divorce doesn't include a continuation of sexual relations between the two of you."

He scowled. "You take it right."

"Fake it."

He blinked. "Pardon?"

She chuckled. "You heard me, Captain. Pretend. Buy twin beds if you have to, but make sure you and your ex-wife sleep in the same room."

He nearly groaned. It had been bad enough just sleeping under the same roof with Ree. He wasn't sure he'd come out of this sane if he had to listen to the soft sounds of her breathing night after night without being able to touch her.

"You really think this will work?"

"The literature cites several instances of remarkable results in other cases of amnesia." There was a pause, then she continued in a softer tone, "Your son needs you, Captain Hardin. And he needs his mother. More now, I suspect, than he ever did before. But I feel I must warn you, it's very possible he might always think of *you* as the one who stole him away from his parents. He might actually hate you."

"He already does. Told me so a couple of times already. He blames me for putting his...parents in jail."

"Hate and love often share the same space in a person's heart."

He thought about the cases of domestic violence he'd rolled on when he'd been in uniform. He'd never quite gotten his mind around the idea that a man could beat his wife bloody one moment, then swear up and down he only did it because he loved her so much.

"Are you saying I should stay out of my son's life?"

"No, that's the last thing I think you should do. Just the opposite, in fact. James was definitely intrigued by you, but then, young males tend to be fascinated by other powerful males, especially ones like yourself who have an edge of danger to their persona."

Grady frowned. Was that good or bad? he wondered. "And his mom? Ria, I mean? Do you think he could come to hate her, too?"

She sighed deeply. "I don't know, Captain. I simply don't know."

Grady pulled into the driveway and parked behind his dad's vintage Studebaker. Fat raindrops pelted his head and shoulders as he raced from the driveway to the shelter of the back porch. The door was unlocked, the way it had always been. He smiled a little when he walked past the irregular spot in the kitchen wall where he'd put his fist through the lath plaster. At the time it had been his brother's face he'd been aiming to pound, but Kale had always been a step faster, even then.

It had taken him half a block before he'd caught up to the smirking bastard and sent him sprawling into Mrs. Genarro's prized peony bush. Kale had ended up with a broken nose, and he'd ended up with a month's restriction and a sore butt.

His mom had clucked over both her boys, dispensing ice for her firstborn's nose and iodine for her second son's split knuckles—along with copious hugs. His dad had given them both hell—Kale for taunting his brother about flunking first grade again, and Grady for being suckered into losing his temper.

His dad had shown him how to patch up the damage, then had taken him out for ice cream, just the two of them. Mason had talked, about baseball and fishing and the difference between winners and losers. By the time Grady had packed away two banana splits, he'd decided to take another stab at the exercises the special ed teacher had given him.

It had taken him four years to catch up with the rest of the kids his age. In spite of the hours of study he'd put in every night—twice as many as his brothers—he'd never made better-than-average grades, but he'd won the battle for his self-respect.

The kitchen was empty. In all the years since he'd been walking through the back door, he'd never failed to feel a sense of comfort and warmth in this room. According to his mom, her kitchen was the heart of the house. The place where hungry bodies were fed and aching souls were soothed.

His mom had been baking, and the scent of ginger and spice hung in the air. He grinned when he saw the gingerbread men lined up to cool on the baking sheet on the counter. Jimmy loved gingerbread men almost as much as he did. His stomach growled, but he fought off the urge to filch a bite.

"Anybody home?" he called as he went through the swinging door into the dining room.

"Grady!" His mom's voice came from above, and he headed for the stairs off the old-fashioned entry hall. "Mason, wake up. It's Grady."

Grinning because it was good to know he would always be welcome in this place no matter how many times he messed up, he rested his hand on the square newel post and waited for his mom to appear at the top of the stairs.

It took less than a wink before she was rushing toward him, her smile as happy as he'd ever seen it.

"This is such a wonderful surprise," she said as he caught her up in a hug. It gentled him some to breathe in the clean scent of plain soap that had been one of his earliest memories. Then as now it promised security and love. His grin dimmed as he wondered if Jimmy would ever feel similar feelings for his mom again.

As soon as he set her on her feet, Sarah was looking behind him, her eyes as bright as stars. "Is Jimmy with you?"

"Nope. Does that mean I have to leave?"

"Don't be a smart-ass, James Grady," she ordered before tucking her arm in Grady's. "Come sit in the kitchen while I pack up the treats I made for the little angel. I want to hear everything that happened from the moment you left for California. Don't leave out a thing."

Thirty minutes later Grady finished both his story and the bottle of beer his dad had handed him as soon as he'd settled into the bench built into the breakfast nook.

"Of course you can have the cottage for as long as you want it," his mother said after exchanging looks with his dad.

"Sounds like a damn minefield to me," Mason muttered

before tipping the long-necked bottle to his mouth for a long, satisfying swig. "Pretending to be man and wife. Seems like a sure way to get yourself in a tangle."

"Hush, Mason. Grady knows what he's doing." Sarah furrowed her brow. "What does Ria think?"

Grady felt a sudden burning in his belly. The beer had been a mistake. "I haven't discussed it with her yet."

His father lifted his left eyebrow, the skeptical one each of his sons had come to dread. "Any idea when you might get around to it?"

Grady studied the label on the bottle as though his life depended on memorizing it. "I figure I'll pour her a glass of wine as soon as Jimmy goes to bed, and then when she's feeling nice and mellow, I'll work the conversation around to it nice and slow like."

His dad's eyebrow edged higher. "I'd make that glass a big one, and do your edging at a snail's pace."

"Oh, for heaven's sake, Mason. You know Ria's still in love with our boy. It sticks out all over her whenever they're in the same room together."

Grady had never wanted to believe anything more in his life. "How come if she loves me so much she acts like I have something catching whenever I try to talk to her?" He picked at the label with a fingernail clipped too close to do much good. But it helped him concentrate.

"For heaven's sake, you men can be obtuse sometimes." His mother got up from her seat across from him and started packing up the gingerbread men.

"What about it, Pop? Are we obtuse?" Grady asked, meeting his father's amused gaze.

"Don't know about you, son, but I figure I have to be, seeing's how your mom has this all-powerful need to tell me at least a dozen times a day that what I just said wasn't what I meant at all."

His mom waved a graceful hand. "Don't pay any attention to your father, sweetheart. He's just in a funk because the Cubs have lost seventeen straight.''

''Eighteen,'' Mason grumbled before getting up to snag another beer from the fridge. Grady wasn't surprised when his dad neglected to offer him one, too. Mason was scrupulous about never having more than one when he knew he was going to get behind the wheel, and he'd hammered that rule into each of his sons.

''Cottage phone's not hooked up,'' Mason said after chugging a satisfying third of the bottle. ''Something's wrong with the wiring.''

''Mice,'' Sarah muttered, glancing over her shoulder. ''The same mice your father promised to trap for me this spring.''

''Didn't figure there was any hurry, what with darn near every member of this family hauling around cell phones.'' He slanted Grady a grumpy look. ''Where's yours?''

''In the truck.''

Mason's mouth quirked. ''There you go, Sarah. Who needs wires when you have satellites?''

''I do,'' she muttered, her brow puckering as she concentrated on layering the gingerbread men carefully into the flat plastic container. When she was finished, she glanced up, her expression softening. ''It'll work out, Grady. Jimmy comes from good stock, and I include Ria in that.'' Her lips curved in a fond smile. ''I meant what I said, son. I've never seen two people so smitten with each other as you and Ria. I told your dad right off, after you brought her home that first Christmas Eve, that you'd finally found the other half of yourself. Nothing that's happened since has changed my mind.''

''Don't take this wrong, Mom, but it's Ria's mind that needs changing.''

''So change it.''

He shifted on the hard seat. "It's not that easy," he muttered, dropping his gaze.

"Of course it's not easy. Nothing worthwhile is. But that doesn't mean it's impossible."

Damn near, Grady got to his feet and rinsed out the bottle, then upended it in the drainer. "Thanks for the use of the cottage. I'll take care of the phone wire—and the mice," he added when his mother opened her mouth.

"Thank you, dear heart. It's nice to know there's one thoughtful male in this room." She shot Mason a look that he returned with the same boyish grin that had stolen sixteen-year-old Sarah Smith's romantic heart fifty years earlier.

Grady watched the melting look come into his mom's eyes and ached. Ria had looked at him like that once. He'd walk hot coals stark naked in front of God and the entire Lafayette PD to see that look in her eyes again.

"Give that little one a big hug and kiss from Grandma," his mom said after giving him the same. "And be sure to tell him I can't wait to see him."

"I will and thanks for understanding. You know Ria and I would never keep him from you if it wasn't necessary."

She smiled, a little sadly, Grady noticed. "Lay the container flat on the floor so it doesn't slide," she ordered as she handed over the gingerbread.

"Yes, ma'am."

"I'll walk you out," his dad said as he put his beer on the counter.

"Stay under the overhang," Sarah called after them as they left.

By tacit agreement, they stood shoulder to shoulder on the porch, two large Hardin men, one who'd made his marriage work, one who hadn't. "Your mom never could stand unhappy endings."

"To tell you the truth, Dad, I'm not all that crazy about

them myself.'' Grady glanced up at the low overcast. The rain came down in a monotonous drizzle. He hated rain. It made him edgy.

"It was raining like this the day Ria and I decided to file. I walked out of the house and started running. I don't know how many miles I did. Just rabbited across one field after another until I couldn't run anymore.'' And then he'd leaned against the trunk of a gnarled old oak and cried.

His father turned his head and looked at him as though he'd never seen him before. "It's not like you to give up on something you'd set your heart on. Ria, either, for that matter. In fact, she's just about the most tenacious little gal I've ever met. The way she risked her life to hang on to that youngster of yours—'' Mason broke off, drawing in a slow breath. "From that time on, she was my daughter, same as Manda.''

Grady glanced down at the sodden walk. Ria's obstetrician had given her no more than a fifty-fifty chance of surviving if she carried Jimmy to term. She'd refused to consider any other option. Her grit had humbled him. Maybe it had even made him feel, well, unworthy.

"I didn't know how to be a husband, Dad. I thought it was all about being faithful and providing a good living. I figured making myself successful would prove to her how much I loved her.'' He glanced up at the heavy clouds riding just over the treetops. "She got tired of fixing gourmet meals I never ate and planning picnics she and Jimmy went on alone. She wanted to eat popcorn in front of the fire and watch it snow. I was so whacked out from three straight nights of stakeouts I fell asleep while I was kissing her.''

He felt the heat bleeding into his face. "After a while, she just stopped planning.''

His dad kicked at a maple leaf floating in a puddle at the edge of the walk. "Like I said, son, Ria can be tenacious.

I figure she's hanging on to some leftover feelings of hurt that maybe she doesn't even know about. Women take great store in feeling cherished by the men they give their heart to.'' He lifted his gaze and looked Grady straight in the eye. ''Want some advice?''

''If you got some to give, yeah, guess I do.''

''This time you do the planning. Court her, like the men in those books your mom has stacked all over the house.'' His grin flashed. ''You're a Hardin, son. Through and through. Of all our boys you're the one's most like the first Grady Hardin. Man was flat-out bullheaded in some things, but folks who knew him swore he had half the ladies in Lafayette County in love with him. Charmed all their *no*'s to *yes*'s, sure enough. Guess if you put your mind to it, you could do the same with that sweet little wife of yours.''

''Ex-wife,'' he corrected absently, his mind already wrapping around those *yes*'s.

''Maybe the court says she's an ex, but the way I see you acting, I figure you're still wearing that ring, even though it's no longer on your finger.''

Grady didn't bother to deny it. ''Almost forgot,'' he said glancing away from his father's too-perceptive gaze. ''I need to borrow your sleeping bag, if that's okay.''

''Sure. It's in the garage.''

Grady glanced at the sky. ''I'll get it.''

''More trouble to tell you where it is. Be right back.''

Ducking his head, Mason stepped in the drizzle and walked across the drive to the detached garage. He returned a minute later to hand Grady the bedroll.

Side by side, they walked to the truck. ''Nothing like sleeping under the stars,'' Mason said, his lips twitching.

''I can think of better places.''

''Guess you can.''

Grady opened the door and tossed the sleeping bag inside.

Mason waited before he'd leaned in to deposit the cookies on the passenger-side floorboard before saying with a smile, "Give Ria and the boy a kiss for me."

Grady grinned. Ria adored his dad. She wouldn't dare refuse a kiss from the old man. "Yes, sir. I'll do that."

Grady stood at the railing of the small balcony overlooking the river. The storm that had battered the city for most of the afternoon had moved on, leaving the air washed clean and the sky as clear as black ice.

It was nearly nine. Ria was putting Jimmy to bed. If anything, the boy's surly mood had gotten worse during the hours he'd been sprawled on the floor in the den, watching TV and kicking the scuffed toes of his high-tops against the carpet. The gingerbread cookies were still in the container, untouched. According to his son, he hated gingerbread.

He hated cats, too, Jim had declared with a sneer when Trouble had poked a cautious nose out of his box. Especially ugly ones. From the way Trouble had eyed the boy, Grady figured the cat wasn't all that crazy about smart-ass little boys.

It was the desperate look in Ria's eyes that had had him suggesting McDonald's for dinner. When she'd leaped at it the way Trouble had once leaped at a decent meal, he'd figured her day had been a lot worse than his.

He heard the whoosh of the sliding door and turned. She looked discouraged and pale as she came to stand next to him.

"Need a hug?" he asked a little gruffly.

"Desperately," she said, with a stab at a smile, "but I think that would be a lousy idea for both of us."

"Just a hug," he promised. Keep it light, he told himself. Don't spook her. Just in case, he tucked his hands in his back pockets. It was safer that way.

"Keep it on account. I have a feeling I'm going to need it."

"When you do, honey, I'm your man." He managed a self-deprecating shrug. "Once, anyway."

She folded her arms and leaned her hip against the railing, facing him. She'd changed from the tank top into a tidy knit shirt for the trip to McDonald's, and the soft yellow cotton gleamed in the semidarkness, outlining her breasts just enough to make his mouth water.

"I hate feeling so helpless," she said in a tight voice. "It was awful when he was gone, but I always had hope to hang on to. Whenever I felt that black pit opening up, I'd tell myself I had to be strong for my son when he came home. Now he's here, close enough for me to touch, and I don't feel strong at all."

"Honey, you're too hard on yourself. You're human. You've been through a hell most moms can only imagine. It's only natural to feel a little shaken until you get your footing again."

She drew a breath. "I want my little boy back, Grady."

"It can't happen, Ree," he said, feeling regret grind in his gut.

"I know." She shifted her gaze toward the sky. The moon was waning, shutting down its light a little more each night. "He needs so much love."

"What he needs is the flat of his dad's hand on his backside."

She jerked her gaze to his, her expression changing in an instant from the tight sadness that he flat-out couldn't stand to a mother's fierce outrage.

"Don't you *dare!*" she declared on a little huff of air.

He knew better than to laugh. But damn, she was cute when she got riled up. "I don't intend to beat him, honey. Just get his thinking reordered a little."

"He was just a little upset. It happens."

"Ree, the kid pitched a fit in a crowded restaurant over a damned milk shake."

"What would it have hurt to let him have another one?"

"If he'd asked nicely instead of ordering you around, I would have bought him as many as he wanted."

"He was just being a little boy."

"A little boy who called his mother a gutter name. If that had been me, I'd be soaking my butt in Epsom salts for a week."

"That's different. You always knew your parents loved you, no matter what you did. Jimmy doesn't know us at all."

Grady smiled a little to himself. His mom had always claimed the Lord provided opportunities. It was up to him how he used them.

"Ree, I talked to that child psychologist this afternoon."

Her eyebrows drifted up. "The one in California?"

He nodded. "Dr. Roth. I thought she might give us some direction."

Hope leaped into her eyes. "And did she?"

He nodded. "Why don't I pour you a glass of wine and tell you what she had to say?"

# Chapter 8

At least she hadn't handed him his head on a plate.

Grady considered that a positive sign. On the other hand, she hadn't exactly smothered him with gratitude for coming up with a plan.

Rank coward that he was, he leaned forward to nudge the long-stemmed wine goblet a few inches closer to her reach. Coiled like a wary cat in one corner of the wimpy love seat, with her legs tucked up beneath her and her spine school-teacher straight, she shot him a look he'd seen before—almost always in the mean hours of the night and right before all hell broke loose.

"Now I know why you suggested the wine," she muttered, taking a sip.

He let out the air he'd been holding, and some of the tension eased from his muscles. Since at least one of her hands was occupied, he figured it was safe to reach for the glass of milk. Not because he wanted the damn stuff. Hell, he'd never even liked it as a kid. But the department medic had ordered him to drink it. His stomach lining was in-flamed, the guy had claimed. Too much coffee and stress and not enough sleep. The smug bastard had told him to vent his feelings, instead of swallowing them.

Well, he was trying, wasn't he?

"Dr. Roth promised to use her juice with McCurry, but even if he agrees to slide us into his schedule, it's probably not going to happen immediately. More like a couple of days. Maybe a week."

She rested the goblet on her thigh while she gnawed at the corner of her lip, her brow knit into a frown. He knew the signs. She was working through the positives and neg-atives in her head.

"Maybe Dr. McCurry has a different approach," she said with a hopeful note that tore at his already-sore gut. "Hypnosis, for example."

He pulled up one leg. Just being in the same room with her made him edgy. "I don't know, Ree. Seems like Jim is pretty young for a shrink to go digging into his mind."

"It's obvious we need to do more research."

Well, hell, what did she think he'd been doing? "That's your department. Jimmy and I will do our research in Dad's boat." He risked a grin. "There's nothing like pulling in the big one to settle the mind."

Her smile was a little sad. Still, it was a smile, and he was a desperate man. "I checked with Mom and Dad. They're fine with letting us have the place for as long as we need it."

"So that we can pretend we're still married?"

"For Jimmy's sake, honey." He cleared his throat. "You should have heard Dr. Roth's voice perk right up. She thought it was a great idea."

"Okay, maybe it does make sense. In fact, it makes a lot of sense. Jimmy loved the lake." She took a quick breath. "And I think it's a good idea that we both spend a lot of time with him. I can even see the logic in waiting to tell him about the divorce.'' He opened his mouth, but she forestalled him by raising a hand. ''*And* the logic of needing isolation so that someone doesn't inadvertently slip and reveal the truth,'' she concluded, echoing the argument he was about to make. But then, Ree was always way ahead of him in the brains department.

''So you agree?'' He was damn proud of his restraint.

''With some modifications, yes.''

Hell. ''Like what?''

''Jimmy and I will stay at the lake. We can tell him you're on a case. Night stakeouts, which is why you can only come to visit him during the day.''

''Except I'm *not* on a case, because I don't work cases anymore. And until I can make arrangements to have someone cover for me, I have to work during the day. At least mornings, anyway. And a couple of afternoons a week when I'm locked into meetings.''

She frowned, calculated. Made her decision—and pounced. ''You could be there for dinner and stay to tuck Jimmy in. After he's asleep, you can drive back to town.''

''Ree, think about that. That's two round trips, two hours on the road that I could spend with the boy. Does that really make sense?''

Instead of answering, she shifted her gaze to the window. He didn't need the words to know what was going on inside her. She was frustrated and a little panicky. His lady was only safe when she was in control. The lists she made and checked and then checked again, the separate savings account she'd insisted on keeping when they were married, the need to weigh every decision—they ordered a world that the child in her still expected to shatter into chaos. So he'd let her organize big chunks of his life as well as hers. But not all.

"Trust me on this, Ree." His words were just shy of pleading. "My gut tells me this is what Jimmy needs."

"I don't think I've had enough wine to deal with this," she muttered, taking another sip.

"Give it some time to settle in."

She slanted him a look that had him fighting a need to grin. "Good idea. I'll let you know in twenty years."

"Honey, I'd give you that and more, but I think this is a decision that has to be made tonight."

"Why tonight?" she demanded, her chin up a little more than usual.

Instead of answering, he glanced at the sleeping bag he'd propped against the fireplace. Watching her, he saw the exact moment when she made the connection.

"I was afraid you'd say that."

She took a gulp of wine, then licked a stray drop from her lower lip with the tip of her tongue. His body reacted with a hot, hard speed.

"Even with twin beds it would never work," she declared in a tight voice. "Sharing a bedroom is too...intimate. We wouldn't have any privacy. Besides, you sleep in the nude."

"So?"

She frowned, then exhaled a little puff of air. "So we were always great in bed. It wouldn't be long before we'd start remembering that."

Remember. He'd just spent two and half years trying to forget, with about as much luck as that tired old snowball in hell.

"I won't deny I want to sleep with you, Ree. I do. So bad it's making me a little crazy. But I'm handling it and I'll keep on handling it. You have my word I won't crowd you."

Yes, you will, Ria thought as she smiled again at the cat he'd brought home to her for tending.

His mere presence crowded her. Seeing the way his eyes lit an instant before he smiled at her in that special way crowded her. The brush of his hand when he'd handed her the wine or guided her through the restaurant. Most of all, her memories crowded her. Sweet, special moments like the time he'd come home with a bruised jaw after a dust-up with a whacked-out addict to find her huddled in the middle of their bed, terrified that the spotting she was having was the beginning of a miscarriage.

He'd held her for hours, rubbing her back until she fell asleep. He was still awake the next morning, still holding her, his eyes glazed with exhaustion. And then he'd told her how proud he was of her.

She humbled him with her courage, he'd told her, his voice reverent.

Her heart had tumbled then. It tumbled now.

Steeling herself, she brought her gaze back to his. "I don't know why I'm even bothering to argue," she said, smiling a little to signal her surrender. "We both knew I'd agree before we even started this discussion. I'll do whatever it takes to bring my son back to me." She closed her eyes for a long moment, gathering strength.

"Ree, it'll work out. We both love Jimmy enough to keep whatever resentments we have private."

One side of her mouth slanted as she let her eyes drift open again. "I don't resent you, Grady," she said softly. "It would have been so much easier if I could."

"I wouldn't blame you. I was a jerk." He glanced away, then almost reluctantly it seemed, brought his gaze back to hers. His shoulders eased. "I couldn't stand coming home empty-handed every night, so I ran. It was probably the stupidest mistake I've made in a long line of mistakes." His smile was fleeting, but still potent, she realized when she felt a familiar little flurry in her chest. "I've had a lot of lonely days and nights to regret it."

Lonely?

She felt a splash of cold on her bare thigh and realized she'd tipped the glass. Hastily, she wiped at the spill with two fingers, then licked the moisture from her fingertips. Glancing up, she caught the flash of something hot and needy in his eyes.

The ivory walls she'd painted herself suddenly seemed to pull in closer until she was aware of her own suddenly erratic breathing. It had been so long since she'd felt like a woman. So long since she'd felt his long, hair-roughened legs tangling with hers on sheets hot and slick with their shared passion, so long since she'd thrilled to feel that magnificently male body pressing her into the mattress while his thickly engorged arousal thrust possessively inside her, making them one.

Desire uncurled inside her, an insistent, hungry feeling in hidden places only he knew. She wanted him, and it was useless to pretend otherwise. But that would only stir up all the misery she'd oh-so slowly put behind her.

"Don't, Grady," she said in strained vice. "You're making an already-difficult situation worse."

His mouth slanted into the wry, self-mocking grin that was as much a defense as it was a weapon. "Why not go for broke?" He leaned forward, his body as tense as a predator about to make his move. But it was the fierce look in his eyes that kept her from moving so much as a muscle.

"It's a whole lot more than sex, Ria, what I feel when I look at you. I fell in love with you the first time I saw you, and I'm still in love with you. I've tried every way I know how to shake free, but you're dug in deep. I'd give half the life remaining to me to wake up every morning next to you. With a ring on your finger or without, you're mine. You'll always be mine."

He stood suddenly, surprising her into a soft, gasping breath. "Now I'm going for a run and cool-off before I do

something I'll spend the next fifty years regretting. When
I come back, we'll figure out what happens next.''

On the way to the door he grabbed the Lafayette SWAT
cap he'd tossed onto a chair. He jammed it on his head and
kept going. An instant later, the door clicked shut behind
him.

It had been an hour since Grady had dumped his bombshell on her. As soon as she could breathe again, she'd
dived into the bathroom for a quick shower, then armored
herself in her frumpiest nightshirt and, for good measure,
the robe that was making her feel hot and uncomfortable.

It annoyed her no end that she was still vulnerable to the
man—and very tempted.

The house was quiet as she stalked to her dresser and
glared at her reflection. Her cheeks were stained with color
and her eyes were bright.

Behind her was her bed. Her very ordinary double bed.
No one had slept there except her. But now she saw him
there, stretched out on his back, his legs sprawled in that
loose-jointed way he had, his eyes dark and hungry.

Desire was a gloved fist hitting her squarely in her midsection.

''What a lousy, stinking thing to do,'' she muttered to
the cat who sat on her pillow, staring at her in the mirror
with the unblinking eyes of a born cynic. ''You were there,
Trouble,'' she muttered, picking up her hairbrush. ''You
saw how hard I tried to keep the marriage together. I
*begged* him to fight for us the way he'd fought that horrible
Russian. But you saw how he avoided me, how…how he
flinched when I touched him.''

It had hurt then. It hurt now.

She jerked the brush through her hair, wincing as the
bristles scraped her scalp. ''I adored him, Trouble,'' she
muttered as she ruthlessly twisted her hair into a spinster's

knot at the back of her head. "The blasted man broke my heart at the precise moment when I needed him most." She jammed another pin into the bun and glared at the cat in the mirror. "I won't...I *can't* go through that again."

"Guess I can't blame you."

She spun around to find Grady leaning against the door-jamb with his arms crossed, watching her with hooded eyes. Below the bill of the ratty cap he'd lifted from his SWAT team brother, Elijah, his face was flushed from wind and exertion, and his shirt was sweat darkened in a raggedly triangular patch from his shoulders to his lean belly. He looked hot and virile and very, very male. She held her breath, then realized she was waiting...*wishing* for him to charge across the room and sweep her into his arms.

In spite of the sexless image she had carefully pulled around her, a part of her was desperate to feel the wild exhilaration of his touch, the mindless pleasure that splintered into rainbow shards of bliss when he was hot and hard inside her.

He didn't move. She stopped wishing.

"I think we need to set some ground rules for the next few weeks." She'd tried for stern and ended up with peevish. "For starters, you have got to buy some pajamas."

He didn't smile, but his eyes crinkled just enough to tell her he'd thought about it. "I'll agree to bottoms. No tops."

"And no flirting."

His mouth slanted this time. "You're going to have to define that for me, honey."

"First off, don't call me honey. Secondly, don't...look at me so much."

"Now that's a problem, seeing as how I just can't seem to help myself."

"Well, try."

Trouble chose that moment to sink his needlelike claws into the satin duvet and tug. She saw the material stretch, and lunged. She came up with an armful of startled cat who immediately transferred his grip to her forearm. She shrieked and let go.

The cat executed a graceful leap to the floor, then paused, tail waving like a battle flag to look back at her with an expression of outraged innocence on his funny face.

"Best lie low for a while, buddy," Grady advised as he straightened and unfolded the brawny arms she'd been so eager to feel close around her. "The lady doesn't like to share her bed with scruffy dudes like you and me."

Trouble let out an indignant and decidedly masculine meow before ambling out of the room. Ria watched him go, then shifted her gaze to the other sleek male in the room.

The darkness in his eyes tugged at her. They'd made it work for eight of the nine years they'd had together. That made him special to her. No matter what, he would always be Jimmy's father. They would be together many times during the next decades, marking the milestones of their son's life.

That counted for a great deal. But not enough to risk her cobbled-together peace of mind. She'd spent the first half of her life feeling like an unwanted burden. She refused to feel that way again.

"There's something I need you to do for me," she said as she got to her feet.

"Name it." His tone was suddenly so serious it scared her.

"Don't be so quick to agree," she said with a smile that wasn't quite as steady as it should be.

"Anything you want, it's yours. I love you, Ree."

The house seemed to hold its breath as he took a step toward her. The earthy scent of wind and a powerful man's sweat enveloped her as he cupped his hands over her shoulders.

She felt a nearly overpowering need to burrow into his strength and cling, and it shook her to the core. "That's just it, you don't really love me. You only think you do, and I'm asking you, please, not to say that you do."

His brows drew together. "Not saying the words won't change how I feel."

The mild tone both annoyed and encouraged her. "What you feel is lust. You want me physically, and because I'm the mother of your son and you're a very decent man, you've convinced yourself it's love."

"Sounds like you've made up your mind." His hands were working magic on her shoulders. She wanted to purr.

"Don't," she whispered, her gaze on the pulse beating furiously in the hollow of his sun-bronzed throat. Her own was hammering just as wildly.

"Kiss me, Ree. Just once." His expression was intense, his eyes needy. She could swear his hand shook as he pulled the pins from her hair one by one, dropping them to the floor.

He released her shoulders in order to frame her face with his hands. Inch by slow inch he pushed his fingers through her hair until it was fluffing around her neck.

"Kiss me, Ree. Give me your sweetness."

She felt the heat of him now, and the need, drawing her in. Promising excitement and a soul-shattering pleasure. But at what cost?

More years of struggling not to be hurt when he missed birthdays and anniversaries? Long, lonely nights waiting for him to come home? Emotional upheaval?

Chaos.

"I can't."

His eyes darkened. "You want to. Your eyes are wild with wanting."

She didn't bother to deny it. What was the point? They both knew he could make her burn with merely a look.

"I've wanted your kisses before. I wanted all of you. Your smiles, your laughter. Your love. And more. But it's not enough. I want dependability and stability. And I want those things for Jimmy."

His big hand massaged the spot between her shoulder blades that always made her crazy. Already shivers were sliding like warm rivulets down her spine.

"I'll give you those things, Ree. I'm a desk jockey now. Some weeks I never hit the street at all."

"It's too late, Grady. Maybe if Jimmy hadn't been taken, we might have been able to make it right."

"That's it then? No second chances?"

"I'll always care for you, Grady," she said around the sudden swift rush of pain. "But I don't love you anymore. What we had is gone."

"For you maybe, but not me. I promised to stick and that's what I'm doing." His jaw took on a harder line. "Those words we said in church, I meant them. I still do, though God knows, it doesn't seem to matter."

He let her go so quickly she swayed. "You wanted the divorce."

"*You* wanted the divorce," he said in a hard, clipped tone. "I figured you'd been through enough, so I signed the papers your lawyer stuck in front of me. But make no mistake, Ree, I didn't want to split up."

She stared at him, unable to believe her ears. Not once, during the torturous process of dismantling their marriage had he even hinted he was feeling more than a certain detached relief.

"What choice did we have?" she said when she realized she had to say something. "We were tearing each other apart. A few more months and we would have ended up saying ugly, awful things that neither of us would ever have been able to forget." She took a breath. "Or forgive," she added more softly.

He flexed his shoulders, as though shaking off a blow. "We could have hung in. Gotten counseling. Talked it out."

"How could we talk when you were never there?" She hadn't meant to say that. "I'm sorry," she said, then smiled sadly. "See, it's starting already." She glanced past his shoulder. The house was quiet, the walls well insulated. But the cottage walls were thin.

"We can't do this again. If Jimmy should hear, it would destroy everything we're trying to accomplish." She touched his arm. It went iron hard, but at least he didn't flinch. "Agreed?"

"Agreed," he said with a careless movement of one big shoulder.

"That...that doesn't mean we can't be friends," she assured him. And herself. "For Jimmy's sake."

"Sure, friends." He whipped off his cap and ran a hand through his damp hair before sniffing the air. "Damn, one of us in this room stinks."

She felt a smile tug at her lips. He made it easy to tell herself he wasn't really hurting. "I'm pretty sure it's not me."

"Guess that leaves me." His grin was crooked and almost careless. Almost. "I'll grab a quick shower and then we can work out some more of those house rules."

So much for baring his soul.

Grady stripped off his sodden shirt and dropped it on the floor of the guest bathroom. Even with his eyes open and the light on, he felt as though he'd walked into a black, airless cave where he'd been sent to live out his life alone.

Feeling about as low as low gets, he dropped his jeans atop his shirt and stepped out of his skivvies. He twisted on the hot water, then added enough cold to keep from scalding his butt.

He pressed both hands against the slick tile and ducked his head under the hard spray, letting the water pound at the knot between his shoulder blades. Steam filled the tiled cubicle, making his eyes sting. Out of air, he drew a huge breath that hurt all the way to the soles of his feet. She said he was a decent man.

*She didn't love him.*

She wanted to be friends.

*She didn't love him.*

He opened his eyes and stared at the water swirling around his feet. He was some kind of fool to think he could walk back into her life and with a few stiff words blurted out without more than a few seconds planning, have her falling into his arms again.

Maybe if he'd been the one to rescue their son, she might have forgotten he'd also been the one who'd brought hell down around them in the first place. Women liked heroes, didn't they?

Maybe if he'd kicked down a few doors, busted a few heads. Taken another bullet. Maybe then she'd love him. Maybe…

The pain in his chest ground harder.

Hell.

He'd been wrong. Life didn't give second chances.

Not his life, anyway.

Women wanted the words, his mom had said. Well, he'd given her words, and she'd handed them back to him, along with a prim little speech that had cut all the way to the bone.

With a savage curse that came all the way from the black depths of his soul, he straightened and reached for the soap.

Ria was huddled into her pillow, drifting in the surreal twilight between deep sleep and a restless uneasiness when she was jerked into full awakening by a muted and very male curse in the semidarkness.

Before she could do more than turn her head, Grady had folded into a crouch next to the bed and was sliding the sleeping bag bundle under the frame. In the faint gleam of the hall light shining through the crack in the door, she saw the massive outline of his bare shoulders and the flash of his bright hair as he stood suddenly.

Her heart tripped, flooded her with sharp terror mingled with outrage. ''What—''

''Jim,'' he grated, jerking up the sheet. The mattress dipped as he slid his body in next to hers. Before she could move, he hooked one heavy leg over hers, pinning her fast beneath the solid length of him. Though he'd promised to buy pj's first thing tomorrow, tonight he was wearing running shorts—and nothing else. The heat of his skin was like a brand against hers.

''Stop—'' Her cry was cut off by the pressure of his mouth over hers. She felt an instant of heat, a fast-and-furious jolt of shock and then an instant's fury as he slid one hard arm beneath her neck.

*You bastard!* she screamed silently, struggling. And then she heard it, the almost imperceptible whisper of the bedroom door opening. She froze, her gaze searching his in the dim white glow coming through the opening.

Understanding flooded her and she nodded. The steely muscles of his arms relaxed slightly as he lifted his lips from her mouth and rolled to his back.

''Something bothering you, son?'' he asked, his voice a good octave deeper than normal.

''There's a noise in the closet,'' Jimmy said in a small voice that tore at her. She opened her mouth to offer her baby the words of comfort and love she'd saved up for so long, but Grady beat her to it.

''Want me to go with you to check it out?'' he asked in

the same matter-of-fact tone he'd used to discuss the terms of their divorce. His cop's voice, she realized now.

"I guess," Jimmy muttered, but he edged a little farther into the room, looking anything but eager to face hidden monsters.

"Maybe he should stay here," Ria murmured close to Grady's ear. "Just in case."

"Sure, if he wants to."

Grady squeezed her arm, his rough hand incredibly gentle, before he slipped his arm free and climbed from the bed. Jimmy watched with dark, frightened eyes that tore at her, but he didn't flinch when Grady dropped a hand to his shoulder.

"Do you want to stay here with your mom, son?"

Stevie darted his gaze from one another, his hands torturing the front of the dorky pajama shirt into a twisted knot. He wanted to stay with the lady, even though he was pretty sure she wasn't his real mom, but pride made him shake his head. Guys who wimped out were jerks. Besides, the big guy…Grady…didn't look like he was afraid of anything. Not even guys with guns or knives.

Stevie thought it would be real neat to be like him.

"Guess you might need help," he mumbled, trying his best to make his voice real deep like Grady's.

Grady offered one of those quick almost-smiles Stevie was coming to like a lot because it made him feel special. "Just between us, son, I can always use help, especially when I'm not sure what's behind a door."

Stevie had to think about that. He wasn't sure what was behind that door, either. Only that he'd jerked awake with his heart going crazy and a scared feeling in his head. He thought maybe he'd been having a bad dream, but he wasn't sure. And then he'd heard the noise. The scared feeling that has started to slip away came back in a rush, and he edged closer to Grady's side.

"Maybe you should bring your gun," he said in the off-hand voice he used when he didn't want anyone to know what he was thinking.

"Let's see what kind of problem we're dealing with first, okay?"

"I think it's the man with the funny voice." Stevie hadn't meant to say that, and he felt his face get hot all the way down his neck.

"What man, sweetheart?" The lady sounded awful scared all of a sudden. He figured he must have said something wrong.

"Jim?"

Stevie liked it when Grady squatted down the way he was doing now. Even when the light was dim like now, he could see his eyes real good. They were all crinkly at the corners, like Mel Gibson's. Like he was about to laugh, even when bad stuff was happening. Except when he looked at his wife, and then he looked the way Stevie felt sometimes when he wanted something real bad, only he knew he was never going to get it no matter how hard he wished.

"He's in this dream I have," he blurted out because he knew Grady wanted him to tell. "The guy with the voice."

"Sounds like you don't like him much."

Stevie shook his head.

"Any particular reason?"

Stevie considered this which made a real bad shivery feeling run all through him. "Don't know." He held his breath, afraid Grady would get all mad and yell the way Lance did when Stevie honked him off.

Only Grady just nodded once, real steady like, before standing up again and holding out his hand. "Ready to face that door, partner?"

Stevie darted a look down the hall that didn't seem nearly as long as it had before. He nodded once, and put his hand in Grady's big one.

"Keep my side warm, Mom," Grady told the lady who looked real funny before she smiled.

"Good luck, gentlemen."

Grady glanced down at him and winked. And just like that, Stevie wasn't scared anymore.

# *Chapter 9*

Ria pounced as soon as Grady stepped over the threshold of her bedroom and into the glow of the light she'd turned on while he'd been gone.

"Is he all right?" she demanded, scrambling to a sitting position against the pillows.

Grady allowed his chest to swell just enough to release some of the emotion pulsing inside him. "You should have seen him, Ree. Shaking like a leaf, eyes big as dinner plates, but damn if he didn't march right over to that damn door and jerk it open."

"With you right behind him," she said with a soft little smile that had his mind shooting off on a dangerous tangent. Ruthlessly he shut off the fantasy before it took hold and ruined what was left of an already lousy night's sleep.

"Sooner or later he would have gotten around to doing it on his own."

She shook her head, and the auburn highlights in her thick sable hair caught light. "No, he needed to know you were there."

With hands that were uncharacteristically nervous, she fussed with the nightshirt, tugging on the hem a few times before primly tucking it around her ankles. In his mind he saw his hand reaching for the buttoned-up front, tearing it back to reveal the creamy breasts and sleek curves beneath, ripe and ready to be explored. Just like that, he was desperate to nuzzle his face against those curvy thighs until the scent of her was inside him, wild and sweet, uniquely Ria.

When he felt himself tip toward begging, he shifted his gaze to her face and kept it there.

"Told him you'd be in to check on him."

The surprise had an instant to take hold in her eyes before she scrambled out of bed, an eager smile on her face and her eyes as bright as emerald stars.

He caught a whiff of roses as she rushed past him, the long gown shifting and rippling like water over the curves of her body. He clamped down hard on the moan pushing at his throat, but nothing could stop the blood from pooling in his groin.

He jerked the sleeping bag from under the bed, then stalked into the bathroom. One twist of his wrist had the shower door sliding open, another had the cold tap on full blast.

She wasn't the only woman on the frigging planet. He'd had signals from plenty of other females, hadn't he? Hell, yes. A single guy under forty with a steady job and a face that didn't stop clocks was fair game in this town.

Flynn sure as hell wasn't pining away for his ex. Far as he could see, his brother had women tripping all over themselves. Maybe he didn't have Flynn's silver tongue or Kale's smarts or the twins' humor, but he could hold his own if he had to.

He jerked his shorts over his hips and let them fall. A savage kick sent them flying against the wall. Temper sizzling and blood pounding, he stepped into the stall, sucking in hard as the icy water hit.

To hell with hanging in. With bleeping patience. With giving her time. He'd just been kidding himself. She'd had time, all right. Plenty of it. *Years.* Time to build a wall so thick not even his hard head could batter it down.

Maybe he learned slow, but he *did* learn. About being a man instead of a lapdog. About honor and integrity and keeping your word once you've given it. And about the judgment calls a man makes when he steps beyond black-and-white and into varying shades of gray.

Sometimes a man had to bend a rule or swallow a chunk of pride for a good cause. But there was a line beyond which he sacrificed his self-respect, a line he'd tested a few times but never crossed. Pining for a woman who didn't want him was on the loser's side of that line.

As soon as things shook out, he damn sure intended to find himself a nice lady to woo. No more running laps when the hunger built up inside like a volcano about to blow. No more middle-of-the-night brooding over mistakes he couldn't take back. No more kicking himself over things he should have said or noticed or done.

By the time he was shivering and the ache in his groin had been numbed to a dull pressure, he'd run through an entire lexicon of curses. Most of all he cursed the stubbornness that welded him to a woman who didn't want him.

Ria smoothed the pillow slip away from her little boy's tanned cheek, then because she wanted desperately to touch her baby again, let her fingers dance over the rumpled curls. Instead of flinching, he watched her with sensitive brown eyes that tugged at her with the same intensity as his dad's.

"I hear you guys got rid of the mystery noise in the closet."

He shrugged, but the sudden glint of pride in his eyes

had her heart turning over. "Weren't nothin' in there but a bunch of dumb clothes. Stinks somethin' awful, too. Even the cat wouldn't go in."

Ria blinked, then laughed. "You must mean the moth-balls."

His mouth relaxed enough to curl a little at the corners. "Yeah, that's what Grady said."

Grady, not Daddy? Well, it was a start, she told herself. As for her, so far he hadn't called her anything at all. But he was talking to her now instead of grunting. And there had been that hint of a familiar smile. She would hold that to her heart while she waited for him to trust her.

"Where is Trouble anyway?"

Jimmy frowned, then nudged the bunched covers away from the side of the daybed. Curled into his usual boneless knot, the pampered creature opened one tiger-yellow eye, blinked, then closed it again. As though a switch had suddenly been snapped on, a rumbling purr of contented feline filled the room.

"Grady said Trouble usually sleeps with him...I mean, you guys, you know? Grady's going to teach me how to brush him and feed him and stuff like that."

She nodded, a lump in her throat. "In the house we used to have when you were a baby, I had this perfectly lovely bed for him, with a foam mattress as soft as a cloud, but of course, he preferred a ratty old sweatshirt of your dad's instead."

"Grady said he's real good at waking up if someone comes in."

Ria glanced at the cat who now seemed to be dead to the world. "As watch cat's go, Trouble is the best, no doubt about it," she declared, keeping her expression suitably so-ber. "I also think he's adopted you."

Pleasure fought with a scared little boy's need to play it cool. Her heart gave a little hop when the pleasure won.

"Guess I wouldn't mind having him around. Long as he don't bug me too much."

Jimmy's lashes fluttered down, then jerked up. Her brave little boy was fighting sleep. Just like he used to when he was curled up in her lap, listening to her read his bedtime story. Her arms really did ache with the need to hold him, she realized, on a rush of emotion so powerful she had to take several breaths before it was contained again.

*Just one more, Mommy,* he would plead. And then, when that story was finished, he would offer her that twinkling, sloppy smile that never failed to melt her and beg, *Last more, Mommy, okay?*

The boy who'd been stolen had loved stories, following along with avid interest. The boy who'd returned would rather stare mindlessly at TV for hours on end.

She wanted to do violence, to rage and rant and use her fists—and it terrified her. Needing something to occupy her hands, she reached for the ratty old bear she'd propped next to a stack of Jimmy's favorite books on the floor.

"Poor Pooh feels lonely down there," she murmured, rubbing the spot on the plump belly where the nap had been worn slick. She made her smile easy as she looked for a sign of recognition. Instead, she got a sleepy look of impatience. She tucked the bear into the far corner of the bed frame and folded her hands in her lap.

"You know, Jimbo, I'm not sure I've ever seen your daddy more proud than he is right now. He thinks you're one brave kid."

"Grady's cool," he muttered, his faced reddening.

"Like father, like son."

She leaned forward to brush a kiss over his curls, then gave in to a desperate need and nuzzled her face against his, drawing in the scent of him before she drew back to smile down at him.

He stiffened, but the surly expression refused to take

over. Something settled inside her, and she realized that finally, miraculously, a part of her heart was back where it belonged.

"Sleep tight, my darling," she said, her voice thick. "Daddy and I love you very much."

She was practically walking on air when she returned to the bedroom.

Grady had switched off the lamp while she'd been with Jimmy, and the part of her room that was beyond the reach of the night light's dim glow was thick with darkness.

He was lying on his back atop the bright orange sleeping bag on the floor, his bare feet crossed at the ankles, his hands behind his head. His face was expressionless, his mouth set in a grim line.

"Oh, Grady, he let me kiss him good-night!" she exclaimed when he glanced her way. "And I *smelled* him."

His brows drew together in the jagged furrows that never quite disappeared, even when he grinned.

"You want to run that by me again?" he said, his voice dust dry.

Hugging herself, she did a little pirouette which caused the hated gown to flare around her ankles. He shot her a grumpy look, and she laughed self-consciously.

"It's a mom thing. Nature's way of making sure we can recognize our own baby in the midst of a herd."

One side of his mouth moved. "That *is* helpful, especially in downtown Lafayette."

She was so happy she actually giggled.

"It wasn't that funny, Ria."

Like Jimmy's, his eyes were half-closed, but even in the limited light, she noted that the expression glinting between the outrageously long golden lashes was anything but drowsy. His heavily padded shoulders, too, radiated tension, and his face was shadowed, his jaw like unyielding granite. His hair was even more tousled than usual, as though plowed repeatedly with angry hands. It was also damp, she realized belatedly.

"I thought you'd already taken a shower," she muttered as she slipped into the sheets that were now cool against her skin.

"Go to sleep, Victoria."

It was then, at that precise moment, that she realized the air in the room pulsed with something infinitely more dangerous than the dark.

"Grady, are you angry about something?"

"If I am, it's my problem."

How could a voice so utterly flattened of all inflection seethe? She pulled the sheet higher and adjusted her pillow before glaring at him.

"Fine, be that way. Shut me out."

His snort was pure masculine disgust. "Seems to me you're the one slamming doors around here."

"Don't be silly," she said crisply while giving her pillow another thump. "You're here, aren't you? In my house. In my *bedroom,* for Pete's sake."

"Wrecking my back on the frigging floor."

"That has nothing to do with doors!"

"Yeah, right." His deep voice dripped sarcasm.

Ria hated sarcasm, and he knew it. She frowned, then realized the high collar of the gown was constricting her throat. Stupid thing, she thought, freeing the top two buttons.

"Grady, I don't want—"

"Exactly!" The word was a bullet, hard and deadly. "You don't want me in your bed. You don't want me to love you. Okay. Fine. Your call, your choice." He drew up one leg, then shot her a look that seemed designed to strip the flesh from her bones. "If there's something else you want, tell me now because I'd like to get some sleep."

"Nothing more, thank you," she said with great dignity—and civility.

"You're welcome. Now, can we get some sleep?"

"Yes—provided you stop dumping your bad mood on my head."

"Don't push it, Ria."

His voice was deadly quiet. No reason at all to think he was hurt. And yet she was sure it was hurt she heard. Desperate aching hurt.

Shaken, she sneaked a peek in his direction. Though his eyes were open, he didn't notice because he was staring at the ceiling. So she let her gaze linger on that unyielding profile.

His was a face with hard planes, aggressive angles and a wide, beautifully shaped mouth that had once skimmed hers with the delicacy of a butterfly's wing. She felt a heat that had nothing to do with the weather steal over her until her skin was overheated and itchy.

She was also, she realized in a sudden burst of total honesty, deeply shaken. In all the years they'd had together, the good ones and especially the silent, edgy ones, she'd never thought of Grady as vulnerable.

Not in the way that she was vulnerable, needing reassurance and the security of a love that didn't crack under strain. Needing the freedom to falter and fail and make mistakes without being judged—and rejected.

She'd been wrong. Terribly wrong.

The sudden lump in her throat made it difficult to breathe.

"Excuse me," she muttered, scooting out of bed again. She was out of the room and down the hall before she heard the ripe curse of a man pushed to the limit.

Still flat on his back Grady plowed both hands through his hair, then let his fingers trail down his cheeks.

*She wasn't crying, damn it!* Ria never cried.

Well, not often, he corrected when the memory of the last time she'd broken down reared up to clip him a good one, right in the conscience. He closed his eyes, battled the need to check on her.

His ex-wife had told him that she didn't need him pushing himself into her problems. Into her life. The woman ran a nonprofit business with the skill of a Fortune 500 CEO. Last year she'd been Lafayette's Woman of the Year. No reason to think she couldn't handle this. Except he wasn't exactly sure what *this* was.

"Hell!"

A quick look-see wouldn't hurt, he told himself as he stalked down the hall. He found her in the kitchen, bent over the stove. He heard the hiss of the gas burner, smelled melting chocolate.

His face turned to fire. All the time he'd been working his gut into a hot twist, picturing her huddled in a heap, sobbing her eyes out, she'd been *cooking*.

Score another one for the dumbest of the Hardin boys. He was already turning around when he heard the funny little half hiccup she made when she was upset and trying not to show it.

This time it was his belly that burned.

"Need some help?" he asked, careful to sift just enough careless unconcern into this tone to save her pride.

The elegant shoulders he'd dreamed of tracing with his mouth went rigid. "No, thank you." Her voice was muffled and a little tense the way it got when she was busy convincing herself her life was ticking along just fine.

He started to tuck his hands into his pockets, then realized he was still half-naked. Hooking his thumbs in the elastic of his shorts instead, he ambled closer.

"Smells good, whatever it is."

She cleared her throat, surreptitiously scrubbed her cheeks with her free hand.

"It suddenly occurred to me that I always made fudge to take to the lake," she said, her head still bent over the stove.

"Ah." He'd conducted enough interrogations to know when to push and when to hang back and wait.

"Jimmy—if he remembered being Jimmy that is, which he doesn't but he will—would have expected fudge."

He considered it a mark of his experience in the surreal world of the streets that he understood the twists and turns of her logic.

"Sure would. Heck, he's probably dreaming about his first bite as we speak."

Her laugh almost fooled him. Almost. "Remember how he screwed up his face and made smacking noises the first time you gave him a tiny piece?"

"I remember how you reamed me out when he woke up screaming with a tummy ache," he countered with just enough dryness to let her keep on believing she had him fooled.

"You walked him for hours, even after he was asleep." She stopped stirring. "I wanted to be furious with you. I should have been, but...you were so contrite."

What he'd been was terrified, his own belly full of acid at his carelessness. "Contrite, hell. I was damn deaf. The kid always did bawl loud enough to crack glass."

He shifted, remembering how he'd buried his guilt in making love to her.

"Yes, well..." She cleared her throat, as though she too remembered. "The sense of taste often triggers memory."

She banged her wooden spoon against the side of the pan, then for good measure, banged it again before fiddling with the burner control. When she had it exactly right, she resumed stirring.

"Ree, he'll come back to us. All he needs is some time."

"I know. I've told myself that same thing a thousand times, but it's tearing me apart to be so close to him and not be able to hug him the way I used to. Or kiss him or even nuzzle his neck." She drew a shaky breath.

He wanted to touch her so badly his muscles burned. "You'll do it again."

"I know I shouldn't complain. I'm not, really. It's just that I have so much saved up."

"I know, sweet. But you'll get to hug your little cub soon. He's a Hardin. No way will he be able to resist a pretty lady."

She dropped the spoon and turned, challenge in her eyes and her cheeks an adorable pink. "Make love to me, Grady."

His mind went blank. His throat closed. He opened his mouth, then shut it, almost certain he would stammer something damned embarrassing.

"Is that a yes or a no?" she asked, her voice a little hoarse.

He felt the world tilt as she framed his face with her small hands and tugged his head closer until she could press her mouth to his. Desire had sharp, painful claws, tearing away layers of armor until he was raw with need. Still, he'd been bloodied too often to step blindly this time. So he made himself draw back, his hands cuffing her wrists.

"What's going on, Ree?" he demanded, his body already hard and ready. "Why the sudden change of attitude?"

Her lashes flickered, and her breath stuttered. "I want you. Isn't that enough?"

Not in a million years. But a man who was starving to death took crumbs and was grateful.

"It's enough," he grated out an instant before crashing his mouth down on hers.

He put all the years he'd spent dreaming about this into his kiss. The longing, the regret. The love he couldn't kill.

Her mouth trembled, then met his eagerness with hers. She arched up, her hands diving into his hair, her nails raking his scalp. She was heat and hunger and soft, moaning pleas that fired his blood and shattered his control.

He found a breast, his fingers trembling slightly as he teased the nipple with the flat of his hand. She gasped, then moaned. He drew back, breathing hard, to see the glitter of passion in her half-closed eyes.

"Not here," he managed, his voice thick. "I want you naked and sweaty."

Her breath shuddered out, then splintered into a little cry of alarm as he swung her into his arms.

"Wait, Grady, the burner!" Leaning down, she turned off the flame, then burrowed against him, her breath warm against his neck. Pulse pounding, he carried her to the bedroom, pausing only to kick the door closed behind him before striding through the sudden velvet darkness to the bed. The mattress dipped beneath his knee as he deposited her on the rumpled sheets.

"Lock the door," she whispered, impatience and need in her voice. "Jimmy might hear another scary noise in the closet and come looking for his new hero."

"It's the scary noise in the bedroom I'm worried about," Grady said with a grin that felt cocky as he snapped on the lamp by the bed.

"That's something else that would be familiar," she murmured, blinking like a little owl in the sudden splash of light.

"Somehow I don't think that's what Dr. Roth had in mind."

The door safely locked, he slipped off his shorts with hands that fumbled with impatience.

"Oh, my," she said on a rush of air.

''Well, it's been a while,'' he muttered.

''I'm glad,'' she whispered, lifting her arms to pull him down.

''Not yet,'' he said gruffly, his hands already on the hem of her gown. ''Not until I can see all of you.''

Ria went hot all over, even as she fought down a fast flurry of trepidation. They weren't getting back together, she reminded herself. Simply satisfying perfectly normal urges.

Perfectly glorious urges.

Impatient to feel those wonderfully rough hands on her, she sat up quickly, feeling as awkward as a virgin. His movements were jerky, his expression harsh with need as he pushed the gown over her thighs. His callused palms brushed her skin, arousing little tremors of reaction beneath her skin. Tiny urgent pulses of need, spreading heat.

''Lift your arms,'' he ordered, his eyes glittering.

''Hurry,'' she begged as she obeyed. A flip of his sinewy wrist sent the ugly gown flying, and then he was looking at her intently.

Reverently.

''God, sweetheart, I'm not dreaming here, am I?''

Ria heard the harsh need in his voice a split second before his mouth took hers. Over and over the rough silk smoothness of his lips teased and tempted, while his clever hands stroked her hair, the line of her jaw, the vulnerable skin of her throat.

''So good,'' he whispered before touching his tongue to the sensitive hollow at the base of her throat.

He drew back to look down at her again, his dark eyes hot and hungry before he bent to salute one breast, then the other with a long, moist kiss.

''I love kissing your breasts and knowing I was the first to take those hard little nipples into my mouth,'' he whispered with a catch in his gruff voice.

"There's been no one but you," she murmured, running her hands over the padded steel of his chest. Bending forward, she kissed the curved birthmark on the slope of his shoulder.

He groaned, then sent her reeling with another searing kiss that went straight to the liquid core of her. His hands were gentle yet sure as he found all the secret places, until she was writhing helplessly, swept along on a tide of sweet pulsing pleasure.

Grady heard the pleas she breathed and knew bliss. She was his, only his. No other man had ever made her senses swim. No other man had felt the urgent shivers that grew more and more frantic as he stroked and kneaded.

He knew he should feel humble. Instead he wanted to shout to the heavens. He settled for murmured endearments, whispering praise for the softness of her skin, the sleekness of her thighs, even as his fingertips traced circles just above the indentation of her navel. When she was writhing, he let his fingers trail lower, into the silky curls, over the sweet mound and into the slick, moist heat. He heard the plea in each breath she exhaled, the gathering impatience in the helpless little noises she made deep in her throat.

He slid one finger into her, then two. She gasped, twisted, clawed at him, but he knew there was more he could give her. Much more. Everything he was and hoped to be.

Half-wild with longing, he dug deep into himself for the discipline he'd learned so painfully, narrowing his mind until it was focused on the tiniest shift of breathing, the smallest change in her expression.

Tonight she would accept his love, like it or not.

"That's it, sweetheart, fly for me," he whispered against the perfumed skin of her shoulder. "Let it go. For once, let it all go."

Ria arched upward, close to sobbing, desperate for relief.

Each stroke of his raspy fingers brought her closer to the brink, closer to that moment when sweet ecstasy would be hers. A wanton madness seemed to have entered her body, crowding out the lingering agony of her lost love. Bathed in the heat of his massive chest with its cruel scars, she felt her bones melting under her skin, dissolving under his passionate assault.

She whimpered deep in her throat as the urgency built. Her fingers bit into the hard texture of his back muscles as she arched against him, eager to feel him sliding inside her, hot and thick and potent.

"Please," she whispered, clutching at his arm even as she bucked against his hand. "I want you now."

"Soon," he promised, his voice rasping.

Teeth gritted, sweat making his skin slick and wet, Grady thought about the nights he'd spent alone, aching for her. He'd dreamed of this for so long. He wanted this night to last. Another memory to add to his wall against the loneliness.

"Yes, baby, that's the way," he urged as she let out a low, keening moan that ended in a shuddering gasp. Her eyes popped open and she looked at him with glazed shock.

"Oh," she said. "Oh, my."

He palmed the delta between her thighs, his fingers still slick with nectar, and squeezed, bringing her down slowly, gently.

"You're so dear to me," she whispered, running her palms up his arm.

Dear? Hell, she said that about his brothers, too. Especially Flynn when he was being charming. Selfish bastard that he was, Grady wanted to be special to her. As special as she was to him. More than that, he wanted her love.

Battling disappointment, he bent to kiss the damp curve of her breast.

"Come inside me," she whispered, sliding her hands up his thigh to touch him. "I want to feel you explode."

He groaned as his body threatened to do just that. Reminding himself to be gentle, he stroked thighs already widening to welcome him. He chewed the inside of his mouth to distract himself from the punishing urgency, fought to keep from plunging hard and deep. Because he remembered the last time—each mindless thrust that had hurt her, each bruise he'd left—he settled himself slowly, testing her with his fingers, watching the pleasure gather and seethe in her eyes. Finally, when she was hot and dripping, he pushed himself into her with a slowness that had sweat pouring from his skin and his nerves screaming. Still he let her take him gradually, feeling the velvet walls stretching to accommodate the thick hard width of his need.

"Yes," she cried, clutching at him. "Oh, yes, that's the way. Yes, *yes!*" She arched, writhed. "More, give me more. I need..." Her voice shuddered into a gasp and her eyes widened. "All of you, I need to feel all of you."

And then he was welded to her, a part of her.

Home.

The sound he made was strident and primitive, a man's cry of possession and triumph. His control broke; his patience drained dry. Hands fisted in the sheets, legs braced, he drew back, his muscles shuddering with restraint and his teeth gritted, then thrust into her, alive for the first time in years.

She was his love. His happiness.

Gasping, she matched his rhythm, wildly responsive. He felt her muscles squeeze him, sensed her hover, then flash. Even as she cried out, he came with a splintering force that exploded white in his head. Dimly he heard himself shout her name and then he was spiraling into a sweet welcoming pool of heat.

He had just enough mind left to roll to his back, his arms

still locked around her. "Sleep," he murmured. She sighed, linked her arms around his neck, snuggled. Murmured words he couldn't hear. And then he let himself shut down, taking her with him.

Ria surfaced slowly, feeling wonderfully sated. She was also smashed against the hard wall of Grady's chest, which meant that she was being cooked by the heat pouring from his naked skin.

She smiled into the dawn light filtering through the loosely woven drapes. Sleeping with Grady had always been a battle for space. Even deep in sleep, he was restless, sprawling from one side of the bed to the other a dozen times in the course of the night.

Lifting her head, she looked past his bullet-scarred chest at the clock. It wasn't quite six. She resettled her head on the pillow that was half-buried under his shoulder and drew in the soap and male-musk scent of him—as familiar to her as her baby's, she realized as she exhaled slowly.

Letting her lashes droop, she studied the harsh planes of the face turned her way. Though more relaxed now, he still wore that slightly dangerous look that had fascinated her from the moment they'd met. The eyes that crinkled beguilingly when he laughed could narrow to lethal warning in the span of a thought, and the sensuous mouth that coaxed helpless moans from her throat could harden into an implacable line.

Hard edges on an even harder man, Kate had described it once. Deliciously potent—if a woman was strong enough to handle all that soul-stirring power.

She let out a careful sigh and tried to wiggle her way into more breathing room. He stiffened, his face going hard and the steely muscles already bracing. During his years undercover she'd learned to call his name even before his eyes were open.

Grady dived a hand under the pillow and came up grasping air instead of the weapon that should be there. His gut screamed danger a split second before he heard Ria's voice—in his head, he thought—until he opened his eyes and saw her face.

Her eyes were soft and luminous, her lips a little swollen from the kisses he'd tried so hard to keep gentle—until her wild little cries had driven him past his control into a wildness of his own.

Because his fingers were too clumsy and too rough, he used the back of his hand to nudge the wispy curls away from her cheek.

"Was it all right?" he asked because he had to know. "I didn't hurt you?"

"It was very all right, and no, you didn't hurt me," she murmured with a drowsy smile.

He let out the air he'd been holding, and some of the hot tension in his gut eased. "Not sore?" He stroked her hair and inhaled the faint scent of flowers.

"Only a little." The corners of her mouth curled up in an imp's grin. "How about you? Did I hurt you?"

He lifted the sheet and pretended to look. "He's pretty bruised but still up for a challenge."

She choked a laugh and he felt wild with happiness. Since she didn't want the words, he rolled her on top of him and kissed her forehead.

"How about a morning quickie?" he proposed with a grin.

"Hmm?" She rubbed against him and he groaned.

"Not *that* quick, sweetheart," he begged, earning himself another laugh to add to his hoard.

"Jimmy was always an early riser," she reminded him before nipping his chin with her teeth.

He wrapped his arms around her and rolled to his side.

The sheet grabbed at him, and he jerked free. She giggled, and he wanted to shout.

"Not funny, Victoria," he scolded before covering her mouth with his.

# *Chapter 10*

Since Grady would be commuting to the city from the cottage for at least part of their stay, it seemed logical to take both vehicles. Ria led the way, with Grady and Jimmy following in the truck.

One of two lakes created by damming the Tippecanoe River, Lake Freeman was thirty-five miles northwest. Sunday-morning traffic was light, and the day was sunny and clear. On one memorable occasion, when Grady had come off the night shift hot-wired with too much energy and eager to make love to his bride, he and the Charger had managed the drive in eighteen minutes flat. Even in the truck that had the pickup of a tank, he'd figured twenty-five max once he got the sucker up to speed.

With Ria driving the van as though it had bald tires and iffy brakes, they were working on forty minutes and counting. It was making him crazy. Every five miles or so he reminded himself that he was a patient man.

Besides, any morning that he woke with Ria wrapped

around him like a soft blanket on a cold night was a darned good day, no matter what the weather was like.

"Pretty day, isn't it, son?"

Jimmy answered with a grunt. Belted into the seat next to the passenger door, he was playing a computer game he'd picked out in the Discount Mart where they'd stopped on the way in order to supplement the meager supply of clothing Grady had picked up for him in California.

Grady hated computer games. Forty minutes of electronic beeps and screaming riffs was his personal limit.

"You like rock and roll, Jimbo?"

Shoulders hunched as his fingers flew over the buttons, Jimmy spared him an impatient look. "S'okay," he muttered, returning his attention to the small screen.

Biting off a sigh, Grady grabbed a cassette from the well in the console and shoved it home. His spirits rose even higher as the soul-stirring beat of Chuck Berry in his prime throbbed through the speakers.

It was a good bet Ria would be listening to one of those classical tapes she liked so much. Mozart probably. Something with lots of violins and no real beat. In the early days of their marriage, she'd talked him into driving up to Chicago to attend a concert.

Not only had he been forced to wear a suit and a tie, but he'd also had to cram his oversize body into a seat designed for a midget for three endless hours. Worst of all, in spite of his best efforts, he'd fallen asleep after the intermission and ended up damn near snapping his head off when she'd jabbed him in the ribs with her elbow.

Ticked big-time, she hadn't spoken to him all the way back to the city. Even though he'd managed to coax her into making love when they'd gotten home, it had taken him weeks to get back in her good graces.

But damn, she'd looked like every man's fantasy in that slinky black dress. He'd lost count of the number of guys he'd had to warn off with a look. He let a smile play over his mouth at the thought of making love to her again. Tonight, if he had his way.

"She hates me, doesn't she?"

Not sure that he'd heard right, Grady glanced the boy's way. Jimmy had stopped playing his game and instead was simply staring at the screen. The shoulders that had been hunched in concentration a few minutes earlier were now stiff.

With a snap of his wrist, Grady turned off the music before asking quietly, "Are you talking about your mom?"

When the boy continued to stare, he added more softly, "Do you mean Ria?"

Jimmy looked at him long enough to bob his head. "She hates me 'cause I wanted to ride with you." This time Grady heard the faint tremor in Jimmy's voice and groaned to himself.

Grady waited for the on-coming car to whiz past, then flicked a quick glance at his son.

"Jim, I doubt there's anything you could do in this lifetime that would make your mother—or me for that matter—hate you."

Jimmy didn't look convinced. If anything, he looked more uptight.

Damn, he didn't have enough experience for this, Grady thought as he searched back through his childhood for guidance. Some profound words of wisdom his dad might have tossed at him at some point in his benighted childhood. But he came up blank.

So he did what painful experience had taught him to do. He simply told the boy the truth.

"When you were born and your mom held you in her arms for the first time, she looked at you with so much love I thought my heart was going to pound through my chest. The two of you together…" Grady felt his throat close up, and he had to take a breath. "Sometimes, when I'd come home late, I'd find her in your room sitting by your crib, watching you sleep." He risked a grin. "She seemed to think it was better than TV, though from what I saw you didn't do a lot then but sleep and belch."

That had Jimmy's interest, which both scared and encouraged him. Don't blow this one, hotshot, he told himself, as he slowed to follow Ria's van through the last of the small towns between Lafayette and the turnoff to the lake.

"This is just a guess, but I think Mom's afraid you've forgotten how to love her back." He risked a quick look the boy's way and caught the look of confusion pass over the pinched features.

"If she's my mom and you're my dad, how come I don't remember you?"

Grady drew a breath and sent up an urgent prayer that Dr. Roth came through for them with McCurry, because he was way out of his depth here.

"It's complicated, like most things having to do with life," he hedged.

"That's what grown-ups always say."

Grady marveled at how much disgust a six-year-old could pack into a few words. "You're right, son. I'm stonewalling here because I figure you deserve a dad who has all the answers, and to tell you the truth, I've got darn few." He cleared his throat and laid it all out. "Maybe I don't show it like Mom does, but I'm pretty scared you won't love me, either."

That had the boy staring at him as though he'd suddenly grown another head. "Lance said only wimps get scared," he said in a voice that he tried to make cynical.

"Lance is wrong, Jim. Everyone gets scared."

That shook the boy big-time. Grady saw it in his eyes and figured he'd blown a chance to make progress. Damn.

''Way I see it, you're smart enough to figure out what's true and what's not. It might take a while, but sooner or later you'll work it through.''

When Jimmy lapsed into silence, Grady wanted to pound something.

''This is your room, sweetheart.''

Ria opened the door and stepped back to give Jimmy a good look at the bright yellow-and-blue bedroom. Two sets of bunk beds lined opposite walls. There was an identical room on the other side of the hall. Two more bedrooms opened off the far end of the central hall, the larger of the two serving as the master bedroom. The smaller, where Manda had once slept, had been converted into Sarah's sewing room.

''The bed with the Pooh bear quilt is yours,'' she said when the boy hesitated on the threshold. Sarah had insisted on holding it ready. Ria felt a pang of guilt at keeping Grady's family at bay. But it was necessary, she reminded herself. Tomorrow, though, she would call her ex-mother-in-law and tell her all about her grandson.

Warning herself not to hover, she ambled over to the window to raise the miniblinds. Sunshine flooded into the room, warming her face. She took a testing sniff, drawing in the mingled scents of musty air and Sarah's homemade potpourri that invariably greeted her when they arrived. Years of memories flooded her senses as she unlatched the window and pushed up the sash. Wind from the lake beyond the sloping lawn wafted over her, adding a fishy flavor to the mix.

Located on a spit of land guarding a pretty little cove, the white-painted, frame bungalow Mason Hardin had built with his own hands looked out over a sandy beach on one side and a deep-water pool on the other.

At the end of a long, white pier she'd helped Grady build

one hot, lazy summer sat a sleek maroon-and-white pow-
erboat, bobbing impatiently in the swells. An aluminum
fishing boat covered in canvas had been pulled up on the
beach.

All six of the Hardin kids had learned to swim in the
shallow water on the leeward side of the spit, then tested
their courage in the dark green depths on the other side.
She pictured the legendary four-foot catfish called Old
Whiskerface lurking somewhere beneath the wind-ruffled
surface that looked so serene in the late-morning sunshine
and smiled as she turned.

Jimmy was standing in front of the open closet door, a
thoughtful frown playing over his face as he studied a series
of marks scribbled onto the yellow paint.

"Your grandma calls that the Hardin family history,"
she said when he cast a skittish glance her way. "Every
year, on the Fourth of July, Grandma and Grandpa would
stand each of their children up against this door and measure their heights."

Encouraged by the tiny kernel of interest that flashed for
a moment in the back of his brown eyes, she stepped closer.

"This is Daddy, see?"

She watched his eyes widen as he trailed his gaze upward
to the final line, etched there when Grady was eighteen.

"He's a fraction over six-two," she said, answering the
unspoken question in the light brown eyes. "I have a feeling you're going to be at least that tall."

He absorbed that with a thoughtful look. At least he
wasn't scowling, she thought as she traced her fingertip
downward along the uneven line of horizontal marks.

"Let's see, age nine, age eight…here, age six." She
touched a red line, then turned to measure the top of his
shaggy head against the marker. "I think you have Daddy
beat, sweetheart."

Jimmy's face crinkled into the grin that was a little-boy

version of his dad's—lopsided, dimpled and more than a little cocky. Her mother's heart gave a hard thump of joy— and she wanted to shout. Thank heavens for the always-predictable male ego, she thought on a brilliant burst of hope as she squatted next to him. He smelled like soap and grape bubble gum.

"This is you at age three." She touched her nail to a bold green mark about thirty inches from the floor. "You didn't want to stand still long enough for Daddy to measure you, so I bribed you with a gingerbread man." She smiled. "I packed the ones Grandma Hardin made. Just in case you change your mind about not liking them."

His eyes lighted. "The ones with green buttons?"

Her heart jolted. He remembered! It was the first crack. A beginning. God bless Dr. Roth and her brilliant idea.

"No, she only makes green buttons for St. Patrick's Day." She had to swallow the need to smother him with kisses. "Were those your favorite? The…the ones with the green buttons?"

He considered, then darted a glance around the room, as though afraid to be overheard. "I don't remember," he muttered, glancing down at his new sneakers.

*Patience,* she told herself. *Give him time.*

"Hey, how about we measure you now?" she suggested in her brightest voice. "We can show Daddy when he comes in?"

"Daddy's already in."

Startled, she let out a whoosh of surprise and spun around. Grady had a garment bag over one shoulder, her tote on the other and two suitcases in each hand.

Looking more relaxed than she'd seen him since that heart-stopping moment when he'd guided Jimmy across the threshold, he was wearing khaki shorts and a yellow polo shirt she'd bought him years ago, faded now to a soft buttery color. Frequent washings had shrunk the material so that the cotton knit was stretched over his chest, and the tight ribbing of the short sleeves cut into his biceps. She felt the liquid pull of desire and fought a need to rub up against him.

"What are you two up to here?" he demanded in his best street cop tone. "Plotting against Dad already?"

Ria caught the quick, uncertain look Jimmy sent her way and winked. "I was showing Jimmy the famous Hardin family history."

Grady grinned. "Impressive, isn't it, son?"

Jimmy blinked, and for the tiniest instant, she thought she might have seen a gleam in his eyes before his mouth turned wary again.

"Lance is a *lot* taller."

Grady dumped a stack of briefs into the dresser drawer and slammed it shut. "I gotta tell you, honey, I'm getting damn tired of hearing about that bastard, Lance, and how great he is."

Ria closed the suitcase she'd just emptied. "Jimmy remembered the green buttons on the gingerbread men, Grady. It shook him pretty bad, too, which is why I think he said that about Lance as a kind of security blanket."

His eyes darkened, and a muscle ticked just above the hard knot of tension in his jaw. "You think talking about Lance is his security blanket?"

"Yes, that's what I think."

He sighed, then took her into his arms. "I think you're one smart lady, Victoria Madison Hardin. Gutsy, too." He kissed her forehead, then rested his chin on the top of her head. She smelled sunshine on his skin.

"I figure, with your guts and my stubbornness the kid will make it past this adjustment period in good shape." She heard him chuckle deep in his throat. "If old Dad's patience holds out."

"I'd bet on it." She burrowed closer, needing to lean just a little longer.

"It's damn humbling when a guy's only son thinks a frigging drug runner is some kind of hero." She heard the bleak note in his voice and realized he was hurting. Grady all but worshiped his own father, and she suspected he'd always wanted Jimmy to look up to him in the same way.

At three Jimmy had.

"Maybe he hasn't had any other male adult in his life as a comparison," she said, tightening her arms around his solid waist.

Returning to the familiar room where they'd lain together during their honeymoon talking about the life they would make for their children had shaken her more than she'd expected.

Her dreams had been so bright then, and they'd been so young and hopeful. So full of promises. He would always make her feel special and adored. She would fill his life with strong sons and adorable daughters.

Now they were no longer young, no longer full of idealism and impossible dreams. Jimmy would be the only child she would ever give him. Grady had his work, she had hers.

He stroked her back with the flat of his big hand, and she felt the tension draining away. Little by little she relaxed, letting herself be lulled by his warmth.

"Hey, you're not falling asleep on me, are you?" He drew back to look down at her.

"Mmm." She opened her eyes and smiled up at him.

"Guess you think I'm a jerk, wanting my son to like me better than that...other guy," he said with a smile playing over his mouth.

"I think you're a good man who loves his son and is trying every way he knows how to be there for him."

"I'm not so sure I've done anything to earn many points so far."

She saw a muscle bunch in his jaw and smiled. "I thought I was the impatient one in this family."

His face changed, and his eyes grew very dark. "Is that what we are now, Ree? A family."

She heard the quiet note of hope in his voice and ached. "I don't know, Grady. I just know I like being here with you, even though it scares me. I know you want more, but…"

His lashes flickered, and for an instant he looked disappointed before his grin slanted. "Hey, you ain't seen nothing, honey. Just wait until I turn on the old Hardin charm. Ain't no way you're gonna keep from falling for me all over again."

She laughed because he expected it. But even as she lifted her face for his kiss, she felt the tug of guilt. What if he was wrong? What if she'd built the walls around her heart too high and too strong? What if even the two of them together couldn't find a way through them?

Grady felt her stiffen and made himself pull back from the hunger that grew stronger in him with each minute he spent near her. Hunger to hold her. To kiss her long enough and hard enough to push her past her need to test each step. To earn again the love he'd so carelessly thrown away.

"Relax, honey, I'll hear him if he starts down the hall."

He was giving her an out and prayed big time she would take it. The last thing he wanted at the moment was more talk. After a man spilled out his heart at his feet, anything he added was too damn close to groveling.

"It's just that…I can't make any promises."

"I don't remember asking for any."

"Not in so many words." She sighed, then touched his face so gently it pained him all the way to the quick. "I don't want to hurt you, Grady."

He'd seen enough suffering to last a dozen lifetimes. Seeing it in her eyes nearly laid him flat. Knowing it was because of him had him wanting to bloody someone.

Instead, he found the cocky grin that no one but his mom had ever cared enough to look behind. "I'm already hurting, honey." He cupped her bottom and nudged her closer to the arousal that was already straining his shorts.

Her eyes widened, and her breath hissed out in a little gasp. He gritted his teeth and thrust gently against her. "That's…oh!" She took a quick breath. "That's not, uh, what I meant and you know it."

"I know I want you." He clamped his jaw down tight and rubbed against her. The jagged burst of desire in her eyes was enough for now. "I know you want me. Anything else can wait."

"Be serious, Grady."

"Honey, I don't know how much more serious I can get before I burst."

Her laughter was a gift he cherished. "Hold that thought," she whispered, doing a little rubbing of her own. He nearly lost it before he made himself draw back.

"Tonight," he grated, his voice raw. "Five minutes after Jim's tucked up tight, I want you naked."

It took considerably longer to finish unpacking and coax Jimmy through a shampoo and bath. Then while Ria read him a chapter of the tattered copy of *The Adventures of Tom Sawyer* she'd found tucked into one of the bookcases, Grady had checked the locks on all the doors and windows.

A cop's paranoia, he'd told her. She'd simply smiled, but he'd seen the relief in her eyes. While she showered, he put in a patient half hour watching Jim annihilate galaxy after galaxy while excitedly explaining each complex maneuver that had laid the enemy low. By the time Grady's ears were ringing and Jimmy's eyelids were drooping, it was close to ten o'clock.

"In you go, tiger," Grady ordered, drawing back the covers.

"Moira always lets me watch that funny guy with the cigar who comes on after the news," Jimmy protested sullenly as he climbed between the sheets.

Grady figured Moira wasn't watching much late-night TV these days. Not unless California jails were a lot more liberal than the ones in Indiana.

"One of these days real soon your mom and I will sit down and iron out some rules, but until then, we'll go by the ones my folks had for me." He grinned. "Which means lights out by ten during the summer."

Jimmy's lower lip zoomed out. "That's a dumb rule."

"You're certainly entitled to your opinion." Grady slipped the computer game out from under the pillow where Jim had stashed it.

The sleepy look vanished as the boy reared up. "Hey, give that back."

"Tomorrow." Grady grinned. "Right before old Dad leaves for town."

"Not fair," Jimmy muttered, but he settled down again, only to rear up almost immediately. "Where's Trouble?"

Grady glanced around. "It takes him a while to settle in someplace new. Probably doesn't know where he's supposed to bunk, so you'd best whistle for him."

Jimmy stared, big-eyed and skeptical. "Cats don't come when you whistle."

"I have a dollar that says he does."

Jimmy worried his lip and considered, looking for the kicker. Grady hoped the cat didn't come waltzing in before he got this particular fish on the line.

"Don't have no money to bet," Jimmy declared finally, looking disappointed.

Grady set the hook. "How about this? If you're right, I'll give you back your game and pretend I don't hear those godawful noises in the middle of the night. But if I'm right, you agree to call Ria Mom all day tomorrow." Pressing his advantage, he stuck out his hand. "Deal?"

Jimmy hesitated. "Who gets to do the whistling?"

"Your call."

"I'm not much good so you'd better do it," Jimmy said, before sealing the bet with a quick handshake.

Grady gave it all he had, splitting the air with a piercing whistle, then held his breath. Right on cue, Trouble came trotting through the door, his tail twitching.

"How did you do that?" the boy said, clearly in awe.

Grady wanted to strut. "Patience and bribery." And a long string of empty nights to fill. Training the cat had tested his patience and tired his mind.

Seeing Grady, the cat paused, then executed a perfect leap onto the pillow next to Jimmy's head. Grady made a mental note to buy a case of those gourmet cat meals.

He came to her naked from the shower, with hunger in his eyes and a hint of a cocky smile on his lean face. He was beautiful corded steel and fluid grace layered with bronzed muscle.

Ria felt desire flash inside her like the sudden kindling of a flame. Oh, yes, he wanted her, she thought as she watched him walk toward the bed, his body already fully aroused.

*Magnificently* aroused.

It was a woman's pride that ran through her. It was a heady drug, this power she had over him. Watching his eyes turn hot and needy as his gaze ran the length of her body had excitement dancing in her head and her pulse pounding.

Last night he'd been achingly gentle with her, and

though he'd found his own release, she had sensed the restraint in him. Tonight she wanted him wild and out of control.

"If you're too tired, tell me now," he ordered, his voice raspy.

She summoned a siren smile and let it bloom. "Not a chance."

"Thank God," he grated, his eyes a little reckless as he flicked a quick look at the closed door.

"Already locked," she murmured, feeling smug and daring—and wonderfully wicked.

"Proud of yourself, aren't you?" His grin was lethal, his movements lightning as he grabbed the sheet she'd pulled to her waist and jerked it free of the bed, sending it whipping across the room.

She felt a wanton excitement sizzle across her nerve endings, leaving her jittery and impatient. "I love to see a man take charge," she murmured, raking him with her gaze.

The mattress dipped as he braced himself over her. "How about a man being tormented into a mindless frenzy by a dark-haired temptress?" he all but growled.

"Mmm," she managed, already linking her arms around his neck. His skin was still warm and dewy from the shower, the scent of soap as intoxicating as the musk of climax.

"Hang on tight, honey," he warned an instant before his mouth crashed down on hers.

Her senses exploded, raw heat and brilliant light. Like a roaring wave, pleasure rolled through her, rippling and surging until she was liquid and pliable and hot. His mouth was greedy and clever, his tongue persuasive one moment, demanding the next. His hands were everywhere, sometimes stroking, sometimes kneading.

"Let go, sweetheart, let it go," he urged, even as she bucked and writhed under the onslaught.

He suckled her breasts until she was quivering and weak, then slid his mouth lower, tracing a slow line with his tongue to the hollow of her navel.

She gasped and he looked up at her, amber fire glittering in the heart of his brown eyes. "Tell me what you feel," he demanded.

Her mind clouded, and she struggled to clear it.

"Tell me, sweetheart."

She heard urgency in his tone and more. Something vital she needed to understand. But the blood was pulsing and she hurt. "Grady," she whispered on a moan. "You...I feel you."

"No other man touches you," he grated, and she whimpered.

His breathing grew shallow and rapid as his own desire built, yet he took his time moving lower, using his teeth to tug on the curling hair below her belly until her skin was acutely sensitized and shivering.

"Now," she begged.

"You're not ready yet." He made her wait until she was boneless and moaning, her hands clutching, then limp.

She wanted wild; now he gave her gentle, kissing the heated skin of her throat, the damp underside of her breasts, her belly until she was trembling.

She wanted savage; he gave her sweet, urging her up and up until she quivered, poised and desperate, only to sooth her back from the brink.

Always he watched her, a waiting, hungry look in his eyes. She tried to touch him, to relieve the pain she saw haunting the deepest part of his eyes, but he drew her hands away from between his legs and pressed them over her head, holding her prisoner.

"Say it," he demanded harshly, though it seemed a plea. "Tell me what I—" His voice broke and he dropped his head to her breast.

A shudder ran over him, and she fought to reach past the rampaging need inside her to soothe him.

"Grady please…"

He lifted his head and looked at her with savage eyes as he nudged her thighs apart with his knee, then positioned himself and thrust, taking her breath.

She arched, bucked against the powerful hands holding her. His thighs pressed hers wider as he thrust over and over, driving her higher and higher. She writhed, she gasped, and then she was cresting.

He caught her keening cry with his mouth, muffling the sound so that their son wouldn't hear. She felt his body convulse, his muscles rigid with steely resistance, his breathing wild.

With one last convulsion of muscle and nerve, he was pouring himself into her. She felt the slick heat, the tremors of aftershock, the weight of his spent body as he rested atop her long enough for breath to return.

Pressed against the mattress, she felt replete and quite thoroughly loved. She lifted a weak hand to smooth the rumpled hair away from his wet forehead. He murmured her name on a sigh, then drew his brows together.

"Need to move," he said thickly. "Too heavy."

"No," she whispered, pressing a kiss against the furrows of his frown. "Stay in me."

Groaning, he hooked his leg over hers and rolled until they were lying face-to-face, still joined. She pressed a kiss to his throat, full of feelings she needed to sort through. So many feelings, so much pleasure.

"Okay?" he asked, his eyes slumberous between lazy lashes.

"Incredible," she murmured, touching the hard knot of tension in his jaw with trembling fingers.

"Enough," he muttered, before turning his head to kiss her wrist. "I'll make it enough."

# *Chapter 11*

Grady was gone when Ria woke a little before seven. Though he'd promised to rearrange his schedule in order to spend more time with her and Jimmy, he had the regular Monday-morning staff meeting to conduct. There were other obligations, too, she knew. The routine work of a man who held an important position.

After checking on Jimmy—and finding him still sleeping like an angel with Trouble curled up next to him on the pillow—she stepped naked into the shower. Though her body was still deliciously relaxed, she felt a few twinges from the wild ride Grady had given her. Smiling smugly, she lifted her face to the warm spray and wondered what Dr. Roth would say if she knew what a momentous chain of events she'd set in motion.

Twenty minutes later, dressed in comfortably worn cut-offs and a No Bull tank top that she'd packed in the hopes Jimmy would remember the prize-winning Guernseys that had fascinated him at the State Fair, she padded barefoot into the silent kitchen.

Grady had left her a note propped against the coffee-maker, printed in the block letters he used instead of script because it was easier for him, saying that he'd be back by noon at the latest. Though he figured to be in meetings most of the morning, she could reach him at one of the three numbers he'd jotted down. He'd also left his cellular phone, along with a P.S. that the cottage phone was out of order.

Yawning, she poured a cup of the thick black sludge he'd brewed before he'd left and carried it along with the phone to the screened-in porch facing the cove. Though it was still early, even by vacation standards, the lake was already dotted with boats.

Nothing much had changed in three years, she decided as she sipped. Sarah's petunias still spilled from the boxes below the windows and bushy-tailed squirrels carried on a chattering game of tag in the treetops, leaping from branch to branch in the leafy canopy overhead.

The last time she'd been here was two years ago on the Fourth of July which had also been Manda's twenty-first birthday. Grady had gotten blind drunk and ended up swimming across the lake in the dark. Terrified and furious, she'd waited until he'd staggered out of the water, then politely made her farewells to his family and driven away.

She'd made it to the top of the hill behind the small lakefront community before the tears she hated blurred her vision, forcing her to pull over until she could get herself under control again.

Living with madness had taught her to be strong and independent, yes—but it had also taught her to be cautious in caring too much about the people in her life.

She'd broken her own rule when she'd met Grady, falling blindly, desperately in love. Though he hadn't left her physically, she'd still ended up alone emotionally.

The thought of letting herself feel more than affection and desire was terrifying to her. And yet—

The phone at her elbow shrilled, causing her to let out a little yelp before snatching it up. It rang again before she found the right button.

"Hello?"

"Morning, sweetheart." Grady's voice was husky—and just a little cocky. "How's your day so far?"

"Barely started," she said with a smile she knew he could hear. "How about you?"

"So far the best part was peeling your warm little body off my chest. And that was hell—especially when you rubbed against me like a sleepy kitten."

She felt a quick flurry of pleasure. "Speaking of which, looks like Trouble and Jimmy are best buddies now."

His chuckle was deep-throated and sexy. "That's not exactly what I meant, honey."

"Oh, no? Then perhaps you'd better be more specific."

His groan was soft and private—and bone shivering. "Not a chance, honey. Not while I'm sitting in an office with glass walls."

She laughed. "Coward."

"You got that right." He cleared his throat. "Two things, and then I've got an appointment with the chief. Since I'm trying to wrangle money for two more detectives out of the mean-spirited bastard, I figure I'd best be on time."

"By all means." She heard a noise and glanced up to find Jimmy hovering in the doorway, Trouble draped around his neck like a black-and-white stole. She smiled and waved him in. "Good morning, darling."

"Pardon?" Grady sounded confused.

"Jimmy," she explained.

"Say hello for me."

"Daddy says hello," she told the boy with a soft smile. Jimmy grunted something before ambling over to the window.

"Sent his love, did he?" Grady drawled, and she burst out laughing.

"Something like that."

He sighed. "I got a call from McCurry's office a few minutes ago, and it seems the doctor is in Ireland until the beginning of next month. We're slotted to see him the afternoon of the first." He paused, then went on. "It was the best I could do, Ree."

She shifted position on the vinyl cushion, drawing Trouble's attention, but not her son's. "What about the other two referrals?"

"I can try them if you like, but I figured since things had calmed down a lot, we could wait."

Ria gnawed her lip and weighed the pros and cons. Jimmy was standing at the window with his back to her, watching the squirrels, one hip cocked in a perfect imitation of his father's blatantly masculine stance.

"Dr. Roth did say McCurry was the best, didn't she?"

"Yes, several times." He didn't sound rushed, but she knew, somehow, that he was. "But she also said that the others were good, too, so if—"

"No, I'm sure you're right. We can wait."

The pause was brief, but telling. She suspected that he'd heard the doubt in her voice. When he spoke again, the sexy little growl had been replaced by the careful tone that had marked the last months of their marriage. "Ree, I don't want you to worry, so I'll be happy to give the others a call."

"No, I trust your judgment," she said firmly. It was as close to telling him that she didn't blame him for what happened as she could come.

This time the pause was longer, and on her part anyway, distinctly uncomfortable. "You said two things," she prodded. "What's the second?"

He cleared his throat. "I ran into Flynn this morning and he said to tell you that his nose is itching."

Ria blinked. "Is that supposed to be significant?"

"It is to my brother. Claims his nose starts to itch whenever facts of a case don't add up the way they're supposed to."

The hand holding her coffee mug froze halfway to her mouth. "So he's going to reopen the Benteen investigation?"

"Sounds that way. He also said…hang on a minute, Ree. Got a small fire I have to put out." She heard the brush of his raspy calluses as he covered the phone with his hand. While she sipped, she listened to the muffled sound of angry voices and watched Jimmy playing with the cat in the middle of the woven mat covering most of the porch.

Sensing her gaze, he glanced up. In the wink of an eye, the smile in his eyes turned to wariness before he dropped his gaze again.

"As soon as Daddy and I hang up, I'll fix breakfast."

"Whatever," he muttered, walking his fingers toward Trouble who sat in regal silence, licking one paw.

Ria had a sudden thought. "How about strawberry waffles with whipped cream and chocolate sprinkles?" It was his customary reward for being good on the drive.

Jimmy's head shot up again, his face a study in eagerness. "Really?"

"Really."

"Cool!"

Seeing that his adversary was clearly distracted, Trouble pounced, digging his claws into Jimmy's hand with just enough force to signal victory but not nearly deep enough to draw blood. Nevertheless, Jimmy let out a yowl that was loud enough to shake the windows.

"Ree, what's wrong!" Grady's voice was suddenly low and urgent in her ear. "Was that Jim? Are you okay?"

She laughed softly. "Fine. Jimmy and I were just discussing breakfast, and Trouble was feeling neglected."

She heard him let out his breath in a rush. "Geez, Ree…I thought…" He inhaled a breath, let it out. "I guess you can imagine what I thought."

She felt a jolt of fear. "Grady, you don't think—"

"No, I don't," he said with deadly certainty. "It was just a gut reaction, that's all. I don't want you to worry about it."

"But—"

"You said you trusted me." It wasn't so much an accusation as a challenge.

"I do. Of course, I do."

"Fine." His voice was clipped, and she felt a chill.

"Grady, don't take this wrong, but humor me, okay? No one knows where we are, right?"

"No one but my folks." There was a pause before he said softly, "Do you want me to come back up there? If I have to, I can shake loose now."

"What about your meeting with the chief?"

"Say the word and I'm on my way."

Surprise rendered her speechless.

"Okay, I'll be there in twenty minutes," he said, obviously mistaking her silence for agreement.

"No, wait! That's not necessary." She drew a shaky breath. "But thank you for offering."

Now he was the one taking time to answer. "I meant what I said, Ree. Nothing is more important to me than you and Jim. Maybe someday you'll believe me."

He hung up without saying goodbye. It was only later, as she was grating chocolate that she remembered he hadn't told her what else Flynn had said about the case.

She would call him back later, she decided as she shouted for Jimmy to come to the table.

By the time she and Jimmy finished breakfast and he

was in his room dressing, Grady's assistant informed her that "the captain was on his way home."

Was that what they were making—a home? she wondered, as she hurried into the bedroom to brush her hair. The idea both tempted and terrified.

Grady slipped the padlock from the storage shed and slid the door open. A thousand memories rushed at him along with the smell of boat gas and musty canvas. Jimmy hesitated on the threshold, his body a little tense, his eyes bright with curiosity.

"It stinks in here," he grumbled, screwing up his nose.

Grady drew in a satisfying lungful and savored before releasing it. "Smells like freedom to me."

Jimmy looked up, a look of cautious interest on his face. Grady could almost hear the echoes of a three-year-old's chatter in the silent look, and he mourned the lost years.

"Why?" Jimmy asked finally.

"When I was a kid, I'd started looking forward to the last day of school along about the time that new-book smell wore off, which was usually the end of September."

He glanced around at the stuff piled up over the years. Mismatched water skis, water toys, a broken lawn chair. The tube from a tractor tire he and Ria used to share. Tonight he'd do his best to talk her into taking a moonlight swim, he decided.

So far he and Jimmy had been the only ones in the water. While Jim had been searching the sandy bottom for catfish, Grady had been pumping him for hints about the life he'd led during the past three years.

Yeah, he'd had a pool at his house. A lot bigger than his best bud Jeremy's.

So why couldn't the boy swim?

Naw, he didn't go to a dumb school 'cause Moira was a real good teacher.

So how come he didn't want to talk about his favorite subjects.

No, they weren't his real parents, but they'd been real good to him. The *best*. He never had to make his bed or clean his room or eat anything he didn't like.

"What's that?" Jimmy asked, pointing.

"Croquet set."

Grady grinned at the thought of winning a game with Ria. Hardin rules said that the winner got to claim a prize. He thought of that inner tube that held two and a lakeful of water that was bathtub warm. As he recalled, she'd climaxed twice the last time they'd gone skinny-dipping.

He felt his body stir and reminded himself he'd never lost a game yet.

"You ever play?" he asked, watching Jimmy trail his fingers over the mallet heads.

"Uh-uh." He kicked the stand with the toe of his sneaker. "Lance is gonna teach me to play golf next time we go to Palm Springs."

"Is that something you do often, go to Palm Springs?"

"Sometimes."

Grady grabbed the red mallet that Jimmy used to drag around behind him as he'd followed his dad around the court and handed it to the boy. "Try the feel of this one," he suggested, deliberately keeping his tone offhand. "Maybe this afternoon we can set up the court."

He moved aside the lawn edger and leaned down to open the large wooden cruise box. Two flags lay atop a collection of life preservers. He took out the Stars and Stripes and started to close the lid, only to stop when Jimmy asked suddenly, "What's that gold thing?"

"Purdue banner. Here, hold this and I'll show you." He handed his son the flag before holding up the banner so that Jim could see the familiar Boilermaker logo.

His son seemed less than impressed. "What's Purdue?"

"It's a college in West Lafayette. A pretty famous place, actually, especially in these parts. Your mom and just about everyone else in our family went there."

Jim took a moment to work that through in his mind. "So did you go there, too?" he asked finally.

Grady took in a slow breath. He'd lost track of the times he'd been asked that same question over the years. It never failed to jab his pride.

"I tried, but I couldn't make the entrance requirements."

"What's that mean, they wouldn't let you come in, like in the movies?"

"In a way." He heard a speedboat scream by and glanced through the dusty window at the violent ripples rushing toward the sandy beach. "Entrance requirements are mostly a set of rules they have about who they want and don't want."

"And they didn't want you?"

Grady nearly groaned at his son's obvious disappointment. "Nope. But I got me a real polite letter with a seal and everything."

"*How come* they didn't want you?"

Persistent little cuss, his son. "I have a problem reading, which means I have to find other ways of learning things." He folded the pennant into a neat square before stowing it away. "I can usually figure things out, but it takes me a long time sometimes."

"Me, too, sometimes." Jimmy's gaze slid from his. Something in the angle of the boy's head had his gut tightening. "Guess people mighta made fun of you on account of that."

"Some did, yeah—till I got old enough to make them pay. Then they stopped."

Jimmy looked intrigued. "Did you shoot 'em?"

"Nope. Punched 'em. My brothers mostly. And a few of their big-mouthed friends."

Jimmy kicked the croquet set again. Hard. One shoulder hunched, then the other. He dropped his gaze.

"I did what you said. You know, like for the bet?"

Grady had to grab a minute to catch up. "You mean calling Ria Mom?"

He nodded, and his hair flopped. "I thought, since it was what you wanted and all, it was supposed to be a good thing. I mean, you're all the time trying to make her laugh and watching her to make sure she's not upset and all."

Grady was damn near speechless, blown away by the kid's ability to read him. "You're right. It's supposed to be a good thing." He hesitated, then squatted down to bring his gaze closer to Jim's. "Are you saying it wasn't?"

Jimmy rubbed his ear with a hunched shoulder. He looked miserably unhappy and a little scared, like maybe he was worried about what Grady was going to do next. He didn't want to think about another man punishing his son, especially a man with big hands like frigging Lance's.

"You don't have to tell me anything you don't want to, son, but if something's bothering you, I might be able to help."

Jimmy didn't look impressed, and Grady bit off a sigh. "I admit I don't have all the answers. Heck, sometimes I think I was sleeping-in the morning the Lord passed out sense, but I'd sure give it my best shot."

Jimmy rubbed his ear again, then gradually lowered his shoulder. Grady waited patiently while the boy worked it through. He had all day if that's how long it took. Finally Jimmy aimed another kick at the croquet set and started talking. "She got this funny look on her face, and then she started bawling."

Grady let out the relief in a long breath. "Remember what I told you right before we knocked on Mom's door that first night?"

Jimmy slanted him a wary look. "Some."

"Women, especially moms, sometimes cry when they're happy, too. Yeah, I know, it doesn't make much sense, but it happens."

"You think that's what she was doing. Being happy?"

"I think it's a good bet." He reached up to ruffle the unruly hair that he'd passed down to his boy. "It's not easy for a guy to understand why women do what they do sometimes, especially that crying thing, but when a guy finds a lady as special as your mom, well, he's willing to do a whole bunch of trying."

Jimmy let out a noisy sigh that was almost comical. "Does that mean it's okay if I call her that again?"

"*Very* okay," Grady said with a grin that felt damned wobbly at the edges. "And I'm *very* proud of you for keeping your word and paying off your bet."

His son flushed with pleasure. Grady wanted desperately to hug him, but the instinct honed over a lot of years told him it was too soon. So he took the SWAT cap from his own head and slipped it on Jimmy's, brim backward.

"C'mon, let's go hoist the flag. And then if we ask real nice, Mom might give us a coupla hunks of that fudge she was cooking up when I got home."


The sun was setting over the lake, turning the water to flame. The three of them had eaten outside at the picnic table, then taken a boat ride before tackling the dishes. Falling easily into old habits, Ria washed and Grady dried while Jimmy practiced hitting croquet balls through the wickets Grady had set up on the lawn facing the lake. Every few minutes Ria would lean close to the kitchen window and look out.

The yard had been fenced years earlier to keep the youngest of the Hardins safe. The latch on the gate was not only over the boy's reach, but locked. The fence itself was sound. He'd walked it earlier to be sure and told her twice that it would take a tank to break through.

Still she checked.

Though she professed to hate firearms in the home, she'd packed the Walther .380 he'd taught her to shoot on their honeymoon. It was now on the top shelf of the master bedroom closet. It was also loaded.

"Did Flynn say how he'd found Monk's ex-wife?" she asked as she rinsed the last of the cups.

"Nope. Just that she'd agreed to see him." Grady gave the dinner plate another swipe before returning it to the cupboard. All through the meal he'd waited for Jim to call her "Mom." But the boy had said almost nothing.

Taking an extra loop around his impatience, he'd looked forward to the moment he and Ree were alone, positive she, too, was just waiting for privacy before sharing her joy.

"When I called the Center to give Kate and Tova the number of your cell phone, Kate said that Brenda had left a message on my voice mail, asking me to call her back. I left a message on her machine, but so far I haven't heard from her."

Grady reached for the cup she'd just upended in he drainer. "If there's fault in the thing, Flynn will find it."

"I know. That's why I asked him to look into it."

She checked on Jimmy, smiling a little at something she saw. The smile faded quickly, however, as her brow puckered. "If Monk did murder that poor little baby in her own bed and Brenda knows it, I have to believe it's tearing her apart inside."

"Maybe. Or maybe she handed him the pillow."

She winced, and he hated himself for not guarding his tongue with greater care.

"No, I'm sure she'd never harm a child."

"Keeping silent hurts as much as a fist sometimes, Ree," he said, hanging the mug from a hook in the cupboard.

"You're right, of course. It's just that I hate to think I've misjudged her."

"It happens."

Frowning thoughtfully, Ria scrubbed down the counter, then wrung the dishcloth dry before hanging it from the faucet. "I can't help wondering about that woman. Moira."

Grady plucked a glass from the dish drainer. "What about her, honey?"

"Do you think she really came to love Jimmy or do you think she just put up with him because of the money?"

Grady took his time putting away the glass. "If that woman had an ounce of maternal blood in her veins, I'll put on a tutu and walk the fifty-yard line during the Purdue–Notre Dame game this September."

Ria's mouth twitched, but the shadows in her eyes only shifted aside for a moment, returning full force when her expression sobered.

"Grady, I know I overreacted this morning. I know you'd never let anyone get to Jimmy again."

The words were right. It was the way her gaze slid from his that had his gut twisting hot. "We both overreacted, honey. It's going to take time for us to relax again."

"I realize that, but still, it started me thinking…" She broke off to close the window over the sink. It stuck, and she had to give it a hefty shove which made her fanny wiggle enticingly. Though he managed to keep the groan inside, his hormones drop-kicked him dead center.

"What if Rustakov decides to steal our baby again?" she asked when she was sure they wouldn't be overheard.

"Bastard's dead, Ree." He concentrated on draping the damp towel over the edge of the counter to dry.

She picked up the glass of wine he'd poured her before they'd tackled the dishes, then put it down again without taking a sip. "How do you know? Are you sure? Maybe your source was wrong."

"This source doesn't make mistakes."

"Did...did you kill him?"

"No." It wasn't for lack of trying, but no one knew that but a couple of hard-eyed contacts in Washington. Guys with kids of their own willing to grease a few palms, make a few phone calls in a good cause.

"He was blown away by the head of a rival cartel on the steps of his villa overlooking the Black Sea," he told her when he realized the anxious look hadn't quite faded from her eyes.

"I'm glad he's dead," Ria said, downing a huge swallow of wine. "I hope he died a horrible death."

It had been that and more. It also hadn't been quick. At the time Grady had felt only fury that his best link to his son had been snuffed out.

"He can't hurt you anymore, sweetheart." He said the words quietly, but the knowledge of his own part in her suffering was like acid against his throat. Someday, maybe, she would forgive him. He doubted he would ever forgive himself.

"I hated him." She took another sip. Though she seemed calm enough, he caught the ripples in the wine and realized her hand wasn't as steady as it should be. "He was a horrible man."

"He's gone," he said very quietly, even though he doubted she heard. His brave lady was at the end of her emotional rope. He'd seen the signs often enough. In fellow officers shaken by a particularly bloody crime scene. In Kale when his partner had taken a bullet meant for him. In himself after Jimmy had been snatched.

Days of stuffing her feelings deep inside. Months of denying emotions that had the power to destroy until finally the ability to feel was numbed.

"I wanted to kill him myself," she said in a strained tone he'd heard only once before—on the night she'd asked him to move out.

"I know, honey."

"He was evil. Vermin of the worst kind." The wine sloshed over onto her hand, but she didn't notice, just as she didn't notice when he plucked the goblet from her fingers.

"Tell me," he urged. "Tell me how you hurt. How I let you down and how you hate me for it. Take a swing at me if you have to. Or scream. Just let it out."

"No, I'm...fine now." The words seemed torn from her, and her face was white. She blinked, then jerked her gaze toward the window. "Jimmy?"

"Still whacking the heck out of the ball."

"He's been practicing for hours. He's determined to win, just like his dad." Her voice was a croak, and she cleared her throat. "He called me Mom today. I made a fool of myself and dripped all over him."

"Hey, that's great, honey. About the Mom thing, I mean. Really great."

She narrowed her gaze, back in control. "It would have been if he'd come up with it himself."

He could almost hear the whine of a bullet headed straight for his head. Like all wise cops, he ducked first. "Come again?"

"You tricked your own son—and don't try that innocent look on me. I have my sources, too."

He'd be damned if he'd feel guilty. "I consider it more a case of finessing him in the right direction."

She snorted. "You ran a street con on a six-year-old."

"Hey, now that hurts." He did his best to look wounded. Even pressed his hand to his heart. It didn't faze her. "You know what cats are like. Independent as hell."

"You *trained* that animal to come when you whistled."

"Honey, it takes a professional to train a cat. I'm just...hey, wait a minute. Let's examine this more closely. How is it you know about the whistling?" He crowded her against the counter, his chest rubbing a little against her breasts, and his thighs molding her. She sucked in, her eyes darkening.

"I might have overheard part of your conversation with Jimmy," she hedged, angling her chin at him. Like mother, like son, he realized, smiling to himself.

"Listening at keyholes can get a lady in deep trouble, sweetheart." He bracketed her waist with his hands and held her still.

"It was...inadvertent," she declared haughtily. "And don't try shunting your guilt onto me, Grady Hardin. You suckered your own son into a bet you knew he'd lose." She poked him in the chest. "Didn't you?"

"I'm pleading the fifth."

He bent suddenly to kiss her hard on the mouth before drawing back again. She glared, but her mouth was suddenly as soft as rose petals. "Sneaky, Hardin. Really sneaky."

"Yeah, but like you said, I'm cute."

He inched his hands up higher until he could run his thumbs along the underside of her breasts. Her breath hitched, but she wouldn't yield easily. Maybe she never would. But he knew now he'd keep trying. The alternative would leave him too empty and lost.

"You're impossible," she sputtered, but her gaze was on his mouth. The impact shot him past his troubled thoughts and right into sharp, angry need. Pride had him taking his time instead of yanking down her shorts and driving into her.

"But sexy, right?"

"What you are is exasperating." Her voice was strained and her eyes were going smoky.

"Admit it, honey. You're crazy about me."

She winced. "Don't use that word."

He called himself a few choice names. "Sorry, I forgot you hated it."

"I hate the memories it evokes," she whispered, resting her head against his shoulder, her body still tense. He sighed and pulled her closer.

"How would you feel about a little dip after Jimmy's tucked into bed?"

She lifted her head and looked up at him. The bad memories were still there, deep in the backs of her eyes, but they were dimmer now. "The last time you suggested a little dip I ended up with sand in my bikini bottom and..." Her voice faded.

He lifted a hand to brush back her hair. "And a marriage proposal," he finished softly, aching a little.

"Grady—"

He used his mouth to cut off the sweet little speech he saw forming in her eyes. About how much she liked him, and needed him.

"The only proposal I'm interested in right now is an indecent one." To sweeten the pot, he slipped one hand beneath the elastic at her waist. He felt heat through the damp silk of her panties and bit off a groan.

"How about you, honey? Are you interested?"

She drew a shaky breath. "I just might be—later," she whispered.

"It's a date." Reluctantly he withdrew his hand and straightened her shirt.

She lifted a hand to his cheek, her gaze on his. "About that trick you pulled," she said softly. "Thank you."

Don't thank me, he wanted to shout. Just love me. Instead, he offered her a lazy grin and kissed the tip of her nose. "You can pay me back later, honey." He leaned closer to whisper a very graphic suggestion in her ear.

When she blushed, he kissed her again and felt the tiny shivers run through her.

It was enough, he reminded himself. At the moment it was all he had.

# Chapter 12

**B**renda pulled into the apartment lot, her stomach feeling like she'd eaten something rotten. Her heart was beating so violently she felt faint.

It was almost five-thirty and Monk was due home some-time tonight. He'd been on the road for a week, and like always, he would expect dinner to be ready when he walked in the door.

It wasn't her fault the battery in the old Chevy had gone dead, she told herself as she scrambled out and reached behind the seat for the groceries. With the rain and all, it had taken her forty minutes to find someone to give her a jump start. The old guy who'd helped her had been real nice, too, offering to follow her back to the apartment, just to make sure the rusted-out junker didn't stall out.

Brenda had been tempted, what with the gangs taking potshots at each other in her neighborhood the way they'd been doin' these past months, only she'd been scared that Monk would find out.

Monk didn't like her talking to strangers. He hated any-one knowing their business. Things were real bad right now, so more trouble was the last thing she needed.

Monk had always been moody, but he'd never been mean. Oh, maybe he got a little rough in bed, but that was the way men got sometimes. Her stepfather had been a lot rougher when he'd raped her when she was twelve.

Monk really loved her, she was sure of that. But since Missy had died, he'd been kind of weird, sometimes staring at her with the strangest look on his face. Like he was trying to figure something out in his head.

He'd been having bad headaches, too. Worse than they'd ever been. Which is why he'd come home early a few weeks ago and found the note she'd made to herself after Callie had called, reminding her of the Healing Friends meeting that night.

It was her fault he'd lost his temper and knocked her around in the parking lot outside the Center, he'd told her when he'd finally calmed down. Hadn't he asked her real nice not to go back to the support group? But had she listened? Had she *obeyed,* the way a wife should?

*No, she had not.*

Any man worth the name would have lost his temper when he found out his wife was deliberately defying him. Still, he'd only shoved her a little instead of beating her the way her stepfather had beaten her mother. And then afterward, Monk had turned up real sweet, loving on her so nice she almost forgot how much he'd hurt her.

She felt a sharp pang of guilt and told herself she'd only gone back to the group just one more time after that. She wasn't sure why. Maybe because she'd felt safe there with Ria and Callie and the other women, like she wasn't really alone the way she felt sometimes.

And because she'd been hearing Missy crying in her dreams.

It had gotten real bad for a while. Sometimes she actually thought her baby was in the house. It wasn't like she was crazy, exactly. More like scared, which is why she'd tried to call Ria at the Center. Only Ria wasn't there.

By the time Ria had called back, she'd already calmed down to realize she couldn't ever tell anyone about... things. Not even Ria. Still, she'd felt real bad, hearing the concern in Ria's voice on the machine.

Going to the Center was a dumb mistake, she knew now. No one understood Monk the way she did. Callie was wrong about him. He didn't beat her. He loved her. And he'd promised to make her pregnant again.

Maybe a little boy this time.

Men always liked sons better than daughters. Look at her own father. After he and her mom had split, he'd taken her two brothers, leaving her behind to deal with her mother's drinking bouts. She'd never seen her father again.

Juggling two bulging sacks of groceries, Brenda hurried through the pouring rain toward her apartment. She had her key out, ready to unlock the door and her mind already searching for ways to get a meal on the table as quickly as possible, when suddenly the door jerked inward, throwing her off balance. She lost her grip on the already-sodden sacks, and they fell, sending the groceries flying.

She gave a startled screech before she realized that it was Monk who had his big hands wrapped around her arms.

"You bitch!" he shouted, spraying her face with spittle. "You really done it this time."

"I c-couldn't help it," she stuttered, backing away. "The b-battery died and—"

"I should have killed you, too, while I was at it."

Brenda felt the scream tug at her throat, but some sixth sense warned her not to give in to the terror pounding like a fever pulse in her veins.

"I'm sorry," she whispered. "Whatever I did, I'm sorry."

His eyes were black holes filled with fury, and his face had turned a frightening shade of purple. "I told you to get rid of that brat before she was born. I warned you."

"M-Missy?"

Standing only a few feet away, clenching and unclenching his massive fists, he gave no sign that he'd heard her. "It wasn't my fault."

Brenda tasted bile and struggled to gulp it down. "What…what wasn't your fault?"

"She wouldn't shut up. You said you'd keep her quiet. You promised."

*Oh God, oh God, oh God! It was true.*

Somehow she knew she had to get away from those fists and those terribly hollow eyes. But how?

"Why…why don't I fix you a sandwich and a beer. I got the kind you like—"

Before she could get out a word, he backhanded her, sending her crashing to the floor. Instinctively she braced herself with her arm, only to feel her wrist give way. The pain was crushing, bringing tears to her eyes. She retched, but managed to keep from vomiting.

"Please, Monk, I didn't say anything."

He stood braced, looking down at her for a long, frightening moment before he reached into the pocket of his jeans. He took out a business card and dropped it to the floor in front of her.

Though she'd begun trembling violently, she managed to pick up the card with her left hand. She had to blink a few times to bring the name printed there into focus:

"Detective Sergeant Flynn A. Hardin, Homicide Division, Lafayette Police Department."

Raw terror squeezed all the air from her lungs and her vision clouded. A part of her wanted to give up, but the part that had started hating him the moment she'd realized just how wrong she'd been urged her to fight back.

It was then, at that moment, she heard again the echo of her child's cries. Missy had been the one pure thing in her life, and this man glaring down at her had taken even that from her.

"Where...where did you get this?" she asked, calmer now.

"From my ex-brother-in-law in Gary. Seems this son-of-a-bitch Hardin was up there talking to my ex, wanting to know if me and Arlene had any kids who died under mysterious circumstances."

Brenda stared. "You never told me you were married before."

"What I done before I met you is my business, just like I never ask you no questions about what you did with that pissant stepfather of yours."

Brenda felt ice form on her skin. "I didn't have anything to do with this, Monk," she said, holding up he card. "I swear I never said anything."

"No? Then how come this cop has the same name as the woman who runs that frigging Center?"

"How do you know he does?"

His face twisted. "Her face and her name were plastered all over the front page of the *Journal-Courier* when that place opened." He sneered a smile that made her flesh crawl. "Them other two, they were real pretty ladies. But Ms. Hardin, now that's one classy broad. Be a real shame if a lady like that ended up with her face burned off by acid, wouldn't it?"

Ria dug her toe into the webbing of the chaise and watched Jimmy hunker down, his face screwed into a knot of concentration as he sighted a line between his ball and his daddy's. From the glee on her son's face, Dad was a dead duck.

The three of them had been halfway through the rubber game of their daily croquet tournament when Flynn had called to fill her in on his progress. Since she'd been losing big-time, anyway, she'd been happy to retire from the field, leaving father and son to battle it out for the "Championship of the World" as her son had put it.

"Is the fact that Benteen had another child who also died from SIDS enough to bring charges?" she asked when Flynn ran out of words.

"Not without more evidence. Evidence we ain't got, sugar." His sigh dripped disgust. "The guy who handled his case originally was three days from retirement when he caught the squeal. From the looks of the file, he interviewed the Benteens' neighbors, ran a check for priors on the parents and come up empty. Bottom line, he did a wash on digging any deeper."

An outraged male bellow sliced through her thoughts, drawing her gaze to Grady's irate expression. His green ball was now hopelessly wired against a wicket. She smiled at the show her husband was putting on for their son, who was loving it.

*Ex*-husband, she reminded herself firmly. And likely to remain that way.

Grady had said he loved her—only not recently. He said he wasn't leaving. He said he wasn't interested in proposing—which should have eased her mind considerably since it was much too soon to think about anything more than Jimmy's well-being. Instead, she got a funny, sinking feeling inside when she thought of telling the boy that his parents had been divorced for nearly three years. That they'd been living apart and would continue to live apart. That when they left the lake he would be living with each of them in turn, according to whatever custody arrangement they hammered out, passed between them like a football.

She felt a deeply buried pain struggle to take hold and fought it down.

"What about Monk's ex-wife?" she asked, shifting her gaze to a sailboat tacking into the wind in the mid-lake channel.

"The poor woman's terrified. She only agreed to talk to me off the record and even then, she only hinted that she suspected Monk."

"What about the similarities? Both babies left in his care while the mothers were gone. Both dead when the mothers returned."

"Without hard evidence, even a lousy defense attorney could make a case for coincidence."

Ria worried her lower lip and let her eyes go out of focus. "Somehow we have to get Brenda to testify." She was stating the obvious, but it helped cement things in her mind.

"Agreed. Any idea how to make that happen?"

"One of us will have to convince her."

"Right. Problem is, she seems to have disappeared. I've been by her place three times in the same number of days, and none of her neighbors have seen her. Her car's not in its space either."

"What about Monk?"

"His employer claims he's hauling liquid fertilizer to California. Won't be back for three days. I thought maybe he'd taken the wife with him, but the dispatcher swears it's against company policy."

"What about Brenda's family?"

"A mother and stepfather in Richmond. Claim they haven't seen her since she left the morning of her sixteenth birthday."

Ria worried her lip some more before admitting, "I

should have tried harder to reach her when she didn't return my call, but I was so caught up in my own stuff that I let it slide.''

''Understandable, sugar.'' His voice lightened. ''So how's my nephew adjusting?''

''Better, thank goodness. At least he calls me Mom now, and sometimes he sounds as though he means it. Last night, when I went in to check on him, he had Trouble tucked under one arm and his old Pooh bear under the other. I think he's starting to remember things, too.''

''That's good, right?''

''According to the therapist Grady talked to in California, yes.''

''Then I'll hold a positive thought.''

''Thanks.''

''For family, anything, sugar.'' He cleared his throat. ''What about Jimbo's mom and dad? Are you and my brother still snarling and snapping at each other like two puppies in a sack? Or have you finally admitted you belong together?''

Ria watched Grady line up his ball. She had to admit the man had the best set of buns she'd ever seen. Tight and hard, with just enough curve to fill out the seat of his hacked-off Wranglers. He was also patient to a fault, unfailingly polite and a tireless lover. If given a thousand chances to find the one man who fit her girlhood dream of Prince Charming, she would still choose him. So why couldn't she make herself love him again?

''That's three questions,'' she said when she realized she was listening to static in her ear. ''Which do you want me to answer?''

''Your call, sugar. I'm easy.'' It was apparent to her now that Grady wasn't the only Hardin willing to indulge her. It both touched and annoyed her.

''We're not snapping. There's not a chance under the

sun that your brother could be mistaken for a puppy. As for belonging together, neither of us wants to make another mistake.''

She gazed out at the two males with identical swaggers walking toward her. Both her men needed haircuts. Grady's was almost long enough to make a tiny tail. Definitely non-regulation.

''You still talking to my brother?'' Grady asked before plucking the glass from her hand.

''Yes, why?''

''Need to have a few words with him when you're done.'' He drained what was left of her tea in two swallows before setting the glass on the patio railing with a hard thump.

''We're done,'' she told him before adding for Flynn's benefit, ''I'll keep trying Brenda's number. If I leave enough messages on her machine, she might get tired of hearing my voice and call me back.''

''Good plan. In the meantime I'll run by her place on my way home tonight. I might just get lucky.''

''Thanks,'' she said before handing Grady the phone.

While Grady ambled toward the house, his voice too low to be overheard, Ria watched an aluminum fishing boat easing around the point. Seated in the rear seat, with one hand on the outboard motor was the same determined fisherman in camouflage vest and orange cap she'd seen fishing the point before, two or three days in a row at least. He was certainly patient, trolling back and forth parallel to the shoreline, staying just at the edge of the channel about fifty feet from the beach.

The second time he'd appeared, Grady had checked him out, swimming out to hang on to the boat with one hand while they'd spoken. Her fears had subsided when he'd returned to assure her that the guy was a mechanic from Indianapolis visiting his sister who lived across the lake.

"Guess what, Mom? Grady said he heard from the lady at the marina that a guy fishing the dam hooked Old Whiskerface but he snapped the line."

She flipped up the bill of the SWAT cap he'd appropriated as his own. "Do I sense a heavy-duty fishing expedition forming here?"

His eyes shone as he dug into the bag of chips he'd left by her chair. "Grady has a neat idea for bait."

"He does?"

He crunched chips, spraying bits as he rushed on. "You know that macaroni gunk you made for lunch?"

She huffed. "Watch it, buster," she protested, her expression fierce. "I'll have you know there are people who would *kill* for the recipe for my pasta salad."

He went white, his hand frozen halfway into the bag. "I didn't mean it," he said quickly, his voice thin, his gaze darting and nervous. "Don't be mad, okay? I won't say it again, I promise."

Ria's stomach clutched. "Oh, baby, I was just teasing," she said quickly. "You can call everything I cook gunk and it wouldn't bother me."

"But you said...I don't want to get killed."

*Oh, God. Oh, my God.*

"Sweetie, I love you. Your daddy loves you. People who love each other sometimes say the wrong thing. They even hurt each other sometimes, but because they love each other, they forgive each other, too."

"They do?"

"Oh, yes." Though she wanted to wrap herself around him and hug him close, she kept her hands curled loosely around the chair arms.

"So it's okay if we use your, uh, pasta salad? Well, not all of it. Just the parts that look like bow ties."

"Of course."

He cheered, then grabbed the bag and headed for the

door. "Did you hear, Grady? Mom said we could use those yucky bow tie things for bait."

Ria twisted around to find Grady standing at the edge of the patio, watching her. "Great," he said, his hand on the boy's shoulder, but his gaze was fastened on her face.

"I'm gonna pick out some really smelly ones right now, okay? So we'll be ready to shove off as soon as the sun sets."

Without waiting for permission, he slipped from his dad's grasp and went inside, slamming the screen door behind him.

Only then did she exhale the breath she'd been holding. "How much did you hear?" she asked quietly.

"Enough to fill in too many blanks about the people he's been living with."

She nodded, her insides shaking. "It seems like every time I open my mouth I say the wrong thing."

"Sounds to me like you said exactly the right thing."

"About the pasta?"

"About loving someone enough to forgive." His mouth slanted just enough to push a shallow crease into his hard cheek. "It's a hell of a thought."

He saluted her with a quick grin before following their son into the house.

Stevie tucked his tongue between his teeth and pulled on the rope real steady like, one hand over the other the way Grady had taught him. Above his head, the flag snapped in the wind.

It was his job to run the flag up the pole at the edge of the water every morning and take it down every night when the sun went behind the trees on the other side of the lake. After the first time, when Grady showed him how to fasten the clip things through the metal holes, he'd done it all by himself. Sometimes Grady never even watched. And he never nagged him about remembering or doing it right or calling him a dumb head if he messed up on the time or stuff, like Lance used to do.

Stevie thought it was way cool the way Grady treated him like a grown-up. Mostly he thought Grady was way cool, too. It was like, if he said he'd be home to go for a boat ride at four o'clock, he was there right on time. Most times he was early. Sometimes, though, he'd come blasting down the driveway at the last minute, looking kinda hassled. But he always came.

He let Stevie drive the boat, too. And not just real slow, but fast enough so's the boat sort of lifted up out of the water. Stevie loved going fast.

He thought maybe he might even love Grady a little. He was pretty sure Grady loved him a lot. Nobody ever said they loved him before Grady did that first day in California when he came into the pink house where they'd taken him after Lance and Moira had gotten arrested.

It was that way with Mom, too. She was really neat. He knew he loved her. He was even thinking of maybe admitting he liked being called Jimmy. Maybe he even sort of remembered her calling him that before. Only, whenever he thought about that, he got that funny sick feeling in his belly.

It was the way he got sometimes watching scary movies right before something real gross happened.

"How come we have to take the flag down every night and put it up every morning?" he asked as Grady came ambling up carrying his tackle box, the poles over his shoulder. "How come we don't just leave it up?"

Grady glanced up, his face kinda soft like as he watched the flag coming down. "Because the flag is special and needs special rules to show that." He glanced toward the water and the guy fishing off the point. Jimmy had seen him pull in two already.

"Lance said he burned the flag once. Said it gave him a high."

Grady's face got so hard it was scary. "It's a funny thing, Jim. In some countries, Lance could be shot for burning a flag. But here all of us including Lance are allowed to say anything we want about the government or the flag, just as long as we don't break any laws while we're doing it."

"How come burning the flag isn't against the law?"

"Because the men who thought up this country figured we were all smart enough to get along with one another without loading us down with a bunch of rules."

"Did you ever say bad things about the government?"

"Sometimes, especially when I have to pay my taxes every year. But I would never burn a flag or spit on it or do anything but respect it. My mother's dad was killed fighting for that flag." Grady looked a little sad for a minute. "Need a hand with folding?"

"Wouldn't mind."

Grady put down the tackle box and poles and reached up to haul in the flapping material. "There's something else that's pretty neat about the flag, too," he said as he handed Stevie one end. "It can be used as a signal."

Stevie concentrated on folding the side along one red stripe. "What kind of signal?" he asked when he had it right.

"You ever hear of Mayday? Or maybe SOS?"

"Sure. There was this war movie and this ship got torpedoed. They sent out this signal."

"If you hang the flag upside down, with the stars down, it means that you're in trouble and you need help."

"Hey, that's gnarly."

"Guess it is." Grady handed over his end, and Stevie finished folding. "One thing, though, Jim. Don't ever do it unless you really need help. But if—let's say someone came around looking to hurt you or your mom—do it as quick as you can, and then hide someplace and wait for help.'' Grady glanced at the lake again. And then at the hill where the road was. ''Is that clear, son?''

Stevie nodded, a little scared. ''I can run really fast if I have to.''

''Good man.'' Grady ruffled his hair before grabbing his stuff. ''You put away the flag and I'll meet you at the boat. Old Whiskerface is waiting.''

# Chapter 13

*He was a big boy, now. Three years old. He almost never sucked his thumb anymore and pretty soon he was going to ask Mommy to turn off the night-light when he went to bed. He knew there were no such things as monsters because Daddy said so, and Daddy never lied. But Daddy also said that there were some really bad guys in the world who liked to hurt little kids, which was why he wasn't ever s'posed to talk to grown-ups he didn't know. And he hadn't.*

*He'd gone to his room to get Pooh when two men with funny masks on their faces had snuck up behind him. Jimmy had tried to scream for Mommy, but the big man in the black clothes had shoved something into his mouth, then dragged him off to the van with no windows.*

*Jimmy had kicked and punched at the guy's chest, but the guy just laughed and stuck an awful needle in his arm. Jimmy didn't remember anything else until he woke up in the back seat.*

*Jimmy was trying his bestest to be brave, but he was so*

*scared his throat felt funny and his head was all fuzzy. He wanted his mommy, but the two bad guys just laughed whenever he asked how long before he could go home.*

*Jimmy really wished Daddy was here now.*

*He felt real safe when Daddy was in the house. When Mommy and Daddy tucked him in and told him to sleep tight Jimmy knew everything was okay. Sometimes he'd wake up and hear Mommy and Daddy laughing in their room down the hall, and he'd laugh, too, 'cause he felt so warm and safe.*

*"My daddy's a p'liceman and he'll shoot you if you don't let me go h-home," he told the man with the funny mask in his best scary voice.*

*"Forget it, kid. Ain't nobody coming for you, no matter how long you bawl."*

*The man's name was Nikolai and he was big, like Daddy. Only the man's eyes were mean, like the rattlesnake in Jimmy's favorite book about bugs and reptiles and dinosaurs.*

*Jimmy scrubbed the tears off his cheeks. He didn't know what to do. His Daddy was s'posed to be here by now. His mouth trembled, and the tears spilled out of his eyes again.*

*"I want to go home!"*

*"Shut your yap, kid, or I'll shut it for you."*

*Jimmy clamped on his cheek between his teeth but he couldn't stop crying. The little man jerked around, then cocked back his fist...*

The scream was earsplitting, jerking Ria from the warm cocoon of deep sleep. Heart pounding at a frightening speed, she fumbled for the light, even as the high-pitched sound reverberated through the cottage.

Grady was already up and tugging on his shorts. An instant later, he was gone, the weapon he'd taken from beneath his pillow in his hand.

"Oh, God, *Jimmy!*" she cried, even as she struggled to free herself from the sheet. In her haste, she tumbled to the floor, banging her elbow on the nightstand as she fell.

"Mama's coming," she called as she somehow scrambled to her feet.

Grady reached Jimmy first. He'd turned on the light and tossed his pistol onto the top bunk. Half lying, half sitting on the bed, he was holding the obviously terrified little boy who was kicking like a wild thing, his brown eyes round with terror.

"Let me go-o-o-o-o!" Jimmy shouted, his voice little-boy shrill. "I want to go home."

Grady wrapped his arms around Jimmy's lanky body and brought his face close to his. "Jimmy, look at me, son," he commanded in a low, insistent tone that somehow pierced the shrill cries. "You are home, son. It was just a dream. No one's ever going to take you away again."

"They put tape over my mouth and I c-couldn't breathe. And then...and then they made me drink awful stuff and then that guy Nikolai, he said I'd never see my m-mommy again."

Grady glanced her way, his eyes bleak, his jaw tight. "Jim, look. There's your mom. Right there by the door."

Jimmy stopped struggling and jerked his head toward her.

"Here I am, baby," she said in a soothing tone as she approached one slow step at a time. "Mom's here."

His face crumpled, and he jerked away from his father. "Mommy!"

Looking achingly like the baby he'd been once, he held out his arms. She gathered him to her breast as he started to sob.

"It's all right, baby. It's all right." She stroked his hair, ran her hands over his shaking little body. Finally, after endless, miserable months, her baby was home again.

"D-Daddy didn't come. I w-waited and waited."

Grady went white. "I would have come, Jim. I couldn't find you."

"Moira said you didn't want me 'cause I'm too dumb to learn to read and write."

"That's not true. I swear it's not true."

Grady looked destroyed. Ria's heart broke for him. He *had* found their son. "Sweetheart, Daddy wouldn't lie to you. He did everything he could to find you. Tomorrow I'll show you the folder with the flyers he sent out every six months. Every day he called other police departments and talked to lots and lots of people."

She broke off to take a quick breath. "We were so sad when you weren't here. For years before you were born, Daddy and I prayed to have a little boy just like you. And when we did, we were so happy we just kept smiling and smiling, so you see we'd never, ever do anything to hurt you. We certainly wouldn't send you away."

"But Moira said—"

"Jimmy, look at me," she ordered. His lashes were stuck together, and his innocent mouth trembled, but he looked. "Have we said anything since you've been back with us that would make you think we don't want you?"

His shoulder aimed for his ear in his version of his father's quick, impatient shrug. Ria brushed back his hair and kissed his forehead. "Sweetie, your daddy has been getting up at four in the morning and going to work early so he can come home early. So he could teach you to play croquet or how to fish. Having you back was the most important thing in the world to him. To both of us."

She glanced at Grady's face and saw anguish beneath the stone. He needed to be reassured as much as their son. Right now, though, the son they both adored needed her more. "Jimbo, if you could choose right now, would you really want to go back to California and live with Lance and Moira?''

His lashes flickered as he looked from one of his parents to the other. She saw the conflicting loyalties, the terror that he would be tossed out if he wasn't good enough or nice enough or quiet enough, and her heart ached.

Suddenly she was six and her mother was screaming obscenities as a stranger dragged her away. Ria had screamed, too, and tried to fight off the arms holding her. Her mother had been crazy, yes, but she'd been the only security Ria had ever known.

Terrified and lonely, Ria hadn't been able to stop crying. Her foster mother had finally given up and called social services, who'd found her another home. By then Ria had figured out that people threw you away if you cried, so she stopped. She had nightmares too, screaming in the dark. Her foster parents tried, but they had a new baby, and Ria's screaming made the baby scream, too.

The social worker she'd had before Alice had lectured her sternly about controlling her emotions. No one wanted a little girl who was out of control. Besides, look what had happened to her mother when she couldn't control herself. By the time she'd started college, she'd gotten very good at controlling herself.

Oh, God, she thought. What have I done?

''I want to stay here with you,'' Jimmy said softly. ''If it's okay.''

''Very, very okay,'' she said through the tears that were suddenly blinding her. She hugged him tightly, feeling love flood her. Finally he'd had enough and started to wiggle. A good sign, she thought, letting him go.

''Since we're all up, why don't we have a snack.'' She smiled at the glint that appeared in Jimmy's eyes. ''Cookies and milk okay with you?''

"I wouldn't mind." Jimmy dashed his hand over her face, then shot a hesitant glance at his father. "Is it okay?"

"Sure thing." Grady cleared his throat and smiled. "Okay if I give you a hug first?"

Jimmy shrugged, a young male uncomfortable showing emotion to the leader of the pack. "I guess, if you want."

Ria saw the flinch deep in Grady's eyes. But the look on his face was pure Hardin bluff. "Hey, no problem," he said as he ruffled Jimmy's hair instead. "We'll do it later."

Looking relieved, Jimmy scrambled to his feet. "I'll get the cookies," he said, before racing from the room, his hair standing on end and the nightmare forgotten.

"Looks like our son is back," Ria said with a shaky laugh.

"Looks like." Careful to duck his head so he wouldn't bang the upper bunk, Grady stood up. Ria stood as well.

"He was only three, Grady. He didn't understand that daddies aren't superhuman."

His mouth slanted into a bitter line she'd seen only once—on the day they'd faced a judge in divorce court. "Especially his, right?"

"You did all you could. It's finished. Let it go."

His gaze froze, then seemed to bore into her. She felt his tension, saw his mouth soften. "I would die for you if that would prove how much I love you," he said quietly.

"I don't want you to die."

His grin flashed, a little cocky. "Works for me, honey," he drawled before retrieving the .45 that was such a part of him. "I'll just put this up."

He started to step past her, but stopped when she put out a hand to touch his arm. "Are you all right?"

"Sure. Why wouldn't I be? Jimmy's back where he belongs. With his mom." He leaned forward to brush his mouth across her cheek. "Best move those gorgeous buns, honey. Your son's waiting."

* * *

"Fish not biting, little brother?"

Grady glanced up from the arrest report he'd been reading to see his brother on the threshold, looking every inch the deputy chief in a conservative gray suit and tie. Shiny stockbroker shoes, too, he noted with a sardonic quirk of one corner of his mouth. The only shoes he owned with laces were his sneakers and the ugly black brogans that went with the uniform hanging in the back of his closet. But then he was at the end of his climb. Kale was still heading up.

Word was Kale was a lock for chief when the present one retired in three or four more years. Grady was proud of his brother, even if he was dreading the day when he had to salute him for real.

"You know how it is with us dedicated types," he tossed off with a grin that was only a little forced. "We'd rather push papers than sit on a shady bank and toss out a line."

Kale snorted as he stopped propping up the door frame and limped to the chair opposite Grady's cluttered desk. For the past week he'd been in San Francisco attending a conference of senior law enforcement officials. Before that he'd spent a week in Florida visiting his teenage daughter who lived with her mother in Miami.

"You get tired of the fast lane on the left coast, Bro?" Grady asked, leaning back.

"Got tired of my butt going numb is more like it. Never did like listening to bull, no matter how pretty it's packaged."

The chair suddenly seemed a lot smaller as his brother settled six feet four inches of lean muscle and heavy bone into the seat. Kale's face tightened as he stretched out his legs. Though big brother would never admit it, his bum hip was obviously acting up.

It had been seven years since he'd taken a header from a second-story window while trying to rescue a three-year-old hostage. In one of life's more painful coincidences, Grady had been at Home Hospital when they'd brought Kale in, darn near every bone in his body busted. While the rest of his family had huddled outside the OR praying for his big brother, Grady had been upstairs in the birthing suite with Ria, coaching her through thirty hours of hard labor as she struggled to deliver the child they'd been awaiting so eagerly.

Once Jimmy had been safely delivered, Grady had rushed to the nearest pay phone to call his folks, only to get word from the sympathetic nurse that the brother he worshiped was downstairs battling for his life.

The doctors hadn't given him odds worth spit, and it had taken him a full year before he was steady on his feet, but Kale being Kale had muscled his way back to health.

"I damn near shouted down the roof when I heard the message you'd left on my machine." Kale cleared his throat and glanced at the bulletin board where the last of a series of flyers was still pinned. Grady intended to leave it there as a reminder never to lose sight of his priorities again. "You done good, Bro."

Grady frowned. "I did diddly and you know it."

Kale lifted an eyebrow. "I know a man who needs a reason to keep beating up on himself will always find one. The question is why the need."

Grady shifted and told himself he wasn't squirming. "You always did have a wild imagination."

Kale was silent for a moment. Beyond the glass partition the usual Monday morning circus had taken on a fourth ring. Already Grady had made a couple of judgment calls that hadn't sat well with a couple of his detectives. A "no" on asking a judge for a search warrant that was too shaky, a "no way" on an elaborate sting that wasn't ready to be put in place. His In basket was buried under a stack of stuff his assistant had flagged as priority, meaning, he'd be lucky to get out from behind his desk before noon.

Ria's vacation officially ended in three days, but she was planning to do a lot of her work from the cottage. On the days she had to be in town, Grady would stay with Jim at the lake.

Neither had talked much about the future. By tacit agreement, they were waiting to talk with McCurry one week from today before making any changes.

"So...how's my nephew, besides being bigger and older?"

"A hell of a kid." He glanced at the photo on his desk. He needed to take some new ones. "He's dyslexic. Can't read more than a few words. The bitch keeping him couldn't be bothered to get him help."

Kale's comment was savagely raw. "Does DEA have a positive ID yet?"

Grady lifted an eyebrow. "Did some checking, did you?"

"You think I wouldn't?"

"Nope." Grady wanted to be pissed. Instead he was touched. Kale had the same instinct to take care of those he loved as he did. "Got a call from Mendoza last Friday. Said the guy was a Canadian national with a long list of priors for larceny and fraud. Seems there's a nice fat warrant waiting to be served in Toronto. Mendoza was walking the extradition through channels himself."

Kale nodded. "And the woman?"

"A former hooker from New Orleans. She's wanted for killing a john."

Needing to move, he got to his feet and pulled down the blinds screening his office from the bullpen. "Ria doesn't know that. It would kill her to know what kind of woman had been raising her child."

"Jimmy's your child, too."

''Yeah, well it's doing a number on me, too. I just have more experience handling it.''

Kale's gaze followed him as he paced off a few laps. When he'd worked off enough of the tension that had him wanting to climb walls, he sat again.

''Better now?'' Kale asked, amusement lurking in his eyes.

''Some, yeah.''

Kale shifted awkwardly, his face tightening. ''So are you two working on a second chance or just sleeping together?''

''There are no second chances, Kale.''

''That sounds heavy. Wanna talk about it?''

''Not much to talk about. She needed a shoulder for a while, now she doesn't.''

Kale adjusted the knife pleat in his trousers. ''The way you were after the divorce, we all pretty much figured you were still in love with her.''

''Was and am.''

''So what's the problem?''

''It takes two. Bottom line, I can't make her love me again.''

''You gonna keep trying?''

''Nope.''

His big brother pinned him with a look that never failed to peel away a few layers of protective camouflage. ''In that case, how about a drink?''

''You buying?''

''Guess I am, yeah.''

Grady glanced at his watch. He and Ria were scheduled to take Jimmy to the amusement park at Indiana Beach for a picnic lunch.

''What the hell, they won't miss me,'' he muttered, getting to his feet. ''Hope your wallet is fat, brother, 'cause I feel a long afternoon coming on.''

* * *

Monk Benteen parked the stolen van behind a storage shed to the rear of the property. During the week he'd spent watching the house, he hadn't seen anyone but the woman who'd turned Brenda against him and the blond guy she was shacking up with. Damn woman must have left a half dozen messages on his machine, the last one just yesterday, begging Brenda to call her.

It had taken him time to come up with the Hardin woman's whereabouts. He had to grease a coupla palms, threaten to bust a coupla heads, but he'd traced her to this place.

Monk allowed himself a congratulatory smile as he performed a final equipment check. Duct tape. Skinning knife. A really sweet Beretta.

His blood pumped hot as he swept the area with a trained gaze. It couldn't be better. The nearest neighbors were screened from view by a row of thick cypress trees, and the house was set back from the road far enough to prevent observation by a passing motorist. Though he couldn't see the lake, he'd spent enough time cruising by in the fishing boat he'd rented to feel sure he could block any escape in that direction.

Finally, his mental checklist completed, he declared himself ready.

*It's payback time. And I'm just the guy to do it.*

She and the kid were alone. Monk had seen her man drive away just past dawn. Big guy he was, built for strength and speed, and moved like he could take real good care of himself. Reminded Monk of the master sergeant at Camp Pendleton. A tough bastard, Sgt. Ruiz was. Ramrod of the commando unit Monk had been part of for a while— before the bastard had washed him out for beating up a Mexican whore who'd cheated him.

Monk tugged the bill of his cap lower to hide his face as he climbed out of the vehicle. It was frigging ninety degrees, and the new fishing vest he'd bought a few weeks back to help him blend in was damn hot.

Being's as how the sarge was always ramming the concept of prior planning down their throats, he figured Ruiz would be damn proud of him. A clean kill was the mark of a skilled warrior, he'd said.

No noise, no mess. Just the way he'd handled those two brats he never wanted.

Twenty minutes tops, he told himself, checking his watch as he walked toward the door. He would allow himself a moment to enjoy the terror in the woman's eyes, and then with one quick snap of his wrists, it would be done. When he left, there'd be one less interfering woman in the world.

# Chapter 14

It was the fifth time in as many minutes that Jimmy had come into the kitchen to check the new clock with the big red numerals Grady had bought in order to teach their son how to tell time. Every night they put in an hour's practice. Jimmy still mixed up nine and six, and sometimes one and eleven, but he was learning.

"Grady's never been late before," he grumbled, plopping down at the kitchen table.

Ria tucked the container of deviled eggs into the cooler and closed the lid before she allowed herself to check that same clock. Jimmy was right. Grady was twenty minutes late.

"He'll be here," she assured her anxious son.

Jimmy upended the salt shaker and let salt pour out onto the table. When he had enough, he laboriously traced an *A* with a fingertip in the grains. It was an exercise Grady himself had invented when he was a kid.

"Mom, is Grady mad about something?"

"I don't think so, sweetie. Why do you ask?"

He shrugged. "He's real quiet when we go fishing, and he never talks about doing stuff together anymore."

Ria caught the quick flash of hurt in the glance he sent her way. "What stuff is that, sweetie?"

"You know, guy stuff. Like going to the 500 next year so I can see the cars the way he and his dad used to do. Or maybe fixing up an old car together."

"I'm sure he's still planning on all those things."

"Maybe," Jimmy muttered, going back to his task.

Trying not to think about the three nights that Grady had spent watching the late show instead of making love to her, Ria poured herself a cup of the coffee she'd made in anticipation of his return and carried it to the table. Though Grady still treated them both with easy affection, he'd been different since the night she'd come to think of as Jimmy's real homecoming.

She'd seen the hurt stagger into his eyes when he'd realized Jimmy blamed him for not coming to his rescue. It was as though he'd shut down a part of himself at that moment.

She frowned, checked the clock herself, then got up to walk to the sliding glass doors to look out at the lake. The fisherman in the orange cap was gone, she noticed. In fact, the lake seemed surprisingly empty.

"Have you seen Old Whiskerface again?" she asked, turning.

"Uh-uh. Grady said we'd try again this weekend."

"Then you will." She took another sip, then frowned. Maybe he forgot the time they were supposed to leave. Or gotten tied up in a meeting. She glanced at the clock again and then at the cell phone on the counter.

"Sweetheart, would you be a love and fetch me the green-striped beach towel hanging on the clothesline? We'll need it to use as a tablecloth."

"Okay." Jimmy slid from his chair and headed for the side door.

As soon as he disappeared, Ria set down her cup and picked up the phone. She had just punched the last number when the front door opened.

"Oh, Grady, thank goodness—" Her voice faltered, then dammed.

The man standing in the doorway was a bulky, black-haired stranger with dead eyes. "Make a sound and you're history," he ordered, closing the door behind him.

Panic screamed in her mind as he walked toward her. Somehow she battled it down. "All right," she said, praying that Grady would pick up the phone she heard ringing in her ear.

"Captain Hardin's office." It was Grady's assistant.

The man moved like lightning. Before Ria could cry for help, he snatched the phone from her hand and smashed it against the counter.

"Think you can put one over on Monk Benteen, do you, bitch?" His lips pulled back in a snarl, and her stomach lurched. Her mind started to splinter into pure terror. Somehow she pulled back.

She had to get him out of here before Jimmy came back with the towel.

"Of course not, Mr. Benteen," she said as calmly as she could. "Would you like a cup of coffee? I've just made some fresh."

If she could reach the pot—

The blow caught her across the face, sending her reeling into the refrigerator. She hit hard, and pain exploded in her head. Her vision turned gray, and she slid bonelessly to the floor. He was on her instantly, grabbing her by the hair to jerk her head up.

"Where's my wife, bitch?"

"I...I don't know, really I don't. I've called and left messages, but—"

"She's gone. She ain't got no friends but you."

"I swear, I don't know."

He drew a knife from his boot, his eyes animal sly as he slowly drew the tip down her cheek. Her face exploded in fire. "Now, I'm gonna ask you one more time. I don't get an answer, the next cut goes deeper."

Ria felt the blood dripping down her cheek. Her mind hazed, and her throat clogged with bile. Somehow she stayed on her feet. *Don't panic, Ria. Think! What would Grady do?*

Bluff, she thought. He would bluff.

"I...have a number for her," she said, watching his eyes instead of the knife only inches from her face. "It's in my DayRunner."

His eyes narrowed. "You'd better not be lying."

She let him see her fear. "I'm not. I swear I'm not. We'll drive to the Center and I'll get it for you."

His pupils were pinpricks, and he smelled of sweat and stale cigarettes. It was all she could do to keep from gagging. "All right, but if you're lying, I'll blow you and that precious Center to smithereens. I got enough plastique in my kit in the van to do it and more."

"I'm sure you do." Blood was soaking her shirt now and wetting her skin. The spreading stain was making her queasy. She swayed, and he grabbed her arm, shoving her hard against the counter.

"No tricks, bitch."

"It's not a trick. The sight of blood...if we're going, we'd better go now. I'm feeling a little faint."

Please, please take me out of here, she wanted to beg. Anything to get him away from the house. Away from Jimmy.

"All right," he said, "but if this is a trick..."

"It's not."

He grabbed her arm and shoved it up behind her. Suddenly awash in pain, she cried out. "Shut up, or I'll pull it clean out of the socket."

"Please, I'll be quiet," she managed, and he eased off.

"When we leave here, you're gonna walk in front of me real nice like, as though we were good friends. One trick and I'll put this knife through your spine. Might not kill you, but you'll never walk again, neither."

"Whatever you say."

He released her, and she moved toward the door. She heard him follow. She had her hand on the doorknob when he grabbed her hair again. "Thought you said your DayRunner's at the Center."

Before she could answer, he spun her around. "Then what's that?" he demanded, pointing toward the table with the knife stained with her blood.

She didn't need to look. She knew. It was her calendar.


Jimmy knew he had to get help.

He'd seen the strange guy walk in the front door without knocking and was about to yell when something stopped him. Instead, he'd gone to the window and peeked in. He was about to run for help when he'd seen the guy hit his mom.

Scared, he took off running toward the lake. Maybe the guy in the boat could help, only the guy wasn't there. Then he saw the flag flapping in the wind, and remembered what his dad had said.

"Upside down. I have to make it upside down."

Darting glances at the house every few seconds slowed him down some. His hands shook real bad too, but he managed to get the flag down the pole far enough so he could snap it free. His hands shook so bad it took three tries to get the slippery material twisted the right way. Finally, sobbing in frustration, he got the hooks through the holes, and then he was pulling on the rope as hard as he could.

Grady saw the phone company van as soon as he pulled into the tree-lined drive and remembered the chewed line he hadn't gotten around to fixing. Guilt curdled the already-sour beer in his belly.

He slammed on the brakes and killed the engine, calling himself a few choice names as he jerked the keys from the ignition.

Well, she even called the phone company to take care of the wiring. Hell, Ree had managed, hadn't she?

Damn straight she had. She didn't need him to take care of her. Too bad he needed her, he thought as he pulled open the door, his apology already half-formed.

His instinct kicked in one step too slow. Still, he had time to twist into a half crouch before the man's boot caught him a glancing blow in the groin. Pain took his breath, and he went down hard. He took another kick in the ribs and played dead. The odds that the guy would buy it were about as thin as the line between consciousness and oblivion he was riding, but it was all he had.

"Don't kick him again," he heard Ria scream through the white haze.

"Bastard cop was asking questions, putting the screws on the cow I used to be married to."

"No, that...that was my brother-in-law."

"Yeah? How come this guy has a badge clipped to his belt."

Grady knew it was coming and tried to brace, but the pain was murderous. The bastard had steel in the toes of his boots, and he felt his ribs give under the blow.

"Don't hurt him anymore!" Ria begged. "I'll do whatever you say, only please don't hurt him anymore."

"You cost me my wife, you bitch!"

"No, I—"

Grady heard the sickening sound of a blow, heard her scream. Somehow he managed to roll, to get a hand on his weapon.

The next kick caught him in the belly. He folded, even as the bastard slammed his boot down on his wrist. He felt bones splintering.

*"Freeze, or you're dead!"*

Grady heard the harsh rasp of surprise, smelled the bastard's fear.

"Drop the pigsticker, you son of a bitch, or I'll gut shoot you where you stand."

Grady heard the sound of a blade hitting the tile and sent up a garbled prayer of thanksgiving.

"Step away from him, Mrs. Hardin, while I cuff the bastard."

Grady fought blackness long enough to see the lethal calm on Tom Delaney's craggy face. Old Tom sure looked funny in that orange cap, but damn, he was still one fine cop, he thought, just before he let himself sink.

They gave him the same room—416 West. He had a couple of the same nurses, too, who'd laid down the law damn near as soon as they brought him back from the OR after fishing the splinters out of his lung.

*Behave yourself, buster,* they'd warned, *or we'll cuff you to the bed with your own handcuffs.*

He was trying, damn it, but the tube in his side was driving him crazy. Every time he moved, a hot poker stabbed a hole through his chest. Pain he could handle; it was the sick knot in his gut that had him climbing the walls. After all the promises he'd made—to himself, to Ria, to the boy—he'd messed up again.

This time Ria had nearly died—and maybe Jimmy, too. All because he'd been drowning his sorrows in beer instead of keeping his word. A frigging thirty minutes late, only it might as well have been a lifetime.

He wasn't exactly sure when he'd given up trying to measure up. Sometime after the paramedics had dumped him onto a cold table in the ER and before he'd jerked awake to find her curled into a chair by his bed, begging him not to die.

Jimmy needed him, she'd said. Jimmy loved him, she'd said.

For Jimmy's sake she didn't want him to die.

For his own sake he wished he could, so he wouldn't have to face himself in the mirror every morning, knowing he'd let them down again. Hell, maybe he'd just grow a beard, he thought, closing his eyes.

He was drifting, trying to keep his mind blank, when he heard her voice murmuring a greeting to one of the nurses. A split second later she appeared, carrying a huge bouquet of roses that nearly hid her face. Her skin was still pale and swollen around the dark bruises on one cheek. On the other, the deep scratch from Benteen's blade was still bright red. Every time he saw that thin, angry line he bled a little more.

"Jimmy sends his love," she said as she bent to kiss him.

Somehow he kept himself from hooking his good arm around her neck and drawing her against his chest. He'd lost the right to need her the moment he'd stepped inside the cottage a half hour too late.

"How's he doing?" he asked as she fussed a little with the vase before pulling the chair closer.

"Pleased as punch that he'd been the one to bring that friend of yours running full tilt to the rescue."

"He should be pleased. He kept his head."

"He must have told your dad a dozen times how you'd explained about the flag. He thinks you're a real hero."

"Sure he does." He shifted, then remembered why that was a bad idea.

"So do I."

He managed a grin. "You're aiming all that gratitude at the wrong guy, sweetheart. I was the half-drunk jerk passing out on the floor, remember? Tom Delaney's the one who crashed through the door in the nick of time."

"Because you had the foresight to hire him to watch over us when you weren't there."

"Nice try, Ree, but we both know I let you down." Because he couldn't quite meet her eyes, he looked at the roses instead. Do it, a voice prodded. Now, before you lose your nerve. But he couldn't. Not yet.

"Flynn stopped by earlier. He said your friend, Brenda, has agreed to testify against her husband."

"Yes. He admitted to killing both of his daughters. Flynn said he feels pretty sure she'll be a creditable witness." She pulled up a chair and sat down. "All the time I was trying to reach her, she was staying with another member of the support group. She'd sworn Callie to secrecy, and Callie was trying to figure out how to get a message to me without Brenda knowing it when they saw the story on TV about Monk's arrest."

He heard someone laugh in one of the other rooms. Outside an ambulance screamed its approach.

"He could have killed you, Ree."

"He didn't."

"I promised…"

"Grady, I love you."

His heart stuttered. All that was in him yearned to believe her. Somehow he made himself look at her. Because he needed distance, he deliberately evoked the memory of her scream when Benteen's fist connected with that elegant cheek.

"You want to love me," he said, echoing the words

she'd spoken to him once. "Maybe you even think you love me, but you don't."

Her mouth trembled a little, giving his heart a hard jolt, before she controlled herself. "I've always loved you. I was afraid to admit it, afraid that if I did I'd lose you the way I lost my mother and everyone else I let myself care about."

"Honey, I appreciate the gesture, but you're fighting after the bell. You and me, we had our shot. You tried to tell me that a hundred different ways, but I was too stubborn to listen."

"I was wrong. Terribly, terribly wrong. But you wouldn't let me go, and now I'm glad." She put one hand on his forearm, and he flinched. "I won't hurt you," she said with a gentle smile that tore into him.

"No, but I'll hurt you. No, don't say anything. Just let me get it out, okay?"

She drew a breath and nodded. "All right."

"You used to accuse me of putting my job first, and you were right, even though I hated to admit it. Still do, but that doesn't mean it's not true. Me and Kale, we've had this competition all our lives. He's bigger and he's tougher, but I'm sneakier. I've been sucking up big-time to the chief." Somehow he found a grin. "Bastard has an ego the size of Texas. Bought every fawning word I slipped him."

She looked confused. "You hate those kinds of games. You said so a dozen times. You'd rather retire a patrolman first-grade than kiss butt, you said."

He shrugged, sending a jagged slash of pain deep into his side. Absorbing it helped him to focus. "Sure, I hate it, but sometimes a man has to bend a few principles to win the big one."

"I don't believe you."

"Hey, have I ever lied to you?"

"No, which is why I know you meant it when you said you loved me."

Damn, this was hard. Ask anyone in the Lafayette PD about Grady Hardin and the answer would be the same; the man was a tough SOB who took the hits without whining, stayed on his feet if he could. If he went down, he kept the pain inside. And he never, ever, gave up. But this was almost more than he could handle.

"Sure, I love you, honey. I especially love you when you make those little noises in your throat when I have my hands on you."

Shock settled into her eyes before that soft mouth he loved curved into a shaky smile. "I don't believe a word you're saying, Grady Hardin. Not one word. You're just saying this to give me an out, but it's not necessary, my darling. I don't want an out. I love you."

She took his hand and pressed it against her battered cheek. It was all he could do to hang on to his control. "Maybe you don't believe me now, but you will, I promise. We have so much to look forward to now. All three of us."

This was killing him. Flat-out killing him. "Ree, I tried, really tried. But I can't be the kind of husband you want. It's just not in me."

"How do you know what I want?"

He expected relief. She gave him impatience and the simmer of anger. "I know because you've told me a thousand different ways. When I came home late, when I didn't come at all, when I left our son standing on the porch with his football in his hand. When I was too tired to make love to you for weeks at a time."

The doubt was a shadow creeping over her face and dimming the glow of loyalty and gratitude in her eyes. "That was in the past. You're behind a desk now."

"Yeah, but not the right desk, honey." His grin came harder. "Like I said, I'm aiming for that big corner office overlooking the Tippecanoe. I figure two, three more years of pushing my guys to have the best arrest record in the whole damn department and I'll be a lock.''

She stared at him, then very slowly returned his hand to the bed. It took all his strength to let it lie there. ''All right, Grady. I give up. I won't pretend to understand why you're doing this, but I know you well enough to know you're deliberately trying to drive me away.''

He nearly gave in then. Only the knowledge that he would surely let her down again kept him from taking back every lying word. ''Ree, I'll always be glad you were my wife and the mother of my son. If you ever need me, all you have to do is call me, and I'll be there.''

''Thank you. I'll remember that.''

The calm in her eyes should have reassured him that he'd read her right. Instead, it made him edgy as hell. ''Honey, it's better this way.''

''I suppose it is, yes.'' She drew a shaky breath, she squared her shoulders. ''Well, now that we're back to where we were before you found Jim, how do we handle telling him that we're divorced?''

Hell, he'd forgotten that. ''We're scheduled to see McCurry next week, right? The doc said I'll be out of here in a day or two. I'll stay at my place until we go to Chicago, and you can tell Jim I'm still in the hospital.''

She gnawed her lip and considered. ''I hate lying to him.''

''Isn't that what we've been doing all along, lying to him?''

Her smile was a little sad around the edges. ''Yes, I suppose we have,'' she conceded as she got to her feet and slung her purse over her shoulder. Her face seemed paler now, the bruises darker, but her eyes were very calm.

''You know, it's a funny thing, Grady. Every time you've told me you loved me, you looked me straight in the eyes. Now, when you tell me you don't, you look everywhere but straight at me. It makes me wonder why.''

He dug deep and told himself it was for her. Even as he forced himself to lock his gaze on hers, pain was ripping into his gut. ''I don't love you, Ria.''

She nodded slowly, her expression perfectly composed, an indomitable woman who had more character packed into that small body than he would ever have.

''Jimmy's waiting,'' she said with only the slightest hitch in her voice. ''I'll give him your love.'' She didn't wait for a reply, but instead turned on her heel and rushed out.

He lay frozen, staring at the empty doorway until his eyes burned. And then he closed them tight and buried his face in the pillow.


''It smells like a frigging saloon in here.''

Sprawled half-naked and unshaven on the couch with the bottle of cheap tequila he was diligently emptying, sloppy swig by swig, Grady opened one eye and glared at his big brother. ''Who asked you?''

Kale walked to the window and jerked back the curtain. ''When was the last time you had a bath?''

Grady winced at the flood of sunshine and closed his eye again. ''Go away.''

Instead, Kale slid open the window and filled his lungs before exhaling in a disgusted rush. ''Mom would kick your butt if she saw you now.''

''She can try.''

''Tough talk from a guy who looks to be one step from a shroud.'' Kale picked up the bottle of antibiotic tablets on the table and grimaced. ''Still full, you stupid idiot.''

''So?''

''So you could lose that hand if the infection turns to gangrene.''

Because he wasn't as dumb as everyone thought, Grady

slitted his eyes before opening them again. The glare from the damn sunshine seared his retinas big-time.

"What the hell?" he muttered, holding up the hand encased in pristine plaster all the way to his elbow. "I've got another one."

"Yeah, what you ain't got is good sense, Little Brother."

"Go to hell." Because he didn't have anything better to do, he took a long, satisfying pull at the bottle, belched a couple of times and glared at the big man with the hot eyes. "How'd you get in here, anyway?"

"Picked the lock."

"Call a cop," he muttered.

"You've had five of them coming around for days, banging on your door. Six, counting Tom Delaney."

"Good man, Tom. Even if he did go private."

Kale grabbed the wastebasket by the desk and carried it with him to the couch. Glass clinked against glass as he tossed in empties. "He said to tell you he's cutting his fee in half on account of catching Old Whiskerface."

Grady reared up, then yelled at the hammer blow inside his head. "That sucker belonged to Jimmy, damn it!"

"Jimmy was with him when he caught it. They took a vote and decided to let Whiskers go. Seems Jimmy wanted you to be with him when he caught the big one."

Grady bit off an obscenity before carefully lowering his head. "Guess I blew that, too."

"Aren't you beat up enough without hammering yourself for not being perfect?"

"Not even close," he muttered, shutting his eyes.

Jimmy glanced up from the ball he was about to whack, his head tilted to one side and a hopeful look on his face. "Is that Dad's truck?"

Dad. It was the first time Jimmy had used that word.

Mason and Ria exchanged looks. Grady had been out of

the hospital for four days now. He called Jimmy every day, and every day he pretended the doctors wouldn't let him come home. Neither Mason nor Sarah liked the plan she and Grady had come up with, but they'd agreed she had no option.

They'd also had a few choice words to say about their second son's mule-headed thinking. "Sounds more like that fancy German job of your uncle Kale's, tiger," Mason said in his gruff way.

"Your dad's still in the hospital, remember?" Ria said, hating to lie, yet hating the alternative more.

In three days they were to see Dr. McCurry. She had a feeling he would advise them to tell Jimmy the truth. After that, she and Jimmy would move back to her place and start making a life without Grady.

"Looks like another wild-and-woolly croquet tournament," Kale said as he stepped through the gate.

"Hi, Uncle Kale. Wanna play?"

"I don't know, Jimbo. I hear you're pretty unbeatable."

Jimmy beamed. "That's 'cause I'm Champion of the World. Dad said."

Kale gave a low whistle. "If your dad said it, it's bound to be true."

"Your turn, champ," she said with a smile.

"Watch this, Uncle Kale," he said with a cocky grin. The resilience of youth, she thought. Less than two weeks ago he was sullen, withdrawn and antagonistic. He still had his moments, but each day was better than the one before it.

"I'm watching, sport," Kale said, fixing his gaze obediently on the ball.

"You, too, Grandpa," Jimmy ordered before hunkering down. He took his time, then rested his sneaker on his own ball, and gave it a whack, sending her ball flying.

"I give up," she said with an exaggerated sigh of relief.

"Mom hates to lose," Jimmy confided in his grandfather with a gleeful grin, which Mason acknowledged with a thoughtful nod.

"Your grandmother's the same way. Owes me pert' near a hundred thousand dollars in this gin tournament we've had going on since we got married. I keep trying to collect, and she keeps talking me into double-or-nothing."

Jimmy made his shot, then glanced up. "What's double-or-nothing?"

Mason bent to rake a twig from in front of his ball. "You don't know double-or-nothing, boy?"

"Uh-uh."

"Well now, son, that's a real interesting strategy you and me might want to explore, seeing as how I owe you six bits already."

Ria and Kale exchanged grins. "Dad's in his element," he said, slipping his hands into his pockets.

"My money's on my son." Ria leaned her mallet against the tree and walked toward the house. Kale fell in step beside her.

"Heard something today I thought might interest you," he said when they reached the patio.

"What's that?" she asked, reaching for the pitcher of lemonade Sarah had set out on the picnic table before driving into town to have her hair done.

"Grady's put in his resignation," Kale said, hiding a smile when she sloshed lemonade onto the table. "Word I hear is he's going to accept that job in Oregon."

## Chapter 15

"Leave me alone, you bastard," Grady grumbled as he felt the cold splash of a washcloth against his face.

"I can't imagine what possessed that doctor to release you so soon. No doubt you badgered him into it the way you badgered me into loving you again."

It took him a minute, but he managed to pry open his eyes. It was Ria all right. She'd pulled up a chair and was busy wringing out a washcloth into a basin of water.

He thought she looked like an angel, with the sunlight coming in through the window trapped in the dark hair fluffed around her face. Because it hurt too much to look at her and know she would never be his, he closed his eyes again.

"What the hell are you doing here?" he muttered.

"Cleaning you up."

"The hell you are."

"I promised Jimmy he could see you today, and I'm not going to break that promise, just because you look like a bum."

"Forget it, honey, 'cause as soon as my head stops spinning, I'm booting your butt out of here and jamming a damn chair under the knob."

"Try it, and I'll break your other hand instead."

It was a dream, he decided—until the cold cloth slapped him in the face again. For good measure she'd added soap. He sat up spitting and cursing. Only when the pain crashed again did he remember why sudden moves of any kind were a bad idea.

"Go away, Ree. When I'm on my feet, we'll work out custody."

Ria heard the defeat in his voice and wanted to lay her head against that big, horribly bruised chest and weep. "You need a shower and a nourishing meal first, and then I'll help you shave."

His sigh was weary. "If that's what it takes to get you out of here."

"Hold on to me, Grady. We'll do this together."

"I'll do it alone. I'm used to it."

She considered it a measure of his stubbornness that he got himself stripped and into the bathroom without passing out. Even so, he was as pale as death, and his hand shook a little as she wrapped it in a plastic bag, secured with a rubber band she'd found wrapped around one of the newspapers piled up outside his door.

"Hold on, I'll turn on the water," she said, opening the frosted door to the tiled stall.

"I'll do it," he muttered, lurching past her.

"Grady—"

"Go torment someone else," he muttered, closing the door in her face. The water came on hard, and she heard him gasp.

"Serves you right, you stubborn jackass," she muttered, glaring at him through the clouded glass. He was so terribly proud—and so badly bruised, inside was well as out.

The man needed tending almost as much as he needed to be loved.

Like it or no, he was going to have to let her do both those things.

The shower door opened, and she stepped into the spray, crowding him against the corner. "Hey," he managed to get out before his heart wedged in his throat. She was naked, her breasts already pearling with drops of steam.

"Hand me the soap," she ordered, her cheeks pink.

"Ree—"

"The soap, Grady." He used his good hand to fumble it into hers. "I'm taking you back to the lake with me, and then—"

"No. I appreciate the effort, but no."

She worked up a good lather, then reached past him to return the soap to the dish. "You lied to me."

"The hell I did." He grabbed the hand she'd been aiming at his chest. Suds ran down his arm to drip onto the tile.

"You said you wanted to be chief."

He made a decent enough stab at meeting her snapping gaze. "I do."

"Here, not in Oregon."

He bit off a half-formed curse. Even so, it had her mouth firming. "I am prepared to forgive you, however," she said with a stern look.

"You are?"

"Of course. I admit I've never given any thought to leaving Indiana, but if that's what you want to do, Jimmy and I will adapt."

"I don't remember asking you to come."

"Of course you didn't. We're a family. Where else would we be but with you?"

The steam curled around them, warming his skin and

turning her hair to liquid silk. She'd never seemed more beautiful. He'd never wanted her more—or felt more inadequate. All she had to do was look at his wrecked body to know what kind of man he really was. Sooner or later she'd figure out she'd made a mistake, tying herself to a guy who would never be more than average.

"Ree, for God's sake, don't do this."

She moved closer, trapping his arm against her breasts. "No one's going to need you the way I need you, Grady. No one's ever going to want you the way I want you. I love you, you idiot. If I have to say it every day for the rest of our lives before you believe me, then that's what I'll do."

He threw his head back and let the spray pound his face. It sounded as though she was offering him salvation and absolution. Paradise. There had to be a kicker, a sneaky left jab ready to take him to his knees. Happiness couldn't be that easy.

"I don't know how to be any better than I am, Ree, and that's not good enough."

"Because you think you failed us?"

He brought his gaze back to her face and kept it there. He would watch her eyes. And he would know when she finally saw him for what he was. It would hurt, but it was necessary. "There's no 'think' to it. It's a fact. I swore an oath to protect, and I made promises in church. I broke both."

He braced for scorn. Instead she used a word that had his jaw dropping before he slammed it shut.

"What if Monk had killed Brenda? Would that have been my fault?"

"Of course not."

Her eyes were a clear green and full of challenge. "Why not? I asked Flynn to look into it. Monk found out, and he took it out on Brenda. He could have killed her. If he had, it would have been my fault.''

''Ree—''

''Even though I was doing what I thought was right, I would have set events in motion, just the way you did by going after a man who destroyed lives for money.''

She had him cornered. Neatly, ruthlessly backed into a dead end.

On the street, he would already be bracing to dodge the first swing, his fists bunched and ready, his body folding into a street fighter's crouch. He hadn't a clue how to fight a woman who refused to listen to reason. Who used words instead of her fists. Who could melt him with a smile and have him on his knees with a kiss. He took a breath. In spite of the steam that was sapping his strength, his muscles were hot-wired and edgy, his nerves humming. He nearly leaned forward and wrapped himself up in her strength. But that would shame him. A cop didn't lose his cool. It was one of the unwritten rules. Rules pounded into Grady by three generations of cops.

''You're not going to give up, are you?''

''Not on your life, my dearest. I gave up once, and spent three miserable years wishing I hadn't been such a coward. As someone I love very dearly said to me not so long ago, I learn slowly, but I do learn.''

He drew a breath. He'd felt this way twice before. The first time had been on the rainy Saturday morning when he'd walked into an airless, dismal classroom to face a sixteen-page police academy entrance exam. He'd been so uptight he'd barely gotten out his name for the examiner. Five years later he'd nearly thrown up before fumbling out a marriage proposal.

''I'll let you down again. I'll try not to, but I will.''

''I'll let you down, too. But we'll forgive each other and keep on loving each other, like your folks.''

"God help me, I…need you, Ree. Every morning without you I had to find a reason to make it through one more day."

"Oh, Grady, so did I." Somehow she'd worked it so his arms were around her and she was pressing him up against the back of the shower stall, out of most of the spray. The tile felt slick and cool against his back. She felt wonderful, her soft body molding to his. If it was a dream, he never wanted to wake up and find her gone.

"You fight dirty," he murmured, kissing her temple. The smell of steam and soap had never seemed so erotic. "I can see I'm in for a rough ride these next fifty years or so."

She drew back and looked up at him, her eyes full of hope, her mouth vulnerable and pale. "So that's a yes?"

Whatever she wanted, it was already hers. Still, he made himself take his time. Even a man in love should know what the heck he was agreeing to. "I don't know. What's the question?"

She frowned, looking adorable and exasperated and precious. "I believe we were talking about marriage."

Happiness was a hot coil in his belly, waiting to unwind. "We were?"

"Of course. Well, more specifically, I asked you to marry me again."

It took him a minute to fight his way past his need to crush her hard against him. The last thing he needed was another splintered rib. "Guess I could do that," he said past the thick emotion in his throat.

"I still have the ring. Your ring." She drew back to look up at him. Her face was shiny and wet. With tears.

His hand shook as he brought it up to wipe her cheeks. "You're the damnedest woman," he managed, his voice husky with the things he should say. Words that he would offer over the years when the emotion didn't threaten to break him. "You only cry when you're—" He stopped suddenly, still unsure.

"When I'm what?" she prodded, her eyes brimming.

He shrugged. "Nothing. It was just something Jim and I talked about."

"Happy?" she said with a smile that slipped right down inside and grabbed my heart.

"Yeah." He swallowed. "Are you?"

"Oh, yes." She wiggled against him, and the body he thought half-dead suddenly came alive. "Are you?"

"I will be," he muttered, helpless to keep from grinning. "As soon as I get you out of this shower and into bed."

Her smile was loving and sweet—and sexy as all get-out. Just for good measure she arched to her toes and kissed him. Oh, yeah, definitely alive, he thought. Every darn inch of him. "Why wait?" she whispered. "We're almost married. No reason not to start the honeymoon early."

Grady figured he should protest a little. After all, cops weren't supposed to be pushovers. "Nope," he said, pulling her closer. "No reason at all."

\* \*, \* \* \*

# SILHOUETTE
# SENSATION®

## AVAILABLE FROM 21ST JANUARY 2000

## BRIDGER'S LAST STAND  Linda Winstead Jones

*Heartbreaker*

When two strangers met that cold and lonely night something special whispered in the air... But with their affair ruined before it began, that was so nearly the end of it—except that Frannie could identify a murderer and needed Bridger's protection. Suddenly, only Bridger's arms could make everything better...

## THE LADY'S MAN  Linda Turner

Elizabeth Davis believed in relying on herself. The last thing she needed was a self-appointed rescuer—even if he was a gorgeous government agent... Close contact with Elizabeth had Zeke forgetting what was so good about the single life!

## KEEPING ANNIE SAFE  Beverly Barton

*The Protectors*

Dane Carmichael was the only man who could keep Annie Harden safe. From the moment he laid eyes on stubborn, beautiful Annie, he knew she would be his... But Annie had never encountered a man so strong, so dominating, so absolutely infuriating as Dane. And never had she needed—*or wanted*—a man more!

## THE MERCENARY AND THE NEW MUM
## Merline Lovelace

*Follow That Baby*

Sabrina Jensen was prepared to do anything to protect her precious child, but the intruder standing over the baby's crib was the man she'd once loved beyond reason, the father of her daughter. *But Jack Wentworth was supposed to be dead!* What was going on?

**AVAILABLE FROM 21ST JANUARY 2000**

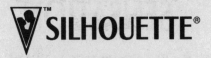

# Intrigue

*Danger, deception and desire*

**LOVER, STRANGER** Amanda Stevens
**RELUCTANT WIFE** Carla Cassidy
**THE BODYGUARD** Sheryl Lynn
**TO LANEY, WITH LOVE** Joyce Sullivan

# Special Edition

*Compelling romances packed with emotion*

**DADDY BY DEFAULT** Muriel Jensen
**WRANGLER** Myrna Temte
**DREAM BRIDE** Susan Mallery
**MARRIED BY ACCIDENT** Christine Rimmer
**IF I ONLY HAD A...HUSBAND** Andrea Edwards
**NOT JUST ANOTHER COWBOY** Carol Finch

# Desire

*Provocative, sensual love stories*

**PRINCE CHARMING'S CHILD** Jennifer Greene
**JUST MY JOE** Joan Elliott Pickart
**THE SOLITARY SHEIKH** Alexandra Sellers
**COLONEL DADDY** Maureen Child
**THE OUTLAW JESSE JAMES** Cindy Gerard
**COWBOYS, BABIES AND SHOTGUN VOWS**
Shirley Rogers

# FOLLOW THAT BABY

Everybody's looking for a missing pregnant
woman in the exciting new cross-line
mini-series from Silhouette®.

Look out in April 2000 for

## *A Fortune's Children Wedding*

and the first book of a 5 part series

## *The Fortune's Children Brides*